Falling for you . . .

"Action!"

Aaron let out a war cry and leapt, still squeezing my hand and pulling me forward.

His arms were flung out from his sides and he held them horizontally, imitating a plane.

We were soaring through the air like birds—only birds on a sharp descent, toward water that looked like a sheet of solid glass.

We were speeding, rushing closer and closer to the water. My breath caught in my throat, gagging me. I fought the impulse to retch.

How close to the water were we supposed to get?

And then, suddenly, my cord pulled taut and my descent stopped. I bounced up, the water receding rapidly.

Out of nowhere a horrific crashing, splashing, screeching sound pierced my ears.

Water shot upward.

I pressed both hands over my mouth and tried to keep the bloodcurdling scream inside, but failed.

Aaron had hit the water . . .

And then there were nine.

Berkley Prime Crime titles by Diana Orgain

Maternal Instincts Mysteries

BUNDLE OF TROUBLE

MOTHERHOOD IS MURDER

FORUMLA FOR MURDER

Love or Money Mysteries

A FIRST DATE WITH DEATH

DIANA ORGAIN

BERKLEY PRIME CRIME, NEW YORK

THE BERKLEY PUBLISHING GROUP
Published by the Penguin Group
Penguin Group (USA) LLC
375 Hudson Street, New York, New York 10014

USA • Canada • UK • Ireland • Australia • New Zealand • India • South Africa • China

penguin.com

A Penguin Random House Company

A FIRST DATE WITH DEATH

A Berkley Prime Crime Book / published by arrangement with the author

For information, address: The Berkley Publishing Group,
a division of Penguin Group (USA) LLC,
375 Hudson Street, New York, New York 10014.

ISBN: 978-0-425-27168-1

PUBLISHING HISTORY
Berkley Prime Crime mass-market edition / March 2015

PRINTED IN THE UNITED STATES OF AMERICA

10 9 8 7 6 5 4 3 2 1

Cover illustration by Bill Bruning.
Cover design by Danielle Abbiate.
Interior text design by Laura K. Corless.

Acknowledgments

Thank you to my wonderful editor, Michelle Vega, and the entire crew over at Berkley Prime Crime for believing in this story, even though it was a bit out of the box. Thanks to my agent, Jill Marsal, for your never-ending enthusiasm and support.

Special thanks to my dear friend, Marina Adair; particularly on this book, you gave me the courage to listen to my heart.

Thanks to all my early readers, specifically Hannah Jayne, Mariella Krause, Camille Minichino, and Laura-Kate Rurka.

Shout-out and hugs to my Carmen, Tommy, Bobby, and Tom, Sr.; you all are simply the best family anyone could ever have.

Finally, thank you to all you dear readers who have written to me. Your kind words keep me motivated to write the next story.

One

The bungee-jumping harness bit into my shoulders and legs as I looked over the railing of the Golden Gate Bridge. To say the water looked frigid was an understatement. The whitecaps of the bay screamed out glacier and hypothermia.

"You're not in position," Cheryl, the producer, yelled.

I felt the camera zoom in on me. They needed an extreme close-up of my every facial expression so they could broadcast my terror to the world. Magnify my embarrassment and mortification.

One of the techs said something to Cheryl and she shouted, "Cut!"

The cameraman lost interest in me.

"Why am I doing this?" I asked Becca, my best friend and the assistant producer on this godawful reality TV show, *Love or Money*.

"To find your dream man," Becca answered.

"I found him already, remember? Then he left me at the altar."

A makeup artist appeared at my elbow and applied powder to my nose.

"Dream men do not leave their brides at the altar," Becca said. "Clearly, he was not the one."

I studied the woman brushing powder on my face. She had beautiful chocolate-colored skin, a straight nose, and eyes so dark and intense they looked like pools of india ink. She looked familiar, but before I could place her, she turned and walked away.

"I thought you always liked Paul," I said to Becca.

"I did until he left me at the altar," Becca replied.

"He left *me*."

"Me, too. I was standing right next to you in a stupid tulle and taffeta dress. Anyway, enough about your horrible fashion sense—"

I laughed.

"Even if you don't find your dream man here," Becca continued, "focus on the cash prize. You need it."

She was kind enough not to add "since you were fired," but I felt the sting anyway. If anyone had told me, six months before, that I'd be on a reality TV show looking for love and/or money, I'd have called them 5150, a.k.a. clinically insane. But here I was, ex-cop, ex-bride-to-be—with a broken heart and broken career—looking to start over.

Ty, one of my "dates," sauntered over. He was wearing jeans and boots and his trademark cowboy hat. A bungee harness crisscrossed through his legs. Despite the harness, or perhaps because of it, he looked hot. Although I was hard-pressed to think of any outfit that he wouldn't look hot in.

"Are you nervous, Miss Georgia?" he asked.

I found myself absently wondering if he'd wear his hat while bungee jumping.

He reached out tentatively and touched the back of my hand with a single finger. "Miss Georgia?" he repeated.

I suddenly became aware of the camera rolling again and snapped to attention. "Yes. I'm nervous. I thought I'd get to pick the dates, but I didn't. I would have never picked this. Only a lunatic—"

I heard the producer, Cheryl, grumble.

I wasn't supposed to say anything negative about the dates, of course. They were supposed to look authentic, so that the audience wouldn't know that I had absolutely zero control over anything. The crew would have to edit out my last comment.

Ty seemed to notice the same thing because he replied smoothly, "I've always wanted to bungee jump." His lips quirked up in an irresistible manner. "And now we get to do it off this beautiful bridge."

Cheryl, who was standing behind him, smiled. He'd just saved the scene. She liked him.

Well, in those tight jeans and boots, and with the cute southern drawl—who could blame her?

I glanced around at the others. They seemed ready to go and had started heading my way. It was inevitable, once someone started showing interest in me, that the others would follow—like a pack of dogs fighting over a lone piece of meat.

Bungee jumping off the bridge was my first date, and I'd selected five of the ten eligible bachelors—or not so eligible. The gist of the show was for me to pick a guy who was emotionally available for a relationship, someone who was on the show for love.

During casting, each guy had given a heart-to-heart interview with the producer, Cheryl Dennison. They'd confessed whether they were ready to be in a relationship. Five guys were searching for love; five guys weren't. Because I'd worked for SFPD, somehow Hollywood thought I'd be able to figure out everyone's motives.

I had my doubts.

If I picked the right guy, we'd split $250,000. If I picked a guy who was emotionally unavailable he'd walk off with the cash prize on his own and, maybe worse, a piece of my heart.

America would be privy to the interviews. I'm sure those clips would expose me as a fool along the way.

I pictured Cheryl's editing staff. As soon as I said someone was cute or hot or sweet, she'd revel in playing a clip of the heart-to-heart where he told America all the reasons he couldn't fall in love. That kind of thing would be great for ratings.

The guys I'd asked on this date were the ones I suspected might be on the show for the cash. Best to eliminate the fakes ASAP.

I'd selected Ty, the cowboy, because at the first night's cocktail party I couldn't actually get him to tell me what he did for a living.

Edward, the hot doctor—tall, with dark hair, a great smile, and a wonderful gentleness about him—had to have student loans from med school up the wazoo.

Scott, the brooding writer, wrote horror stories—I'd been meaning to read some to get an idea about him. He was mysterious and supersexy, with a tight body and a bit of a swagger, and he had a shaved head and dark, piercing eyes.

But who made any money as a writer?

Aaron, the investment banker, looked like the boy next door. Clean-cut, respectable, and polite.

I wouldn't typically peg investment bankers as needing money, but something about Aaron was unsettling, as though he had some desperation vibe wafting off him.

And then there was Pietro, the Italian hunk with an accent that drove me wild.

I'd invited him because I had a weakness for accents, and weakness must be sought out and destroyed at any cost.

Everyone was suited up and ready to go. My harness felt so tight I thought I might explode out of it. It was cutting into my shoulders and crotch—certainly not a woman-friendly look. But I didn't complain for fear they would make it too loose and I'd slip out of it at exactly the wrong moment.

Was there no happy medium for me?

The crew was urging us toward the edge of the bridge. We didn't have time to dillydally, as the show had been granted special access for the shoot. Bungee jumping was not ordinarily allowed off the Golden Gate Bridge due to boat traffic, but the producers had been able to close down the shipping lanes for one hour. Everything is for sale in San Francisco.

Car traffic, on the other hand, was still open on the bridge. Everything may be for sale, but even Hollywood has a budget. It was nerve-wracking and noisy to have the cars whizzing by.

"If you're nervous, maybe someone else can go first," Ty offered.

Cheryl said, "Someone needs to go, for God's sake. We need to get the show on the road. Aaron, want to go?"

Aaron looked surprised and Ty seemed relieved.

"Uh, yeah, certainly. Love to," Aaron said, although he looked unsure.

Cheryl turned to me and shouted, "You, get over here and watch him jump. We need the shot."

I don't know what I'd imagined when I thought about possibly finding love on this show, but it certainly hadn't included this six-foot-tall blond woman yelling at me constantly. In fact, she'd never even entered my mind and now she seemed never to leave.

Aaron took his place near the edge of the bridge and I stood next to him. The crew maneuvered around us, although one camera remained trained on my face, my every expression being recorded for posterity.

I hoped I didn't look nauseous. I certainly felt it.

Despite the tech people assuring me it was safe, jumping off the bridge was the last thing I wanted to do.

Down below I could see the Coast Guard boat hovering, one of the conditions the City of San Francisco had put on our use of the bridge.

Cheryl hadn't cared about the condition. In fact, she'd used it in negotiations for the show, requesting two cameramen be allowed to board and film our jumps.

"Are you ready, Aaron?" I asked, remembering to smile for the camera, but fearing it came off more as a grimace.

Aaron returned my smile, only his seemed genuine. "Oh, yeah. I've been jumping before. It's really a hoot. Feels like you're flying." He grabbed my hand and said, "Georgia, will you jump with me?"

Before I could reply, he turned to the tech. "Is her line ready?"

I heard the tech say, "She's—"

The din of traffic seemed to grow, a car honking at precisely that moment.

Then someone touched the small of my back and Cheryl yelled, "Action!"

Aaron let out a war cry and leapt, still squeezing my hand and pulling me forward. Someone pushed sharply on my back. I was off balance, trying to stay on the bridge.

Aaron didn't release me and his momentum propelled me forward. I slipped off the railing, falling with him, our hands finally disentangling.

The wind howled furiously at me. I howled back. My face tight, completely stretched with the force of gravity, my own saliva streaming across my checks as I screamed. Aaron was screaming, too, only his yells were ones of sheer delight.

His arms were flung out from his sides and he held them horizontally, imitating a plane.

We were soaring through the air like birds—only birds on a sharp descent, toward water that looked like a sheet of solid glass.

Adrenaline surged through my system, everything happening in slow motion: Aaron's expression of pure joy, the sunlight reflecting off the water and blinding me, the sound of the boat nearby.

The Coast Guard.

We were speeding, rushing closer and closer to the water. My breath caught in my throat, gagging me. I fought the impulse to retch.

How close to the water were we supposed to get?

When would the cord tighten?

What had the tech said?

All my mind could process was the water seemingly racing toward me.

And then, suddenly, my cord pulled taut and my descent stopped. I bounced up, the water receding rapidly. The negative g-force playing havoc with my stomach.

Out of nowhere a horrific crashing, splashing, screeching sound pierced my ears.

Water shot upward.

I pressed both hands over my mouth and tried to keep the bloodcurdling scream inside, but failed.

Aaron had hit the water.

His bungee cord finally tightened and snapped to position, but he was already underwater.

I continued flying upward, the distance between Aaron and me an eternity.

It felt as if I would crash right through the bottom of the bridge.

And then my descent began again, water rushing toward me.

Dear God, would I crash into the water, too?

I was paralyzed with fear as the cord tightened and then the water raced away. Then I was falling again, zooming toward the water, now my nemesis beckoning me, luring and tempting me to give up the fight.

The cord tightened one last time and I came to an abrupt stop, suspended above the bay—so close I could feel the salt spray on my skin.

I filled my lungs with air and screamed. I kicked and thrashed about, trying to break the harness that had just saved my life. Aaron was so close to me, I needed to grab him and pull him out of the water. I was vaguely aware of the Coast Guard boat nearby, the sound of the engine revving, the fumes of the diesel gagging me.

I heard the crackle of the Coast Guard's radio and then Cheryl's voice frantically shouting, "Hoist him up! Holy Christ! Hoist him up!"

I raised my head and was surprised to see the Coast Guard boat so close. Without words the entire crew had sprung into action. But one camera was still trained on me. The other camera zoomed in on Aaron.

I felt a jolt and realized I was being raised back toward the bridge.

"No, no, stop! Let me go—I can reach him!" I yelled.

Then the hoist on Aaron's harness began to crank and he was lifted out of the water.

His dripping, lifeless form hung like a rag doll from the bungee.

Two

The journey back to the bridge felt endless. My eyes were glued to Aaron, dangling beside me, and I couldn't stop myself from shouting repeatedly, "Aaron! Aaron! Answer me. Aaron! Respond, damn it!"

Then suddenly I was moving up and he seemed to be at a stand-still, maybe even descending.

What was going on?

Oh, God, was there another malfunction?

Would they drop me, too?

I stopped flailing and gripped the harness, as if gripping it would make me more secure somehow.

Aaron's body made its descent, the Coast Guard boat motoring directly underneath him.

They must have determined that the Coast Guard would have the fastest emergency response.

Taking a deep breath, I realized that I hadn't stopped screaming long enough to inhale. The water was now a great distance away, but I continued to shout in vain, and by this point, I don't think I was saying anything intelligible.

The vague thought that I was in hysterics floated across my mind, as if someone else had put it there, as if I were someone else and not this shrieking woman.

My body was hoisted over the railing of the bridge and, despite the hands gripping at me, I immediately collapsed onto the deck.

Pressing my cheek to the cold metal, I could feel the hum of the traffic reverberate through my body. My screams subsided and I found my voice matching the hum of the bridge in an odd, regressive, self-soothing manner. I was shaking uncontrollably and because I was splayed out on the deck, the sway of the bridge was more pronounced, aggravating my nausea.

Another thought, as if spoken from somewhere outside my head, commanded me to pull myself together. I stopped humming and fought to get my legs under me. I tried to stand up, but hands were pressing me down, a voice calling for a blanket.

"Stay here; don't try to get up," the voice said.

I couldn't identify the voice and I certainly wasn't going to obey it. Not now that I seemed to be getting myself back on track.

I pushed against the hands and flipped over. It was the doctor, Edward, trying to restrain me. I pounded my fists against his chest.

"Let me up. I've got to get to Aaron."

"He's with the first responders."

"I'm a first responder!" I yelled in his face.

"So am I," he said, calmly putting a hand on my forehead and pressing my head back on the deck.

So that was it? I was a victim? Someone in need of rescuing?

"No! No. I'm fine," I said, swallowing back vomit.

"Right, I know," he soothed. He was holding my wrist and I realized he was taking my pulse even as he said, "You had a shock. I just want to be sure."

I leapt forward, shoving my elbow into Edward's chest. This classic self-defense maneuver pushed him far enough from me that I was able to get to my feet. But it didn't dissuade him from charging me and grabbing me in a bear hug.

I punched at his shoulders fruitlessly. "Let me go!"

"No," he said. "I won't."

I buried my face in his chest as sobs racked my body.

He held me and stroked my hair, whispering soothing platitudes into my ear.

I was vaguely aware of the commotion around me. Cheryl yelling into her walkie-talkie, the crew rushing around, and the police sirens, but God help me, I was also aware of my body's reaction to Edward's touch.

His chest felt strong and solid. His body gave off a radiating heat that enveloped me, making me feel safe.

I could barely feel my legs beneath me and I realized Edward was holding me up. I tried to speak but no words came out. I was dizzy and desperately trying to hold on to consciousness.

Don't faint now, for God's sake! a voice inside my head warned.

Nonetheless, Edward picked me up and began to carry me toward the north side of the bridge, where our crew vehicles were parked.

Two police cruisers pulled to a stop.

A different kind of dread flooded me.

Would Paul respond to this call?

I recognized Martinez in one of the cruisers. I squinted at the other car. It was Wong. They stepped out of their respective vehicles as if in an orchestrated dance. Glancing at each other and communicating like cops, without words. Wong ran toward the crew and Martinez cut Edward off.

"Is that Georgia Thornton?" he asked.

Edward nodded. "I'm taking her to her RV."

"Does she need medical attention?" Martinez asked, grabbing at my hand.

I squeezed his hand. "Hey, Marty."

"I'm a doctor," Edward said.

Martinez ignored him and called for an ambulance into the walkie-talkie attached to his shoulder.

The fact that I was on the wrong side of things struck me hard. I was the one who was supposed to be communicating with SFPD, but I was no longer one of them . . .

That realization drew an involuntary noise from my throat, something akin to keening.

"You look like hell, Thorn," Martinez said.

I regained my composure and said, "Thanks. So kind of you to say."

Martinez smiled. "Okay, if you're still able to be a smart-ass, I think you'll live." He raised his eyebrows at Edward. "'Course, I ain't no doctor. Why don't you take her to the RV like you said and I'll check on you guys in a minute."

Edward nodded as two more patrol cars pulled over. I glanced at them: Lee and Schrader.

Everyone would now be responding to the code Martinez had put out.

No Paul yet, though. Thank God.

"Where's Paul?" I asked Martinez. "Will he be here?"

I cringed. The last thing I needed was for Paul to show up and, yet, my voice had semibetrayed me. It almost sounded hopeful.

Martinez's walkie-talkie crackled. "He's in court today."

A shudder went through my body. I took it as relief, but Edward said, "I need to get her warmed up before she goes into shock."

He didn't wait for Martinez to respond.

Inside the coach, Edward wrapped me in a blanket and squeezed my hand. "Do you have any brandy here?"

"What?" I asked.

He shrugged. "It calms the nerves."

"I thought that was an old wives' tale," I replied.

The door to the RV banged open and the horror writer, Scott, stood there.

"How's she doing? The medics are here; they want to take a look at her." He looked around at the white carpet and the mirrored ceilings. "Feels like Vegas in here."

A uniform peeked in. It was a firefighter I didn't know. He asked me a series of questions.

I answered as best I could, while eavesdropping on Scott and Edward.

"Holy cow! I couldn't have written something like that! Did you see him splat against the water?" Scott asked.

Edward frowned and shook his head, motioning in my general direction.

Scott didn't take the hint. "I gotta see the footage the camera crew took. Unbelievable!"

My disgust overtook me and I said, "How ghoulish."

Scott looked over at me, seemingly surprised that I'd overheard him. A lopsided smile filled his face. "You think that's ghoulish? Hell, nobody gets out alive."

I made a mental note: Scott would be the first to get the boot.

The fireman concluded that I had not suffered any physical trauma. Any trauma I felt was purely psychological. What else was new?

When he left, Edward searched inside my refrigerator and pulled out a bottle of water.

Scott peered over Edward's shoulder into the fridge. "What? No beer?"

Edward ignored him and passed me the water along with a small white pill.

"What's this?" I asked, fingering the tiny tablet.

"My personal stash," he replied. "Consider it a fast prescription fill."

Scott oohed. "Give me some of that, man. I've been traumatized, too."

"Undoubtedly, but your trauma was too long ago to fix now," Edward said. He turned to me. "Don't worry, it's only a Valium."

"No," I said.

Why this guy was a walking drugstore?

Ordinarily, I'd have grilled him about it, but since we'd just witnessed a man plummet to his death . . . Oh, God. What if it had been foul play?

The thought made my head ache.

No, it had been a dreadful accident. I kicked off my shoes and climbed under the covers.

The door to the RV popped open again and Martinez stuck his head inside. "We need statements from each of you."

Scott and Edward both got up.

Scott squeezed my foot through the blanket. "I'm glad you're all right."

"Oh, you have a heart after all?"

He pinched my big toe. "I'm sorry; I got off on the wrong foot with you."

Martinez cleared his throat and indicated that officers were waiting outside. Scott and Edward left the RV, the paper-thin door banging repeatedly against the wall as the wind whipped it out of Scott's hand. Martinez reached out and secured the door.

When he was sure they were gone he asked, "What the hell are you doing on a reality TV show?"

I moaned.

"Are those two of the guys you're supposed to be dating?"

I covered my head with the blanket.

After a moment I said, "Are you here on official business?"

"Of course," Martinez said.

"I fail to see the relevance of my dating life, then."

Martinez grumbled. "Okay, tell me what happened."

I cataloged the events for him, as though they had occurred to someone else and not me. I supposed that was some stupid defense mechanism. After all, the last thing I wanted to do was cry in front of him and have that get back to Paul.

Martinez took notes and when I finished, he asked, "You say someone pushed you?"

I frowned. "Pushed me? No, no. Well, not really. I mean, someone did press against me, but I assumed it was Cheryl just trying to get the scene going."

Martinez looked down at his notebook. "Was there an order you guys were supposed to jump in?"

"What do you mean?" I asked.

"Who was supposed to jump first?" Martinez asked. "Was it always supposed to be you and Aaron?"

I shrugged. "I didn't think we were supposed to jump together. I thought there was a safety distance issue. Anyway, I assumed I'd go last, but maybe I made that up."

I was starting to feel fuzzy around the edges.

"I think the cowboy wanted to go first. But the witch told Aaron and me to go," I said.

"Who's the witch?" Martinez asked. "Becca?"

I laughed. Only it lasted a little too long and bordered on hysterics.

I collected myself and said, "I'll tell her you said that. I meant the other witch, Cheryl."

Martinez made a note. "I'll talk to her again."

I sighed. "Yeah, there'll be a lot of talking. Lawyers, insurance people, even the supes from the city will get involved, I bet. Maybe even his royal highness, the mayor. You suppose he'll want a little PR out of this horrible accident?"

"Yeah, you're probably right. Seems like he always wants publicity."

"Who do you think will be the P.I. officer assigned? Kristen?"

"You know we don't get involved with that. Doesn't matter."

"It matters."

Even as the words tumbled out of my mouth I knew Martinez was right. I was no longer a public information officer. I'd been canned for releasing unauthorized information to the public. I'd been asked by the media about departmental overtime and potential steps to remediate the expense. At that the time I thought I was simply giving my opinion, but I soon learned that I wasn't allowed an opinion. At least that's what was made clear to me by the newly appointed police chief. He'd claimed that the overtime forecasts were confidential. City politics at its finest.

First, I'd been put on administrative detail, a.k.a. the rubber gun squad—where careers go to die.

Then, after my Skelly hearing, when the review board found me not guilty and recommended I be returned to my post, the decision to terminate me had ultimately been the chief's. The board only provides "recommendations." The chief, who reports to the mayor, makes the final decision even if it contradicts the review board.

I was asked to turn in my badge and gun.

Boom. Big mouth = career over.

Martinez tapped my arm. "Hey, you sure you're okay? Seems like you're kind of spacey."

My eyelids felt heavy, but I managed a nod.

"How come you haven't called Brandi?" Martinez continued. "She's hurt, you know, that you guys don't talk anymore. She wanted me to tell you that just because you and Paul aren't together doesn't mean *she* dumped you."

I cringed.

Brandi was Martinez's wife. As soon as Paul and I had begun dating, she'd attached herself to me, thinking that because Paul and Martinez were best friends, their significant others should be best friends, too. Problem was, I had a best friend—since middle school—and I'd never liked Brandi.

At that moment, Becca burst through the Prevost coach door. She barely acknowledged Martinez and hopped into bed with me. She scooped me into her arms.

"Oh, my God, Georgia! It could have been you!" She showered the top of my head with kisses. "It could have been you," she repeated.

Martinez mumbled something and left.

I closed my eyes and the entire day flashed through my mind.

It could have been me.

Something nagged at me. The makeup woman I hadn't placed . . . who was she? My mind was becoming increasingly fuzzy.

The coach seemed to be getting darker; either that or I was having a hard time keeping my eyes open.

"I'm exhausted," I murmured to Becca.

"No doubt. It was shock."

I turned over. "I think I need to crash for a bit."

"Yeah. Sleep. It'll do you good," Becca said.

I prayed I'd have a deep sleep and wake up a different person with a different life a million miles away.

Ridiculously, a smile came over my face. "At least I'm done with the show now." I sighed, relief wafting over me.

The last thing I heard before dozing off was Becca saying, "Done with the show? Oh, no, honey, they're not letting you off the show. Do you know what this kind of thing does for ratings?"

Three

....

INT. LIBRARY DAY

Aaron is looking directly at the camera. He's in his late twenties and dressed in a windowpane shirt and has boyish good looks. His foot is repeatedly tapping and his eyes shift back and forth.

CHERYL (O.S.)
So, Aaron, are you looking for love or money?

AARON
Love? Yeah, yeah, love . . . Um, I suppose everyone is looking for love, but if you mean right now, like, here on the show . . . uh, I don't think a reality TV show is the right place to find love.

CHERYL (O.S.)
What if after you meet our contestant you fall madly in love with her?

AARON
Oh. I'm sure she's a wonderful girl. I mean, sure, she's probably great. Nothing against her. It's just that I'm at a point in my life where I really need the money. I mean, I really need it, okay?

I awoke in the RV and peered out the door. We were back in Los Angeles, parked outside the mansion that the men lived in during the shoot. I was only allowed to have dates there, I couldn't move in any of my things. I couldn't cook or shower there and I certainly wasn't allowed to sleep in the incredible master suite.

How cruel was that? So close, and yet so far away.

At least there were no cameras in the bus. I could actually have a moment of privacy. But only a moment, as it seemed that every other second there was someone banging around outside or on my door.

One of the bangs was accompanied by Cheryl's voice singing out, "You awake, Sleeping Beauty?"

I swallowed past the dryness in my throat. "Come in."

Cheryl poked her head through the door. "Good. You're alive. You need to be at the men's house in an hour. Harris Carlson is going to make an announcement." She eyed me. "Christ. Get into hair and makeup. No one wants to see you like that!"

She let the door bang behind her.

I lay back down.

Harris Carlson was the host of the show. Surely "his" announcement was something that Cheryl and the other producers wanted to tell the cast at the same time. What would happen if I refused to go?

How had we gotten to L.A., anyway? Had I really slept the whole way?

And had SFPD really let us leave? The preliminary findings on Aaron must have pointed toward accidental death. Of course. What else could it have been?

Before I could contemplate things further, my door opened again and Becca came in.

"I was told you were given the warning call by the queen herself. You can't ignore her, you know. We need you now. You look like crap and we're not miracle workers."

She pulled me up by the wrist.

I moaned as I got to my feet.

"I don't wanna—"

"Oh, spare me." She pushed me toward the small toilet at the back of the coach. "I don't wanna do a lot of things, either. Most of all I don't want to send you to makeup until you brush your teeth."

I grudgingly stripped and stepped into a freezing shower. Becca was yelling at me, so I didn't have time to wait for the water heater to kick on.

Fortunately, the cold water helped snap the grogginess out of me.

What was Harris Carlson going to tell us? With any luck he'd tell us they were canceling the show. But wait: if that were the case, I wouldn't have to go to hair and makeup.

How could we continue to film after what had happened? How morbid.

My thoughts turned to Aaron. Had the rest of the cast been told about him? How could we possibly play this off for the cameras? The thought made me sick.

I shut off the water and toweled dry.

When I emerged from the bathroom, I spotted the outfit that Becca had laid out for me. It was the same violet halter dress I'd had on the first evening. Why in the world would they put me in the same dress?

I stepped out of the bus into bright L.A. sunlight and felt the sting on my eyes as if I were Count Dracula himself. I looked around for Becca, but didn't see her. I was anxious to pepper her with questions about the previous day and also what was going on now.

I made my way toward the tented area that doubled as hair and makeup. I sat in a fold-up camping chair and a gal with an enviable dye job went to work on my hair. She mumbled something to herself about my posture and I sat up straighter.

The same makeup artist from the day before materialized. She tilted my chin upward and began to apply foundation.

The gal doing my hair gave a garbled command through a mouthful of bobby pins. I figured it had something to do again with my posture, so I pressed my shoulders back and tried to study the woman doing my makeup. Unfortunately, I only got a flash of her face as she immediately went to work on applying my eye shadow.

Who did she remind me of?

They whipped me into readiness in short order and then I was ushered over to the men's house for the announcement.

I entered the mansion and was positioned near the fireplace mantel. The men were all seated and watching me. Had it not been for the unsettling feeling that was already descending upon me, it would have been nerve-wracking to have the nine of them gaping at me. As it was, I felt myself tense, gearing up for a fight. Like answering a call during those few short years I'd been on the beat. You know the news is never going to be good. It may not be fatal, but it's never good.

The guys who'd been on the date the day before—Ty, Pietro, Scott, and Edward—were all a bit ashen faced. The others were smiling and goofing around with each other. They seemed completely unaware of the disaster.

Hadn't anyone told them?

Cheryl entered, but instead of addressing us she put on a headset and made a beeline to the back of the set. She motioned for cameras to start rolling.

Harris Carlson, our ever-fearless host, entered, clicking on a champagne glass with a silver spoon to get our attention, apparently oblivious to the fact that he already had it.

"Gentlemen. Georgia!" He smiled widely, almost blinding me with his overwhitened teeth. "I understand that Aaron had an unfortunate accident yesterday and he won't be returning. So while that is certainly awful news, the good news is that there will be no elimination round." He smiled again.

I surveyed Edward and Scott. They were looking at the floor. Ty and Pietro were looking equally straight-faced and grim.

Nathan, a surfer with shaggy, long blond hair and killer blue eyes, asked, "What happened to Aaron?"

So they *didn't* know.

"Aaron is in the hospital," Harris said.

In the hospital? Was he alive?

My God, how had he survived?

At the very least he was either in a coma or paraplegic or both.

"Did he break a leg or something?" Mitch, a wealthy real estate investor, asked.

Harris toned down the megawattage on his smile. "C'mon, guys, you know I can't disclose his medical information."

Mitch sat up straighter and flashed me his own toothy grin. "Well, don't get me wrong. I hope he recovers fast, but that means I'm one step closer to ending up with this lovely lady." He wiggled his eyebrows at me. "And then there were nine."

"Yeah," Nathan agreed.

I refrained from grimacing. Good God, one had just quoted an Agatha Christie murder mystery and the other had exuberantly agreed. I had to get out of here.

Harris cleared his throat. "We won't be able to use the footage from yesterday. So we're going to refilm the first date. Sort of 're-create' it."

This time I must have visibly grimaced because the cameraman normally trained on me panned to the fireplace. After a moment, he refocused on me.

Re-create?

What the hell did he mean, *re-create*?

I felt my ire rising and I couldn't wait for the shoot to be over to confront Cheryl.

"And I should tell you that we have a new cast member. Sorry, Mitch. Not one step closer to the lovely Georgia, but sort of like a do-over." He upped the wattage on his grin.

Do-over?

Aaron didn't get a do-over. What the hell was going on?

Harris pivoted in his red Berluti loafers and motioned toward the door. "Gentlemen, meet your newest competition."

Two cameras panned toward the door. Another stayed trained on me and the last on the remaining men in the room. Everyone's reaction was sure to be captured and manipulated however Cheryl thought would get the most mileage.

My mouth went dry and I suddenly felt light-headed.

It couldn't be true.

Through the doors walked Paul Sanders, my ex-fiancé. He even had the nerve to wear the tux he hadn't worn to our wedding.

Four

First I fought the wave of nausea that swept through my body, then the urge to punch Paul in the face.

Harris introduced him as "Paul, the Insurance Salesman." Paul flashed a grin at Harris and said, "Thanks for the warm welcome."

He turned to me and outstretched his hand. "So nice to meet you."

What kind of charade was this?

Nice to *meet* you?

There was something in his eyes. A warning. *Play along, Georgia,* it said.

I clenched my teeth and gripped his hand. A zing, on par with a full-on electric shock, zapped through my waist and hips. I didn't trust my voice, so I said nothing.

I glimpsed myself in the mirror over the fireplace and realized that I looked mean. Downright hard. Why would any of these guys want to date me? I forced a smile.

Paul smiled back. He looked every bit as Hollywood-handsome as the others did.

He released my hand and took a seat on the couch next to Ty, who touched the brim of his hat and winked at me.

Harris clapped his hands loudly. "So, Georgia, you've met your eligible bachelors—or not so eligible." He gave a little shake of his head as if he had just amused himself to no end. "You will select five for your first group date and tomorrow the fun will begin."

It dawned on me then: The introduction to Paul was meant to replace meeting Aaron. Redo, re-create. A little Hollywood magic, some snips and edits, and Aaron never existed.

"Cut," Cheryl yelled.

The cameramen took their units off their shoulders and left the area, presumably heading to the craft services area they had set up next door with unlimited coffee and tables overflowing with pastries.

"Okay," Cheryl continued, "gentlemen, go change, then come back to this room and lounge around waiting for the invite card. Georgia, you can go get ready for the date."

It was an order, not a request.

I never did well with orders; my stomach churned at the thought that that very trait had been one of the reasons for the end of my police career and likely even one of the reasons for the end of my engagement with Paul. But, hell, sometimes you can't fight your nature.

"What's going on?" I demanded.

Harris linked his arm through mine. "I know you're probably watching your figure, but they have amazing doughnut holes next door. Why don't you have one? I'll watch your figure for you."

He raised his eyebrows at me in what I was sure was supposed to be a flirtatious way, only it came off flat and sort of like a cautionary signal.

I glanced at Paul. His smile was intact but the warning message in his eyes remained.

Everyone was telling me to shut up and leave the room.

"We'll have you change into your date clothes and then you can get back to hair and makeup," Harris said, as he led me to the craft services area.

I was fuming. "Tell me what's happening."

He looked confused. "With what?"

"With what?" I practically screamed at him. "With Aaron, with Paul, with the do-over, with—"

The cameraman at the craft services table stared at us. Becca appeared at my side and grabbed my elbow. "Hey. That was fast," she said.

Harris ignored Becca. "Well, you were there. You know the poor guy isn't coming back and we can't air what we shot. So we're doing it over on a set, with safety nets."

Becca glanced at her watch. "In about forty minutes, to be exact—"

Harris laughed. "You better skip the doughnuts, cupcake!" he said, proceeding to pop three doughnut holes into his mouth in rapid succession.

Becca rolled her eyes at him, telegraphing that the conversation was over. Then she piled a plate with cheese and crackers, placing two grapes on top. "One for me, one for you. We need to eat our fruit. Come on. We'll take this to go."

"Spill it," I said the moment we were outside.

She shrugged. "We need to reshoot the first date. What was that about Paul, though?"

"He's here. He's the bachelor replacing Aaron."

Becca's eyes widened and her jaw dropped.

I leaned into her personal space. "Yes, Becca, exactly. How *did* that happen?" I mocked her expression of outrage and matched it with my own.

She closed her mouth and stood up straight, taking on an air of indignation. "You're not accusing me of anything, right?"

I squinted at her. "What could I possibly be accusing you of?"

"I . . . um . . . I wasn't for getting him on the show," she stuttered.

I pressed my lips together and motioned with my hand for her to continue.

She glanced around to make sure we were alone. "I told Cheryl it was a bad idea."

"Uh-huh. And how did Cheryl come up with the idea exactly?"

"It wasn't me. I swear."

"Is he undercover?"

Becca shrugged helplessly.

Paul worked on 35 Car for SFPD. It was an undercover detail known to have free range to do what they pleased. But if Paul was here on assignment, why had we been able to leave the jurisdiction of San Francisco?

Further, if Paul was undercover, it could only mean that Aaron's fall hadn't been an accident.

A strange energy surged through my body.

An active investigation?

The door from the craft services room flew open and Cheryl

appeared next to us on the sidewalk. She quickly assessed the situation. "What are you doing still in your evening clothes? Didn't Becca tell you that we're leaving in a few minutes?"

Becca popped a grape into her mouth and gave me a "don't tangle with Cheryl" look.

I ignored her. "What's the deal with my ex-fiancé showing up as a bachelor?"

Cheryl's face registered surprise, then changed into something else. Something along the lines of devilish delight. "Your what?"

I stared at her, then at Becca, who now seemed to have enormous interest in the sole grape on her plate.

"I find it hard to believe you didn't know," I said.

"Well, I didn't." Cheryl smiled and studied Becca, who studied her grape. "But that certainly is a pleasant surprise." She stroked her chin and I imagined her with a goatee much like I would Satan. "We can't let on to the others, you know. It wouldn't seem fair that you've already had a relationship with one of the bachelors."

Before I could protest, she wagged a finger at me. "You should be happy. It's to your advantage that you already know he's *unavailable*. Practically cheating."

She gave a vulgar snicker.

I clenched my fists, reminding myself that while it would probably stop her snorting if I smacked her in the nose, it most likely would lead to problems. I took a deep breath and simply said, "I'm not doing it."

Cheryl stared at me. "Not doing what?"

"The show," I said firmly.

Cheryl waved her hand at me and said to Becca with a laugh, "Pfft. What a prima donna."

I walked away from them. I heard the door to the craft services room open and close and then Becca was at my side. I glanced backward: Cheryl was gone. Becca grabbed my arm.

"Honey, you can't walk off like that. You're under contract, remember?"

"Then I'm calling my lawyer," I said.

"You don't have a lawyer, sweetie, and you can't afford one. Besides, even if you did get one, the network has an entire legal *division*. I mean, who are you kidding? You can't just walk off."

I wasn't listening to her anymore. She was right. I didn't have an attorney and I couldn't afford one, but there was someone.

I turned back toward the bachelor house.

"Where are you going?" Becca asked.

"Richard! He's an attorney."

"Richard? From the show?" Becca sounded slightly hysterical.

I nodded and kept walking.

"You not allowed to go in there without a crew," Becca said.

"Then come with me. You're part of the crew," I said.

"No. It's not the same. I mean, cameras and—"

Suddenly the walkie-talkie at her waist crackled. Cheryl's voice came over the line. "Did you get the *prima* into hair and makeup yet?"

Becca looked at me. I shook my head and said, "No! Tell her I'm not going to do it. I'm done."

Becca grabbed the walkie-talkie off her belt and said, "Yup, on our way."

Becca steered me toward hair and makeup, all the while chatting back and forth with someone other than Cheryl on her walkie-talkie.

We both knew the reason I'd continue on the show was for her. She'd been my best friend since middle school, practically a sister to me. There was nothing I wouldn't do for her. She'd gotten me on as the lead when my life had come unglued and if I bailed on the show I'd ruin her chances to produce her own series down the road.

Not to mention, if there was an active investigation in progress . . . and I somehow managed to help . . . perhaps even resolved the case . . .

Although, how could Aaron's fall be anything other than an accident? Was he really in the hospital? Was it possible he had died and the producers were just placating the cast?

No, that didn't make sense. If Aaron had died, there would be legal implications to the producers for not discussing the information with us. And yet, what was Paul doing here? If he was here undercover, that was one thing, but was I going to have to date him?

"Leave her in the dress," Becca said to a blond woman who had materialized in front of us.

"What? Why?" I asked.

"We need to reshoot the intro scene," she answered.

"The whole scene? I thought we were only doing the first date again."

Becca gave me a strange look. "An intern just reviewed the tapes. Aaron is in practically every shot at the cocktail party. We need to reshoot the introductions so we can match up the lighting. Cheryl wants to rerun the scene from the top."

I stood on the cobblestones in front of the mansion, waiting for the limo to arrive. They were only driving it around the corner. What a joke.

I smiled for the camera and refrained from tapping my foot with impatience. However, clad in the awesome Sergio Rossi shoes that exactly matched the violet of my dress, I think the cameraman might have been happy to zoom in on the tap.

The first time we'd done this I'd been nervous and excited. Had it really been only a few days before? I'd been eager to meet the men, wondering if one really could be my Prince Charming. All certainly were handsome and I'd even felt a little zing with some of them, but now the entire process seemed ludicrous.

I'd quickly lost my patience with the camera. That had been almost immediate. The first night I'd been talking to

Aaron and had completely forgotten where I was, his boy-next-door charm sucking me in and making me feel like I was the only person on earth. Then Cheryl had interrupted us, repositioning Aaron and me. When he'd asked her if his lighting was all right, I'd lost that loving feeling.

The limo stopped several yards away from me. The driver got out and opened the door. Pietro stepped out. He looked as stunning as he did the first time I saw him—his Italian good looks complemented by the tux he was wearing. He crossed the pathway confidently and outstretched his hand to me.

"I am Pietro. So happy to make your acquaintance, *signorina*."

I squeezed his hand. "Thank you. Yes, me, too."

He took my hand and pressed his lips against it. "We will have fun inside, no?"

I smiled. "Yes."

He gave my hand another little squeeze and winked. I couldn't help but feel he was winking more toward the camera than at me. He released my hand and strode off toward the door.

I took a deep breath; the next person out of the limo was Scott, with his shaved head looking sexy as ever. He crossed the cobblestone path and smiled at me. He took my right hand in his and with his left grabbed my elbow. The warmth of his hand sent a shock through my body.

"I'm Scott," he said, his voice smooth and polished, making me flush.

I nodded and squeaked out, "Pleased to meet you."

This was ridiculous. Why was I having such a schoolgirl reaction to a man squeezing my elbow? Especially this one. The gruesome, ghoulish horror writer!

It had to be hormonal.

As if sensing my hesitation, Scott released my hand, saying, "I'll see you inside."

The next person out of the limo was Ty. He was wearing his signature cowboy hat and boots. He put a hand to his hat and tipped it, saying, "Howdy, ma'am."

"Howdy," I said.

He looked me up and down and said, "Sure are lucky, the little lady they picked for us looks good to me."

I looked him up and down in return and I couldn't help but smile. God, he was sexy.

"I'll be looking for you inside," he said as he left.

Next was Dr. Edward. He walked toward me, his gait projecting a certain resoluteness. He stuck out his hand and said, "I'm Edward. It's a pleasure to make your acquaintance this evening."

The first time we'd met we'd had a little repartee about his being a doctor. I'd said something about his making my heart go pitter-patter and he'd promised to give me a checkup.

Somehow I felt compelled to let him make that first impression again with the audience. So I placed my hand over my heart and gave him my corny line. Then he said his line.

We both laughed and he strode toward the door.

The next person out of the car was Nathan, the surfer. He was the only one so far not dressed in a tux. Instead, he was wearing tight-fitting jeans and an orange tee that set off his tan and showed his massive biceps. Under one arm was his surfboard. His smile lit up his face—almost making me forget that the last time around Aaron had been the final guy to step out of the first limo.

Nathan strode toward me and wrapped his free arm around my waist. He easily lifted me off my feet and twirled me. "Wow," he gushed. "When I signed up for this show I was sure hoping the girl would be hot and you are. Doll, you're smoking."

Every alarm signal in my body went off.

The first time around, Nathan had done exactly the same thing, only I'd thought he'd been sincere. How had he managed to do and say exactly the same thing in the same way? Edward had needed prompting and even then it came off flat, but not Nathan. No, this was just an act for him. Now I knew he was definitely on the show for the money.

I pasted a smile on my face. "Nice to meet you."

He gave a little shake of his head and his longish blond curls shook. He licked his lips and headed toward the door.

As soon as he'd disappeared through the door, Harris came out to make small talk with me.

"Cut," Cheryl called. She took Harris aside and whispered something to him.

A team of hair and makeup people descended upon me. One stylist was doing something to my hair and the other woman was touching up my face powder. The one doing my makeup was the same woman I'd been trying to place earlier. I studied her while she fluffed me up.

Suddenly I pictured her in another setting . . . a courtroom.

My stomach lurched.

This woman touching up my makeup bore a striking resemblance to Teresa Valens, a woman I had put behind bars five years before.

"Clear the set!" Cheryl yelled.

Teresa flitted off.

Good God. What would Teresa be doing here? And she'd been on the set in San Francisco. My breath caught as I recalled standing on the railing of the bridge and the hand pressing against my back just at the moment when I needed my balance most. Could that accident have been intended for me?

Before I could process the thought the limousine arrived again, with its second load of passengers.

Richard, the attorney, stepped out. He wore an ascot and a top hat. I smiled inwardly because he looked like the type of guy my dad would want me to end up with.

He oozed class. He introduced himself, kissed my hand, and walked into the house. I liked the simple introduction.

Next was Bruce, the techie geek. He smiled, revealing a slightly crooked front tooth, which reminded me of my first boyfriend in fifth grade. I had trusted him immediately.

Then out of the limo came Mitch, the real estate investor. He walked with confidence and then read me a cheesy poem from one knee. I laughed and thanked him for the poetry.

Next out of the limo was Derek; he used a cane and slightly hobbled. He had a military crew cut and I learned the first night that he'd been injured in Afghanistan and had a few bolts in his ankle. He was expected to have a full recovery but it was still early for him, thus the cane.

Finally, Paul got out of the limo. Unexpectedly my entire body began to shake. I wanted to run into his arms and tell him about Teresa Valens and finally feel like there was something in my life that I didn't have to go at alone.

Paul walked over to me and smiled stiffly. He said, "I'm Paul."

My breath caught and I felt a pain in my chest as if my

heart had just cracked. I fought the tears threatening to spring into my eyes. I wouldn't give him the satisfaction of seeing me cry. He gripped my hands. "Georgia, you're shivering." He released my hands and immediately took off his coat and wrapped it over my shoulders.

"Here, this will keep you warm."

My heart sank. He'd misunderstood me yet again.

He put his arm around me and led me toward the house.

"Cut!" Cheryl yelled.

Six

INT. LIBRARY DAY

Bruce is looking directly at the camera. Behind him are some nondescript bookshelves and a small low table with a lamp. He is about thirty, wearing a green polo shirt with khaki pants. He has a few days' stubble on his checks and his hair is slightly long and unkempt.

CHERYL (O.S.)
So tell us, Bruce, you're a Silicon Valley guy?

BRUCE
(*smiling*) Yup, yup. Living the California dream. I have a high-tech company in Palo Alto. We design video games. Our latest release is Mad Bees. Have you heard of it?

CHERYL (O.S.)
No.

BRUCE
(*sitting up straighter and jiggling his legs*)
Oh, sure, sure. Not everyone's heard of it. But, you know, we're exploring the plight of the bumblebee.

CHERYL (O.S.)
Like in *Fantasia*?

BRUCE
No, no. *Plight*, not *flight*. And anyway, *Fantasia* was . . . uh, never mind. The point is the declining population of the bumblebee is alarming–

CHERYL (O.S.)
Bumblebees or honeybees?

BRUCE
Both, really, but our first merchandise release was about the bumblebee. It was more of a marketing decision rather than ecological, I'll admit. Bumblebees are brighter yellow and our focus groups consistently kept picking the bumblebee over the honeybee, and, hey (*flashes a winning smile*), you gotta listen to focus groups, right?

CHERYL (O.S.)
Right. Right. So, your business is doing well. You said you're living the dream?

BRUCE
Business is booming, yes. More than I'd ever imagined. But there *is* something missing in my life.

CHERYL (O.S.)
Let me guess. You're on the show to find love.

BRUCE
Now, that would be a dream come true.

The crew ushered us to the back of the mansion, poolside. The sun was setting lower in the sky, casting a romantic feel around the patio. Everyone was handed a fake cocktail by a crew member and told to mingle and smile.

My drink was blue-colored soda water with a lime on top. Cheryl had positioned herself behind me, within earshot but out of camera range. I sipped at my drink and tried to clear my head, finding it difficult to concentrate with Cheryl breathing down my neck.

The men were clustered around, talking to each other. When Edward saw me alone, he broke away from his group and approached me. "Can I steal you away for some chitchat?"

"What are you hoping to get out of this?" I asked him.

I heard Cheryl snort behind me.

Battle-ax.

Edward smiled. "Love, of course."

Well, they were all going to say that, now, weren't they? They weren't going to tell me to my face that they were in it for the money. No wonder Cheryl had snorted. I was an idiot!

Edward gazed at me and I felt a mild nervousness.

Were those butterflies in my stomach?

A huge splash came from the pool. Edward and I turned toward it. Nathan had flopped into the pool and now was climbing on top of his surfboard.

"Come on, guys. I need some waves," Nathan yelled.

It didn't take much; within seconds Bruce and Mitch were in the water splashing about and causing a tidal wave. Nathan did a backflip off his board with a great wallop.

"Someone is going to crack their head open on the side of the pool," Edward said.

An involuntary shudder coursed through my body, as images of Aaron slamming into the bay filled my mind.

Edward placed a soothing hand on the small of my back and I was vaguely aware that the cameras seemed to zoom in on us.

I swallowed past the horrific images in my head and said, "It's a good thing we have a doctor nearby."

Edward laughed. "Guys will do anything to get your attention, right?"

I shrugged and took a deep breath. "Tell me about yourself."

"I'm from the Bay Area. I graduated from Stanford Medicine two years ago and now I'm an intern at UCSF."

If he was from the Bay Area and had lived and worked in San Francisco, then it was possible that he knew about my humiliating departure from my job as a public information officer. My termination had been all over the local news. I stuffed down the feeling of disgrace that threatened to surface and focused instead on the butterflies.

Edward was kind and warm, and I already knew his bedside manner was appealing.

Before I could speak, a crew member thrust a towel in my hand. I watched Nathan climb out of the pool, his wet shirt clinging to his chest. He made a point of disrobing and tossing the sopping clothes aside.

I broke away from Edward and tossed the towel to Nathan. "Here. You're all wet behind the ears."

Nathan laughed. He made no move to catch the towel; he simply let it hit him in the chest and slither to the floor.

We locked gazes, him daring me with his incredible blue eyes to pick the towel up from around his feet.

"Unfortunately for you, I stoop for no man," I said to Nathan.

He lunged at me and gripped me around the waist. "Unfortunately for you, I love being wet." He lifted me in his arms and jumped into the pool. We went under for a moment, and I struggled to break his hold, but he held tight as we surfaced. I shook my wet hair out of my face and was ready to scream when he planted a kiss on my lips.

He pressed against me and the kiss lasted longer than I expected, sending a chill throughout my body.

He grabbed at my boobs and I pulled away, angry.

He grinned. "I guess you don't mind getting a little wet, either."

I disentangled myself from his arms and swam to the side of the pool. My eyes caught Paul's, shooting daggers at me.

Pietro was standing at the edge of the pool with a towel. I reached under the water and freed my feet from the beautiful designer shoes. I handed first one and then the other to Pietro. He grabbed the shoes and made a cute little pout, saying, "Poor Sergios."

I laughed.

Earlier in the evening I'd thought a close-up of the shoes would have been nice, but now everything seemed hopeless.

I hoisted myself out of the pool, the halter dress dripping and clinging to me.

Pietro wrapped the towel around me and whispered in my ear, "Georgia, we need to find a place to speak without cameras or microphones. I have urgent information."

I tensed.

Pietro made a fuss about rubbing my back. "Oh, you are cold! We must go inside and sit by the fire."

"Cut," Cheryl yelled.

The cast seemed to move about quickly, more or less disappearing immediately. Pietro gave me a discreet look to make sure I'd understood him. I nodded.

The only remaining people on the set were myself, Cheryl, and a cameraman.

The towel fell from around my shoulders and slipped to the ground. As I reached for it, I noticed my breasts protruding rather scandalously from the dress.

"Crap," I muttered to no one in particular. "I'm practically falling out of this dress."

Cheryl raised an eyebrow at the cameraman. "Maybe she'll make an okay bachelorette after all."

Seven

Cheryl gave me curt instructions to get back to my RV and rest. The reshoot of my first date would take place early the next morning.

I was happy to be done for the day; my head seemed ready to explode. I wrapped the towel tight around my shoulders and walked around the mansion toward my coach. As I walked, I thought about Pietro's comment. What could he need to speak to me about that was urgent? Did it have anything to do with Aaron? Perhaps he had seen something, but if so, surely he'd have told the police.

I heard my name called and I turned to see Becca running down the walkway toward me. "Hey, Georgia, the scene was great! Cheryl is very happy."

"Really?"

"Hell yes. Your boobs flew out of your dress when you jumped into the pool. How could she not be happy?"

"What?" My hands instinctively flung toward my chest. My cleavage seemed intact. "No," I said, relieved.

Becca nodded emphatically. "I was monitoring camera one from inside the studio. The girls showed up. They're already editing the scene for the promos."

"But it's impossible—it's some phony camera angle or something."

Becca laughed. "Oh, please—"

I opened my towel and showed her my dress. "Come on, how could my boobs fall out of the dress and then magically fall back in? I mean, I didn't fix my—"

I stopped short, recalling my kiss with Nathan.

"What?" Becca asked.

"Nathan. I thought he was copping a feel, but he was actually—"

"Aww. How sweet! He was trying to protect your dignity."

I buried my face in my hands. "Unbelievable! I'll never live it down!"

Becca pooh-poohed me. "Ah, a little skin, so what?"

"Can you lose the scene?" I asked.

Becca looked at me incredulously. "What do you mean, lose the scene?"

"I don't know, pour coffee on the film or something?"

"We're digital—"

"Well, erase or delete or whatever." I shrugged. "Come on, it happens all the time, I'm sure."

Becca straightened. "We're not cops, you know, who can just tamper with evidence any ol' way they choose."

"What? What's that supposed to mean?"

"Now, that probably happens all the time—I'm not saying you, but you know. Dirty cops. Like—"

I grabbed her by the arm. "Shh." I glanced around us to make sure we were still alone.

Becca stood frozen a moment and then whispered, "I can't lose the scene. I'd get fired."

I nodded.

I knew what being fired was like. Regardless whether you're innocent or not, it still sucks.

"Never mind. I'm sorry I asked. Of course you can't do that. I wouldn't want you to do anything that would get you in trouble."

Becca nodded. "Thanks."

"Speaking of trouble, though, Teresa Valens is here. She's one of the makeup artists."

Becca frowned. "Who?"

"Teresa Valens!" I whispered. "Do you remember? I put her behind bars for murdering her husband."

Becca shook her head, confused, then covered her mouth with her hand and spoke through her fingers. "I remember vaguely. Was she the lady who shot him dead and then stabbed him for good measure?"

I nodded. "That's her."

Becca suddenly looked frightened. "What is she doing out? I thought she got twenty years. And you think she's here?"

"She's the makeup lady!"

"Which one? We have several, but no, no, we don't have a Teresa Valens."

"The one who does *my* makeup. She did my makeup today and yesterday."

"That's Florencia. Not Teresa."

"She's going by a fake name, then. I'm sure it's her."

"What do we do?" Becca asked.

"Can you look into her file for me?"

Becca grimaced. "You just said you weren't going to ask me to do anything that could get me in trouble."

"Sorry. Sorry, I know. Can you get me onto the Internet?"

As part of the standard contract for the show I'd agreed to have no Internet or phone access. Apparently, they didn't want me spilling my guts to any media outlets before they could control the story.

Becca shook her head. "No. I'd definitely get in trouble for that. I'll look her up."

"And Aaron, too. Find out what happened. If he's dead or in the hospital or what."

Becca nodded. "Okay, let's get you out of the wet dress before you shake yourself to death."

She put her arm around me and I realized I was shivering.

I bundled myself tighter in the towel. "One more thing."

"Crap. What?"

"Pietro—"

"Pietro, mm-mm. Now, he's hot, isn't he?" She steered me toward my RV. "You want some time alone with him, off camera, is that it?"

"He said he needs to talk to me."

She raised an eyebrow. "After you flashed everyone I'm sure he wants more than just—"

"Can you arrange it?"

She sighed. "For someone who says she doesn't want to get me in trouble, you're certainly asking for a lot of favors."

I cringed. "I know."

"I'll see what I can do," Becca said.

I held up my hand and placed my forefinger and thumb an inch apart. "And one more teeny tiny thing."

"You want me to run to the liquor store?"

I laughed. "Weren't you going to do that anyway?"

Becca looked at me through her lashes. "What else do you want?"

"I'd like to see the tapes from yesterday."

The following morning I awoke to an incessant banging on the door to the coach. It was a production assistant, there to usher me into hair and makeup.

This time I was given a proper dressing room inside the studio where we'd refilm a new first date.

I was given the tightest jeans I've ever managed to shimmy myself into and then a top with a deep V cut. Clearly they were hoping to replicate the bosom sensation from the day before.

When I complained to Kyle, one of the stylists, he shrugged and said, "Girl, if you got it, flaunt it. Ain't nobody ever made it in this town by being a prude."

I hadn't seen Becca all morning and now I was beginning to worry that I might have gotten her into trouble. Curiously, Teresa Valens was nowhere to be seen, either, and Kyle moved from my hair to my makeup.

"Where's the other lady?" I asked, trying to sound as nonchalant as possible. Fortunately, sounding nonchalant is practically mandatory for public information officers, so it was a skill I had honed over the few years I'd had the job.

Kyle shrugged and dabbed a small brush into a black tin and, sounding more nonchalant than I did, asked, "Who?"

Clearly, I hadn't mastered the skill as much as I'd thought.

"The lady who did my makeup yesterday. Florencia, is it?"

"Close your eyes," Kyle said, tipping my chin up with his hands. "Don't know. Don't worry, doll face, I can do makeup better than anyone."

When Kyle was satisfied with my "look," I was taken to the set. There was a huge faux rock-climbing set over fifteen stories high; it was awe inspiring. The cast members were instructed to stand on a platform that was designed and painted to look as if we were outdoors, climbing the Marin Headlands with the Golden Gate Bridge in the background. We waited while the safety crew set out commercial-grade air cushions and a safety net.

I noticed none of the technicians helping us this time had been present during our bungee-jump fiasco at the Golden Gate Bridge.

Cheryl pulled me aside. "I'd like you to flirt with each bachelor before they begin the climb. You can go last."

"If I'm a good girl, you promise you'll let me live?" The words tumbled out of my mouth before I knew I'd said them.

Cheryl looked appropriately offended. "What?"

I shrugged. "Someone gave me a little shove off the bridge the other day. I sure am lucky my bungee wasn't the one that failed."

Her face turned beet red. "What do you mean? You were supposed to jump. We couldn't wait all day for you."

"It was you, then, right? A little push in the right direction?"

She leaned into my face and through clenched teeth said,

"Listen, the authorities are looking into it. It was an equipment malfunction. The subcontractor is being served as we speak. Now, you'll do as I say. Flirt, be cute and sexy, be someone America can love."

I snorted. Someone America could love? I was barely someone a single man could love, let alone an entire nation.

Before I could reply Cheryl turned and started calling out places for the cast. Pietro was supposed to go first.

Pietro and I approached the faux rock wall. Silent fans were turned on and suddenly my hair was flipping about my face.

Pietro easily smoothed down my hair with his large hands, cradled my face, and looked me in the eyes. "*Cara mia*, I will climb to the top and proclaim your beauty for the entire world to hear."

I smiled at him, completely disarmed by his handsome face.

"You promise me a glass of champagne, no?" he asked.

According to the producers, I'd have to eliminate someone that night at the cocktail party. In order for a bachelor to stay I had to offer him a glass of champagne. One man would not be offered a glass and would have to leave immediately.

"We'll toast," I said.

Pietro smiled, although he looked at me intensely. I nodded at him, hoping to reassure him that I'd find a place for us to talk.

He began his ascent up the rock wall.

My stomach clenched, despite the safety net below, and I had to look away. My heart pounded against my chest and I forced myself to calm down.

Pietro proceeded sure-footed up the wall, making it look easy. When he reached the top, he was greeted by two techs who pulled him onto the landing.

"That was amazing!" he said, his face flushed with excitement as he yelled down toward me.

"Cut," Cheryl called.

"Can we do something about her?" Cheryl asked Kyle. "She looks green."

Kyle shrugged. "Honey, I can fix green, but what about her expressions? I can't do anything about that."

I pressed my lips together to keep myself from shouting obscenities at them. Paul stepped into my range of sight. "Why don't we film our moments with Georgia and then let her go have a coffee or something? She doesn't have to watch us climb, right?"

Cheryl studied Paul a moment. She looked at him like a cat watching its prey: salivating and bloodthirsty. "Good idea, hunk. Let's have her do her moments with everyone and then we can let the diva rest."

I tensed. Did this mean I wouldn't have to rock climb? The last thing I wanted to do was hover in the air, even over a safety net. At the same time that I felt relieved I was angry. Why did Paul have to speak up like that? Like I was some stupid little girl and he was my protector.

"I'm okay," I lied.

Cheryl laughed. "Sure, honey, but what matters to the camera is how you look." She held a hand up to ward off my argument. "And, listen, I'm being nice here. You don't look *okay*."

Scott, Edward, and Ty stepped up onto the platform.

"I think it'll be for the best," Edward said with a note of diplomacy in his voice.

"No one wants you to have another shock, sweetheart," Ty said.

Paul crossed his arms over his chest, but only glared at me.

Scott shrugged and laughed. "I wouldn't blame you for taking the easy way out."

I stared at Scott. The easy way out? He was calling me a coward to my face.

"I'm not scared—"

Cheryl stepped in. "I make the decisions around here," she snapped. "You all have your moments with her and then I want her off the set!"

The crew magically got into place and I found myself face-to-face with Edward. He made a bit of small talk with me and held my hand a moment. Cheryl ended the scene with Edward climbing into position on the rock wall.

Next was Ty. He said something about southern hospitality that I barely registered and then climbed onto the wall.

My scene with Paul was stopped and started several times because the techs were having problems with the wind fans. If they couldn't get that right, what were the chances of everyone being unscathed from the climb? Safety net or not.

They finally had the fans back up and running. My hair was flying about my face and Paul reached out to pull a strand off my cheek. I grabbed his hand and, before I could check myself, begged, "Paul, please don't climb it."

He squeezed my hand and said, "Honey, I'm going to be fine."

Hearing him call me honey constricted my throat and I felt a rush of emotion. I grabbed at his wrists, but he evaded me and climbed onto the rock wall.

Cheryl stopped the scene and called for Scott to take his place. Before he did she whispered something to him.

Scott approached me with the cameras still rolling.

"Wish me luck," he said.

"Good—"

He reached around the back of my neck and pulled me into him. He pressed his lips eagerly to mine.

Was he only kissing me because Cheryl had told him to? When was she going to call "Cut"?

He released me. "Thank you. At least if I die now, I'll die happy."

Despite the fact that he was an awesome kisser, he'd definitely be the first to leave tonight. I couldn't let his sex appeal distract me. Not to mention, he'd been callous about Aaron's fall and likely he was probably in it for the money anyway.

Scott climbed onto the wall and made it halfway up before Cheryl ended the scene. He rappelled down the wall and stood next to me.

"I think we got what we need," Cheryl said, looking to the crew for confirmation.

"We'll film a picnic lunch later, where you all can celebrate your 'amazing climbs.'" She made air quotes with her fingers, clearly wanting to emphasize how pathetic she thought we all were. She turned to leave.

Becca, who was huddled with a cameraman, called out, "Take a break, everyone."

The cast and crew dispersed. I looked around for Pietro. Where was he? I hadn't seen him since he finished the climb.

Scott joined me. "I'm sorry this isn't actually a date. I'd love to spend more time with you."

I laughed. "Yeah, right. Did she put you up to the kiss?"

"Who?"

"The producer. I saw you two whispering."

"Do I look like the kind of guy who'd kiss someone if I didn't want to?" he asked.

"You look like the kind of guy who wants—"

Paul stepped between us. "Hey, Georgia, can I get a moment?"

Scott turned to me. "I'll catch you later. We'll drink some champagne." He winked at me and walked off.

Paul lowered his voice. "Is there somewhere we can talk?"

"This way." I guided him down the corridor toward my dressing room. "What are you doing here, Paul?"

"You know that I'm on task force 35."

I eyed him. "So, you've been assigned? Is Aaron dead?"

"Not dead. Coma."

"But it's an open investigation?"

"You don't think it was an accident, do you? Guy's equipment malfunctioning like that."

Nerves overtook my stomach and I struggled to identify whether it was because Paul was standing so close to me or because of what he was saying. "You think it was a setup?"

"Yes," Paul said.

My breath caught in my throat. I thought about Teresa Valens. "Do you think it was intended for me?"

Paul looked surprised. "For you? Why?"

I shrugged nervously. "I think Teresa Valens is one of the makeup ladies."

He stared at me. "That's impossible. She's incarcerated."

"Can you see if she walked, got parole, appealed, something? I'm sure it's her."

He cleared his throat. "I'll look into it. In the meantime, I need you to keep the guys who were on the first date around. Get rid of the surfer tonight."

Anger burned the back of my throat even though I had a feeling that Nathan was in it for the money. "Why do I have to do that? I don't have to follow your orders anymore." Paul had always been domineering and expected me to follow lockstep. Well not any longer!

Paul's face reddened. "I don't know why you're on this stupid show, Georgia." He looked at his feet. "I'm just here . . . I'm here to make sure you don't ruin your life."

"You ruined my life when you left me standing me at the altar."

Before he could respond, I pushed open the door to my dressing room. A piercing scream that I barely recognized as my own sprang from my body.

Inside the room, dangling from the ceiling fan with a noose around his neck, was Pietro.

Eight

"Stop screaming. Calm down," Paul said.

The room seemed to do a strange imitation of a Tilt-A-Whirl ride and I felt like I was being shoved off. I grabbed at the chair nearest me but before I could cling to it for support, Paul took hold of me and ushered me out of the dressing room.

"Don't touch anything. Out, out."

"I . . . oh, my God . . . poor Pietro," I cried.

As we emerged into the hall, Scott and Edward tore down the passageway toward us. "What's happened?" they yelled.

"What's going on?" Becca shouted. She was directly behind them, her sneakers with the green soles glowing in the darkened hallway. Behind Becca I could see a cowboy hat flapping in the air, and soon Ty had joined us in the hallway, too.

"What's go on?" Ty asked.

Paul held up his hands. "Hold up, gang. We got a situation on our hands here. Becca, call police dispatch, tell them we got a 10-55."

Scott and Edward both frowned at Paul and I realized his cover as an insurance guy was probably in jeopardy.

Becca's eyes went wide. "What's a 10-55?" she screeched.

"Never mind. Give me your phone," Paul said.

Becca made a face. I knew she wasn't supposed to let the contestants use any phones, but she didn't seem to want to tangle with Paul. She unclipped her phone off her jeans and handed it to him with a grim face.

"Get Georgia out of here," Paul said. He gestured toward Scott, Edward, and Ty. "And them, too."

"I'm a doctor," Edward said. "Is there something I can do?"

"This one's too late for you, Doc."

I whipped around, suddenly regaining myself. "Are you sure? We didn't get him down. We just . . . no. Not we, you! *You* just closed the door on him!" My voice sounded too shrill in my ears. I reached for the door, some strange impulse in me demanding to know what Pietro had wanted to tell me, as if my reentering the room would magically make things different and he'd be alive again.

Paul stepped in my way before I could reach the doorknob. "Come on, G. You're getting hysterical. You know the drill. Stay outta my crime scene."

"What crime scene?" Scott asked. "Who's in there? What's going on?"

Paul ignored the battery of questions and dialed Becca's phone. He made a sweeping gesture with his hand as if he was done with us and we were dismissed.

He mumbled something into the phone as I turned to the group. "It's Pietro. He wanted to tell me something in private and now he's dead, hanging by a noose from the ceiling fan."

Becca gasped and clapped a hand over her mouth in shock.

Paul let out a roar so fierce, one would have thought I'd stabbed him. "Christ! Georgia!"

Scott stepped between Paul and me. "Hey, man. What's going on? Why are you going all postal on her? She's a former cop. She knows—"

At the word *former* Paul looked like he would come out of his skin and I knew it was all he could do to contain himself and not pounce on Scott.

"I thought you were an insurance guy," Edward said. "Why are you acting so strange? Let us in the room, maybe I can help!"

"Back off now!" Paul said, enunciating every word. "No one leaves the building." He glared at Becca. "Got that? Secure the premises. LAPD is on its way."

In the break room it was as if someone had silently drawn battle lines. The contestants—Scott, Edward, Ty, and I—were in one corner, while the crew and producers were in another. While Scott, Edward, and Ty chatted among themselves, I took silent stock of the others.

Cheryl looked annoyed, acting like someone dying on her set was personally offensive.

Becca seemed rattled sitting next to the dragon lady and kept looking over at me and the cast. I knew in her heart she'd rather have been in our gang than in hers.

Kyle, the makeup artist, picked at his nails as he listened to Cheryl complain. He tsked in all the right places and looked completely sympathetic to her plight.

"Behind schedule again," she shrieked.

The two cameramen, one a man on the larger side and the other on the smaller side, were fidgeting with their coffees and seemed generally impatient. Then there was the sound engineer, who had a Zen quality about him. His eyes were closed and he repeatedly stroked his black beard as if meditating.

At another table were a few interns and runners, all of whom looked like wet pups. They seemed to be listening attentively to one of the runners, a blond girl with multiple piercings in her eyebrow and tattoos down each arm, recant tales about her latest trip to Vegas.

Basically we were all hostage while waiting for LAPD to come and question us.

I wondered about access to the building. Could someone have slipped in and out without our knowledge?

"Where's the other guy?" Ty asked. "What's going on with him?"

He meant Paul, of course, but I ignored his question. If Paul had blown his cover it would be up to him to regain it. I didn't need to be involved.

Edward's hand brushed mine and we made eye contact. "Are you okay?" he mouthed.

How could I be okay with two accidents in the span of a few days, especially when I had the sickening sensation that they could be related to me? Was the woman I'd put behind bars, Teresa/Florencia, husband-killer, responsible?

Becca stood to refill her coffee cup. The counter was a

good distance away from the group. Out of earshot, if we were careful. I sidled up next to her.

"I'm freaking out," I whispered.

She grabbed my wrists. "I know!" she whispered back.

"What's access to the building like?"

She frowned. "What do you mean? We all have key cards."

"Who's we?"

"Everyone who works for the studio."

"You mean, beyond everyone that's here?" I asked.

She nodded. "Oh, yeah, there's probably about fifty of us or more."

"Do you have to use your key card when you go from one section of the building to the other?"

Becca shook her head, her auburn curls bouncing around like crazy. "No, only to come into the main building. This is a newish studio. They should have the dressing rooms and greenroom secured, but they were having problems with the wiring and stuff, so they made it general access."

"Well, it's something. LAPD will be able to pull the access records, see who all was in the building. Does Florencia have access to the building?"

"Sure. I looked her up last night, though." Becca glanced at Cheryl to make sure we weren't being monitored and then lowered her voice a notch. "I asked her hiring manager for a favor and she pulled her personnel file, said everything looked fine."

I nodded. "Thank you. I'll let Paul know. He can run a background check."

At the mention of his name, Paul strode through the break room doors accompanied by two uniformed cops. The dragon lady jumped out of her chair as soon as she saw them.

"Well, it's about time. You've had us all waiting forever! What is going on?" Cheryl demanded.

One of the officers stepped forward. "Sorry about that, ma'am. We have an unfortunate situation developing. We'll be needing to speak to each of you individually. If you'd all please have your identification ready—"

"Wait a minute!" Cheryl shrieked. "You can't come into my studio and start barking out orders—"

"You'll never work in this town again," I joked, imitating Cheryl's voice and manner of speech.

Everyone laughed, except the dragon lady herself. She gave me a look that would freeze hell over.

One of the cops held the proverbial olive branch out to me. "Shall we start with you, miss?"

He may have been trying to save me from the dragon lady, but I felt like I was going straight from the frying pan into the fire.

The officer who escorted me down the hall into an empty room was tall and lean, probably in his midforties. He looked haggard and just as bitter as every other officer I'd served with. Paul followed us inside the room and took his usual cop stance, feet hip-width apart and arms folded across his chest.

Part of me wanted to back right out of the room. What? Was I here to answer Paul's questions?

I was annoyed at how fast he'd become all buddy-buddy with the L.A. cop.

They called it a brotherhood, not a sisterhood, for a reason.

I suddenly missed the protectiveness of Edward; hell, I even missed Scott's stupid ghoulish and inappropriate behavior.

I patted the pockets of my skin-tight jeans. "I don't have my ID. I don't have anything on me—"

Paul waved a hand. "We all know who you are, Thorn."

I bit my lip. I was no longer Georgia to him, sweetheart, fiancée, whatever. I was back to my cop nickname. Always the surname, and usually a shortened version or derivative of it. Mine was Thorn and, at this moment, Paul had a pained expression on his face as if my presence were literally a thorn in his side.

I took a deep breath. "All right. Well, then, fire away. What can I help with?"

The LAPD officer pulled out a black notebook and asked me a string of predictable questions. When had I last seen Pietro? How well had I known him? Did I know if he was severely depressed or suicidal?

"Is that what you think? He killed himself?" I asked.

The officer said, "We don't know anything yet. I'm only covering what's in the realm of possibility. People who go on these reality shows . . . well, no offense, but most of 'em don't have their head screwed on properly."

Paul seemed to laugh a little too gregariously at the joke and I felt like I was about to lose what little patience I had left.

"What about the other guy? Aaron. Seems to me maybe Pietro knew something about the bungee-jumping accident and that maybe—"

The officer held up a hand. "Right, right. Everyone's got theories. We'll see what the coroner says."

"Don't cut me off," I snapped.

The officer shrugged. "Look, whatever happened in San Francisco could be related, but S.F. isn't my jurisdiction." He glanced at Paul, who nodded in agreement. "I've got techs in your dressing room right now. What I'd like you to tell me is if anyone else was in there today with you."

"Kyle, the makeup guy; no one else that I know of."

The officer made a note while the walkie-talkie on his shoulder beeped. A series of police codes went off from dispatch, which he ignored. Apparently a burglary on the east side of town and a domestic violence call downtown weren't as exciting to him as the call he was on now.

Paul leveled a look at me. "Georgia, did Scott or Dr. . . . whatever his name is come and see you in your dressing room?"

There was something in his look. Was it jealousy?

Yes! He is jealous of the others!

My heart did a stupid little fluttery thing.

"No one came to see me," I said.

The officer and Paul exchanged glances, disbelief wafting off of them.

"Really?" the officer asked, then snickered.

I frowned. It wasn't fun being on the outside of a joke. What the heck were they snickering about? "You can ask the makeup guy if you don't believe me. We were alone. Why are you guys pressing me on this?"

"Both of those two were gone from the mansion for a while this morning and, come to think of it, so was the cowboy. But it's not that—"

"We found something in your dressing room—" The officer stopped himself short and glanced at Paul.

The walkie-talkie chirped again. The officer was needed. Which was a good thing. I wanted to grill Paul in private.

The officer excused himself and walked out of the room.

"What did you find?" I asked.

"A note."

"A note? From whom? What did it say?"

Paul leaned close to me. "'Your indifference to me has made all the difference.'"

"What is that supposed to mean?" I asked.

"I don't know, but you need to watch your back, G."

Nine

INT. LIBRARY DAY

Pietro is looking into the camera, his dark hair gelled back away from his face and his eyes gleaming. He has a stubby beard and is dressed in a cerulean blue silk shirt with a red and white scarf around his neck. His legs are crossed and a bright red Italian leather shoe peeks into the frame every three seconds as Pietro shakes his foot around.

CHERYL (O.S.)
Hi, Pietro, can you tell us a little about yourself?

PIETRO
(*shrugs*) Of course. What would you like to know?

CHERYL (O.S.)
How long have you been in the country?

PIETRO
Five years.

CHERYL (O.S.)
Italians are big into love and families, right?

PIETRO
Sì.

CHERYL (O.S.)
So are you hoping to find your dream girl on the show?

PIETRO
(*laughs*) Ah, what a world it would be if we could just go on a show and find a wife!

CHERYL (O.S.)
You don't think that can happen?

PIETRO
Perhaps, but not for me. I've already found the one.

CHERYL (O.S.)
Oh. So you're on the show in hopes of winning the prize money?

PIETRO
(*waves his hands around*) *A rubar poco si va in galera, a rubar tanto si fa cariera.*

CHERYL (O.S.)
Care to translate?

PIETRO
(*laughs*) It's an Italian saying. "Steal a little, go to jail; steal a lot, make a career of it."

CHERYL (O.S.)
You're going to steal the money?

PIETRO
No, but it feels a little like that. I have to steal the girl's heart.

The police finished questioning everyone and we found ourselves escorted back to the mansion. Cheryl had requested that the cast gather back in the main living room for another meeting. This time I was sure the show was canceled.

I was so relieved.

I could barely contain my excitement. I was planning my immediate departure from L.A.

Although I actually had no plans.

What would I do? Where would I go?

San Francisco no longer seemed like home and I found

myself daydreaming about my hometown of Cottonwood. I'd grown up on a small farm in northern California. Could going home—going back to that small town—be an option?

I entered the room and surveyed my surroundings. Becca and the crew were across the room in a huddle. There were no cameras on and the set felt strange without the warmth of the lights, almost as if someone had turned off the sun.

Paul was absent; presumably he was working with LAPD.

Dr. Edward and the cowboy, Ty, were seated next to each other in aluminum folding chairs that had been vacated by the ordinary crew. Ty was leaning in close to Edward, discussing something with him, in a manner that could only be described as urgent and hurried. Ty's hand was covering his mouth as he spoke and his head bobbed up and down as he rapidly whispered something to Edward.

I cleared my throat as I crossed the room. Ty's eyes flashed toward me, but he continued his intense talk with Edward. Edward, for his part, glanced up at me and offered me a soft smile.

In the center of the room was Scott perched in the middle of the brown leather couch, his legs crossed with an ankle over his knee and his arms spread open on the back of the couch. He looked about as comfortable and secure as a guy could get—his confidence annoyingly sexy.

God, Georgia, don't fall for the biggest jerk on the set!

I took a seat on far right end of the couch, but Scott scooted closer immediately, his right knee pressing against my left. Heat surged between our bodies and I involuntarily jerked my leg away. Scott lowered his eyes toward the gap that now existed between us.

After a moment, he whispered, "It's too much of a coincidence, isn't it? Two guys dead in within a couple days?"

"Aaron isn't dead. He's in a coma," I said.

Scott shrugged. "You know what I mean, though. It's like the show is cursed."

"Cursed? Come on. You're not superstitious, are you?"

He rubbed at his shaved head and flashed me a crooked smile. "Not at all. That's why I said it couldn't be a coincidence."

The sound of a woman's hurried footsteps followed by more footsteps brought a close to the side conversations in the room, each of us looking up expectantly. Cheryl flew into the room followed by the other male contestants. The men looked confused as they filed into the room.

Nathan, the surfer, smiled when he saw me and took a place behind the couch where he could stand directly behind me. He put a hand on my shoulder. "Is everything okay? You all look shaken."

Before I could reply, Harris Carlson entered the room and spoke with Cheryl in hushed tones; the rest of us were quiet, watching their interaction. Nathan's hand fell away from my shoulder and finally Cheryl turned to the cast. "Listen, we had an unfortunate incident today on the set. Pietro committed suicide—"

I jumped up. "What? Wait a minute!"

Cheryl put a hand up. "Hold on, Georgia. Let me finish—"

"No!" I said. "We don't know that he committed suicide! He was—"

"The police are investigating. Certainly," Cheryl said. "But right now the main thing they're looking into is suicide." She flashed me a strange look, a cross between pity and something else, as if she thought I came from another world and she wasn't sure what to do with me. "Given that this is the second incident on our show, I've spoken with our attorneys and they've instructed me to give you all the option of resigning."

The cast stood frozen. It felt like a cold gust of air had hit us; my skin pebbled and I shivered involuntarily.

"What do you mean, resign?" Derek, the Afghanistan vet, asked.

At that moment, Paul stepped into the room and crossed to where the cast was seated. He said, "The production staff is giving us an opportunity to get off the show."

Yes! What a relief!

I would get to go back home to Cottonwood, or even San Francisco if I wanted, but mercifully I would be off the show.

I jumped off the couch. "Thank you!"

All eyes in the room traveled to me. I nervously smoothed down my jeans, staring back at the cast. "What?" I asked.

"You can't just bail out!" Nathan said.

"I'm not bailing out. Two guys are . . . this is wrong. We can't keep going with the show!" I said.

"Why not?" Richard, the attorney, asked. "Obviously, Aaron had an accident and Pietro was severely depressed. All that is sad and all, but what really does it have to do with us?"

"No! I'm not staying on the show. This is totally morbid and I don't buy that suicide thing someone is—"

Paul stepped toward me. "G, can we talk?"

I felt more uncomfortable now than before. Not only were all eyes on me, but it felt like they were boring holes right through me.

Can I say no?

"Uh . . ."

Paul wasn't actually waiting for an answer, though; he'd already crossed the room and had a hand on my elbow.

Scott stood up. "Hey, no private one-on-ones! It's a rule. I mean, if we're going to continue with the show, then we should be following the rules!"

Edward nodded in agreement. "Yes! Why does he get one-on-one time? That's not right!"

Paul held up his hands in surrender. "Okay, okay. No problem." He smiled conspiratorially at the other men on the cast. As if he wanted them to think he was just like them. I figured he'd probably been about to pressure me to stay on the show, perhaps so he could continue to investigate, but now he'd struck a nerve with the other contestants. He must have thought I'd feel the peer pressure and stay.

I glanced around at the men's faces. "You all want to stay on? I mean, seriously? Every single one of you?"

"I do," Scott said.

"Me, too," Richard chimed in.

There were various nods and agreements, but I noticed that Bruce, the techie, and Mitch, the real estate investor, were both silent.

"You two don't want to stay on?" I asked hopefully, reaching for a lifeline.

"Well," Mitch said, "it's definitely been an adventure, but I have to be honest, I really would like to be off the show."

"Me, too," Bruce said. "No offense to you, Georgia. You'd be any man's dream, but I don't think I'm the reality show type of guy."

"Especially when the reality is that people are getting hurt or worse," I said, flashing an angry look at Cheryl.

She studied her hands for a moment, as if searching out an answer from her nails. Suddenly she looked up. "You both don't have to stay on the show. We'll have a champagne ceremony tonight. You can choose to be eliminated. Will that work?" she asked.

Bruce and Mitch exchanged glances.

"I don't see why not," Bruce said.

"Wait, wait," I said. "Is any of this up to me?" I felt the warmth of Scott's hand on the small of my back.

"It's okay. Let them go," he said.

"But I don't want to stay. *I* want to go."

Edward turned to me. "Oh, Georgia," he said. "We've all had a big shock, but really you came on the show for a reason. Don't you want to see that through?"

Paul was upon me. I could feel the weight of his frenzied energy pushing at me. "Georgia, you need to stay on."

I don't know if I imagined him saying it through gritted teeth or if he actually did, but either way it seemed like it was another *order*. I glanced around the room and saw Becca, her face a mixture of pleading and support. I knew she'd be my friend no matter what I decided to do, but finishing the show would probably launch her career and bailing out on it meant she would have to start over.

Cheryl's eyes seemed to bore holes through me. "We can get everyone into hair and makeup right away," she said. "Film the scene and then take the night off."

The men around me nodded.

Cheryl smiled. "Besides, we have a special guest arriving tomorrow and I know you'll want to see him."

"A special guest? Who is it?" I asked.

"Someone who will help you through all the decisions

you have to make." Cheryl dangled the offer in front of the others, baiting me to ask again.

Normally on these shows a best friend was brought in to consult with the bachelorette on her choices, but my best friend was already here. Cheryl glanced at Becca. She knew I'd stay on the show for Becca's sake, no matter what.

"Who?" I asked again, pressing.

"A *very* special guest." Cheryl smiled triumphantly, as if declaring she had the ace in the hole.

Ten

....

INT. LIBRARY DAY

Mitch is looking directly at the camera. He is seated in the library on a gold wingback chair. His ankle is crossed over a knee and he picks an imaginary piece of lint off his pants. He has a chiseled face, with a strong chin and nose, and is alarmingly handsome.

CHERYL (O.S.)
Hello, Mitch, can you tell the audience a little bit about yourself?

MITCH
(*nods slowly, his expression calculating*) I'm from Los Angeles. I am a real estate investor and I've done pretty well in the market . . .

CHERYL (O.S.)
Good for you.

MITCH
Until recently . . .

CHERYL (O.S.)
Sorry to hear that.

MITCH
Well, everyone has ups and downs. And it's certainly not fatal. All I need is a quick infusion of cash and I'll be right on track.

CHERYL (O.S.)
Are you hoping to find that here?

MITCH
Cash?

CHERYL (O.S.)
Yes. Are you on the show for love or money?

MITCH
(*laughing*) Well, love would be great, if she was rich, too. Can't beat that combo.

CHERYL (O.S.)
Let me be clear. Are you searching for love?

MITCH
Well, ultimately yes. But I'm too young to settle down right now, plus I'm sort of in a bind. (*He makes a pained expression.*) Need the cash right now. So I'll pass on love if it gets me the prize money. (*He nods repeatedly to himself.*) I'm on the show for the money.

We were taken to hair and makeup. Florencia was curiously absent again and I longed to talk about that with Becca, but she'd been dispatched to the control center, a studio where she'd watch the live feed from the various cameras during our elimination ceremony.

Kyle did my makeup quickly and even though I wanted to talk to him about Pietro, I felt oddly self-conscious, not sure who to trust or confide in. Someone dropped off a rack of dresses and Kyle picked through them.

"What do you think? Green sleeveless chiffon or do you prefer a slinky gold gown?" He held out the dresses for me to look over.

I shrugged. "Whatever."

He made a face. "Whatever?"

"Sorry, I'm just not feeling it, Kyle."

He swirled my chair so I could see my reflection in the mirror. "Come on, girl. Look at your face. I've made you stunning! Well, even more stunning than you normally are. Smile! You got a squad of hunks who wag their tongues every time you walk into the room."

I looked into his eyes through the glass. "I'm spooked."

Kyle shook a finger at me. "I won't talk negative. *No, ne, nyet, nein.*" He fixed a glare at me in the mirror. "You shouldn't, either."

"He was in my dressing room, Kyle! Do you know if anyone else went in there?"

"Oh, honey, don't you know all good stylists have a mantra for success?"

"And what is that?" I asked.

"See no evil, hear no evil, speak no evil."

"Come on, this is a serious matter. If you saw something, you have to tell me."

"I just told you I didn't see anything."

"You're infuriating, you realize that, don't you?" I said.

He cupped a hand around his ear. "What?" he asked. "You prefer the gold gown?" He flung it at me, saying, "Me, too."

When I stepped back into the mansion, candles were glowing from every corner and rose petals were strewn around the furniture, creating the ultimate romantic illusion for our TV viewers. The scent of the roses was cloying and I was almost able to ignore the crew members busily darting about, duct taping cords to the floor and adjusting lighting.

Except for the fact that I was shaking.

How were the producers going to explain Pietro's absence?

Harris Carlson was already in the room, primping and preening as he stood waiting for me.

"I discussed the situation with Cheryl," Harris said. "We're going to be up-front with the audience about Pietro. His suicide is already on some of the news channels—"

"We don't know that it—"

He held up a hand to quiet me. "I'm following marching orders." The look he gave indicated I'd be smart to follow the same orders.

Cheryl sauntered into the room. "All set?" she asked, then a strange expression crossed her face. "What's that smell?"

"We got an active leak. I've called a plumber," one of the techs who was working on a light answered.

Cheryl scrunched up her nose, but didn't say any more about it. She stepped toward Harris and me. "All right. We got Harris to give the audience a brief rundown about Pietro. So you don't need to address that, Georgia. Just give us a quick recap about your dates and how torn you are to have to choose between all these great catches, *capisci*?"

Yeah. I capisco, *all right.*

She was closely guarding how the information about Pietro was released and she wanted to be sure I had nothing to do with it. She gave a whole new meaning to *public information officer*, and I'd already proved I couldn't do that job.

Cheryl stepped away from us and called, "Action."

Harris proceeded to ask me about the rock-climbing date. I gave a lame answer, something to the effect of, "It went about as well as could be expected."

Then one by one the men came into the room. They were dressed in formal wear, each looking more handsome than should be legal.

I was to call the men's names and ask if they would accept a glass of champagne. If I offered a man a glass and he accepted, he would remain on the show. I called out to Paul, Ty, Edward, Scott, Nathan, Richard, and Derek and handed each a glass of champagne. When the seven flutes were handed out, Mitch and Bruce were left standing with their hands folded in front of them.

What should have taken a few minutes to film seemed to take forever. Cheryl kept interrupting us and readjusting the camera angles. Then she'd instruct the men to look either overly confident, charming, or distressed. The distressed look seemed to be the easiest for the guys to master because they all looked completely frazzled by the time the scene was finally done.

Harris took a step forward and said, "Mitch, Bruce, I'm sorry. Please take a moment to say your good-byes."

Mitch and Bruce shook hands with the other men. Then Mitch stepped away and approached me. "Georgia, it was a pleasure to meet you. I'm sorry it didn't work out."

"I'm sorry, too," I said sincerely. And then I had to ask him the question that Cheryl had instructed me to ask. "Mitch, I have to know. Were you looking for love or money?"

He took a deep breath. "Georgia, I was looking for money."

I smiled, relief wafting over me.

At least that's one Mr. Wrong gone.

Mitch turned and walked out of the mansion.

Bruce moved closer to me, took my hand, and kissed it. "It was nice meeting you," he said.

I nodded and asked him the same question I'd asked Mitch.

He tilted his head to the side and said, "I'm looking for love."

My breath caught. I'd just lost one of my eligible bachelors.

"You'll find it," I said.

He pressed his lips together and nodded. "I hope so. Good luck to you." He turned and walked out the door, and part of me—well, most of me—wanted to follow him right out.

Harris Carlson clapped his hands together. "Well, Georgia, seven men remain. You've eliminated one who was in it for the money and one who was in it for love. And, as our viewers are aware, we lost Pietro." He glanced down a moment and the cast joined him in an unrehearsed silence. "Our confessional videos reveal that Pietro was on the show for the money."

I surveyed the remaining men. All were holding their champagne flutes and looking at me expectantly. The odds had tipped in my favor. Now of the seven men remaining, four were in it for love.

I held up my glass. "Well, gentlemen, thank you for accepting this toast. May we all live long, happy lives."

Everyone clinked their glasses together.

"Here's to you, Georgia," Paul said.

"Tomorrow there will be a group date for five of you and a one-on-one," Harris Carlson announced. "You'll all receive your date cards in the morning."

That was my cue to leave the mansion alongside Harris. I walked next to him, feeling completely numb. Somehow, I'd agreed to continue on this godawful show and now I felt more alone than I'd felt when I'd been abandoned at the altar.

My life had truly reached a low.

I slept a fitful night, reliving the image of Pietro hanging from the ceiling in my dressing room over and over.

Did his death have anything to do with me?

My worst fear was that he'd seen or known something and had been silenced for it.

I couldn't believe it was suicide, but what about the note they'd found?

I finally drifted off to a deeper sleep, only to have the alarm jolt me awake. Bright Los Angeles sunshine was peeking through the blinds, but my head hurt and I still felt fatigued. I stumbled toward the miniature kitchen and fumbled for coffee. Someone on the production crew had stocked the refrigerator for me and I pulled out some cream for my coffee and some fresh raspberries to top my cereal.

As the smell of coffee wafted through my trailer, there was a small sound from outside. Gravel crunching in a slow and even pace. Not a cat or a raccoon.

This was definitely human.

Why was someone creeping up on me?

Through the blinds, I could make out the figure of a woman and she seemed to be dressed like my best friend, Becca, with a billowing jacket and skin-tight yoga pants. The woman's long curly hair bounced as she walked.

My shoulders dropped and air rushed back into my lungs.

Yes, this was definitely my friend Becca.

"G?" she called as she rapped softly on my door. "Are you up yet?"

I pulled open the trailer door. "You scared me."

"Sorry," she said, tumbling into the trailer and seating herself in the tiny eating area.

"Why are you sneaking around?" I asked.

"I wasn't sneaking."

"You were kind of skulking."

"I was? I don't know—I'm totally freaked out. I thought

I heard something behind me, but I think it's just my mind playing tricks on me."

I remained standing and peeked out of my windows. I couldn't see much and I tried to shake the spooked feeling.

"Anyway, I came over to get the list from you," Becca said.

"What list?"

"Your date list. I have to make out the date cards now. Who are you going to take out?" Before I could answer, she added, "Is that coffee I smell?"

I poured her a cup, then one for myself, and took a seat across from her. "I can't believe we're going to continue this charade."

She put a hand over her heart. "I know. Poor Pietro. I tried to talk Cheryl out of continuing, but when you all voted to stay on—"

"I didn't! I didn't vote to stay on."

"Well, you were outvoted, but what can I say, she thinks the ratings are going to be through the roof. We're already getting press inquiries like you wouldn't believe and, man, these people are vultures."

"I can believe it. Remember I was the public information officer in San Francisco. I know how the press can get. Speaking of which, were you able to get copies of the footage we shot in San Francisco?"

Becca shook her head. "No, sorry. I asked around and everyone seems to think we gave the footage to SFPD."

"All of it?"

"Yes." Becca sipped her coffee, then asked, "So, who's it going to be?"

"Where are we going for the date?"

"Amusement park."

I quirked an eyebrow. "Disneyland?"

Becca smiled. "Girl, we are low budget. We don't have the dough to close Disneyland for the day."

"We got the bridge in San Francisco."

"That's different. The city encourages producers to film there. They want the business. Disney doesn't need our business. Do you know how much they pull in a day?"

I buried my head in my hands. "Actually, I don't want to know. I'm sure I'll only find it depressing. Besides, if what happened in San Francisco—"

Becca clapped her hands over her ears. "Don't even say that!"

"Scott's worried the show is cursed."

"La, la, la," Becca sang.

"You're going to ignore me? You're just like the makeup guy, Kyle! What is this Hollywood denial?"

Becca shut her eyes and continued to sing to herself.

Well, what did I expect? It is *the land of fairy tales and make-believe.*

"You have to face reality, my dear. Something weird is going on with the show. Do you think it's me?"

When she didn't answer, I closed my mouth and waited her out. After a moment she opened an eye and peeked at me.

"Are you done with the nay-saying? I don't want to participate in any bad juju."

"The juju is here, darling. Whether we participate in it or not."

She ignored me and pulled out a pen. "Who do you want on your date?"

"How many guys do I need to invite?"

"Five of the seven. You get to pick one guy for the one-on-one and someone will get left out. Who are you liking the best?"

I thought about it for a moment. Deep down I didn't really think I'd find love on the show, but since I was stuck here, I'd better come up with a plan. After all, I had a chance to split the money with someone if I picked the right guy.

"Paul is out. We know he's not on the show for love or money," I said.

"No, no. That's not how it works. He took Aaron's place, so you can't think of him as Paul. You have to think about him as Aaron."

"What?" The cereal I'd poured took on a soggy, unappetizing texture and I suddenly felt sick to my stomach.

"You have to guess if Aaron was in it for love or money. Paul agreed to that with Cheryl. We had to keep the balance on the show—you know, five guys in it for love, five in it for the money."

"Do you know?" I asked, picking a raspberry off my cereal.

"Nope, and even if I did, you know I can't tell you."

I shrugged. "I know. I guess it doesn't matter, though. I want him gone."

She studied me a moment. "So, are you going to eliminate him next?"

"Hell yes," I said.

She made a face.

"What?" I challenged.

Becca shook her head and found immediate interest in her coffee. "Nothing. Got any sugar?"

"You don't take sugar in your coffee. Now tell me what's up."

She played with her coffee cup. "It's just that I think he's still in love with you, G."

It was my turn to make a face. "Puh-lease!" I said. "He doesn't love me. He loves his job."

"He loves you and you know it."

Arguing with Becca was actually pointless. I've never won an argument with her.

Ever.

"Well, maybe I don't love him anymore, Becca," I said. "He's not . . . he's not . . . husband material."

Becca laughed. "Of course he is! He's got a great job, he's got a great ass—"

I held a hand up to stop her. "Having a great ass is not on my list of criteria for making a good husband."

"Liar."

"Okay, well, maybe it is. But *having* a great ass and *being* a great ass are two different things and I just think our ship has sailed. Every time Paul opens his mouth I feel totally misunderstood. I'm not on the show to go backward."

She nodded, a serious expression on her face. "Right, right—and you shouldn't. You've got some great guys on the show and every one of them is just as handsome as Paul. I shouldn't be so superficial."

We burst out laughing together.

She held up a finger. "But before you eliminate Paul, remember to think carefully about Aaron. Paul only agreed to what Aaron agreed to."

I sighed, then took a sip of my coffee. "You really can't tell me?" I pried.

She shook her head.

We drank our coffee in silence for a moment, engaging in one of our time-tested staring contests. When she didn't budge, I asked, "You got any favorites?"

"For you? I think—"

I laughed. "What do you mean, for *me*? Do you have your eye on someone?"

She giggled. "No. Well, you know, I don't want to unduly influence you. You need to be able—"

"Oh, come on, girl. I have more than enough to choose from. Who are you eyeing?"

"The cowboy."

"Ah! I should have known."

Becca had a soft spot for anything western. In fact, I couldn't count the number of times she'd made me sit through old movies with John Wayne or Clint Eastwood or even *Big Valley* reruns.

"You can have him."

She clapped her hands together. "Really?"

I fanned my fingers at her. "Totally, honey. He's up your alley. You have my blessing to make goo-goo eyes at him."

She laughed. "Oh, I'll make more than goo-goo eyes at him."

"I'm sure. So, who do you like for me?"

"The writer or the doctor."

"The writer, Scott? No way," I said. "I swore to myself he'd be the next one gone. He's out of here!"

"Really?" Becca played with the salt and pepper shakers on my small table. "I think he's so funny and you totally light up when you see him."

"I do?"

She nodded. "The surfer guy is hot, too."

I thought about it for a minute. The one who had piqued my interest was the doctor, Edward. He was strong and compassionate, although I wasn't sure about the walking pharmaceutical part of him . . .

Why not take a chance?

"Let's say for the one-on-one date I'll go with Edward," I said.

Becca made a note.

"And then for the guy left behind, I'll leave Ty."

She placed a hand over her heart and fluttered it back and forth. "Thank you!" she squealed.

"No problem. So, that means the others go on the group date," I said.

"Including Paul," she said.

I groaned.

She stood and jutted her chin out at me. "That means you need to get ready. Remember to flirt like crazy. Cheryl will make you redo everything if you don't spice it up a bit."

Eleven

Hair and makeup were getting easier and easier for me to sit through. The first days I thought I was being tortured or doing some sort of penance, but somehow I'd gotten used to it. Today, the woman doing my makeup was the same lady who ordinarily did my hair, the one with the enviable dye job, whom I'd learned went by Ophelia.

"Have you seen Florencia?" I asked.

"Florencia? Yeah. She's over at the studio today doing makeup for *Peril*."

Peril was the game show that was supposed to steal ratings from *Jeopardy*. So far, it was halfway through its pilot season and rumor had it its future was in "peril."

Ophelia fiddled with her makeup case, holding several bottles of foundation against my skin, seemingly trying to decide if I was tan enough for the darker color or if she should just accept reality.

I was as pale as a ghost—thanks to years of living in foggy San Francisco.

"Have you worked with her long?" I asked.

She applied foundation to my face with a small sponge, then topped it off with powder. "Sure, I guess. Why?"

"Do you know much about her?" I asked.

She shrugged and turned to pick up a blusher brush. She dipped it into the pot of color and then dusted it on my cheeks, telling me to smile. "Uh, I think she's single. Works late. Always wants overtime. Says she's got no one to go home to and gets kinda mopey about that, but who doesn't?"

I bit my tongue. It certainly wouldn't help matters to say, "Oh, she's got no one to go home to because I put her behind bars for killing her husband." Instead I said, "How long have you worked for the studio?"

"Six years. Florencia came on board about a year and a half ago or so. I have to say she's a quick learner and mostly keeps to herself."

Eighteen months.

Had Teresa gotten out on parole? Considering she'd probably have served five years of the twenty-year sentence, it was possible, but it didn't seem plausible after the brutal murder she'd committed. I'd have to find Paul and see if he'd found anything out.

The woman finished my makeup and moved on to hair. "Terrible about that Italian hottie, huh? What was his name, Pietro?"

I nodded.

"I'll never understand what drives someone to kill himself," she continued. "Can you imagine what would drive a man to do that?" She didn't wait for my reply; instead, she blasted the hair dryer and our conversation ceased.

I was dropped off outside another studio. Maybe the execs figured that going back to the same studio where Pietro had met his fate would be too much for us to bear. Either that or LAPD had it closed down as a crime scene. I guessed it was probably the latter, but, hey, Hollywood would try to score points where it could.

Becca was waiting for me outside. "G! You look beautiful."

I laughed. The costume team had laid out skin-tight pink jeans for me, along with an animal print top reminiscent of a corset. I wore stiletto sandals that could have been weapons on their own.

I reached for her arm. "I can't walk in these things!" I complained.

She grabbed my elbow and waved her free hand around. "You don't need to walk; just hobble onto the set and have a seat. We've laid out a gourmet picnic for you and you can take off the sandals and flash your beautiful toesie-woesies for the camera." A worried expression suddenly crossed her face. "They did give you a pedicure, didn't they?"

After years of wearing police uniform boots my feet were hammered, and no one knew that better than Becca. Fortunately, once I'd been promoted to public information officer, I'd been allowed to wear plain clothes, including normal footwear, and my feet had healed.

"Yes, the beauty team gave me a pedicure a couple days ago. And besides that they also waxed me to within an inch of my life. They gave me a touch-up today." I wiggled my eyebrows at her. "See?"

"Oh, yeah. I know those brows weren't the only things waxed!" Becca said.

There was a catering cart parked in front of the studio doors and Becca grabbed a powdered doughnut from a tray of decadent pastries.

"It's painful," I said. "Can't you request I get laser hair removal? I wouldn't mind never having to shave my legs again!"

"It's not fast enough for TV," Becca said, taking a bite out of the doughnut and then wiping the sugar from the corners of her mouth. "That process takes months. Plus I heard it hurts, too."

I made a face and she added, "Why does it have to hurt to be beautiful?"

"Not you," I said.

Becca had a natural beauty that always seemed easy. Curly hair that looked even better when unruly and curves that forgave if she took an extra bite from a sugary treat.

She waved a hand at me. "Aww, shut up. I'm not gorgeous like you. I could never be the on-screen girl." She pushed open the door to the studio. "You go take your spot on the picnic blanket. The men are backstage already, but we want to capture you greeting them each on camera." As I turned to go, she called out, "Hey, want to hook up for cocktails tonight? I'll smuggle you out of your coach, but don't tell anyone."

I laughed. "Of course I want to go out with you tonight! But I have the one-on-one date."

Becca waved a hand. "After that! I'll pick you up." She put a finger over her mouth to remind me of the secrecy.

I nodded. "Mum's the word."

Twelve

The set was made to look like a carnival-style amusement park. There was a huge Ferris wheel in the center of the set and on both sides of it were additional rides: one was a canoe ride and the other bumper cars.

A popcorn stand and cotton candy booth were on display and in the middle of everything was a picnic basket laid out on a plaid blanket. I took off the stilettos immediately and flopped onto the blanket, although I was nervous that the skin-tight jeans might give if I moved too erratically.

I peeked inside the basket: a crusty baguette, warm cheese, and chilled fruit. There was a bottle of wine opened and several glasses ready to be filled. I marveled at how the set resembled the outdoors. On flats were painted trees that were so realistic they actually looked three-dimensional.

Cheryl appeared from between the popcorn and cotton candy booths, startling me. I sat up straighter; somehow her mere presence put me on high alert.

"Hello, Georgia." She attempted a smile. "Have you already been prepped for the scene—I mean, date?"

I nodded. Cheryl nodded back, seemingly satisfied with my response, and muttered, "Good."

Several cameramen followed her and took up positions surrounding the picnic area. Cheryl put on a headset, then walked out of sight. Suddenly the amusement park came to life. Actors playing the parts of vendors took positions at the popcorn and cotton candy booths and a few more actors manned the rides and game booths, including one where you had to throw a ring around a bottle in order to take home a stuffed penguin the size of a small child.

The entire scene was a bit surreal and creepy. I half expected a clown to jump out and scare the bejesus out of me.

Cheryl called, "Action!"

Nathan, the surfer, suddenly peeked his head out from between the popcorn and cotton candy booths. I jumped up and raced toward him. More than anything, I was happy to be able to talk to someone.

Nathan grabbed me around the waist and swung me around. "Hey, girlie!"

My feet lifted off the floor and I enjoyed the feeling of weightlessness. I pressed my cheek against his shoulder and tried to surrender to his joyful energy.

What would it be like to go through life so carefree?

"Are you always so happy?" I asked.

He looked puzzled, then laughed. "Sure. It beats the alternative."

He was quickly followed by Scott, the writer, who seemed genuinely pleased to be there. Richard, the attorney, who undeniably had a beady-eyed look about him. Derek, the Afghanistan veteran, who was reasonably sure-footed with help from his cane; and Paul, who didn't seem the least bit happy to see me.

I hugged each one of them and when I got to Paul he whispered in my ear, "I was hoping for the one-on-one date."

"Be glad you even got this date," I whispered back.

He frowned at me, his expression clearly showing his dismay.

I ignored the look and asked the group, "What do you all want to do first? Picnic or rides?"

There was a mixed shout from the group and we decided that it'd be a shame not to sample the fine wine while it was chilled. Richard took charge of pouring the wine, while I broke the bread and passed it around.

Nathan popped a handful of grapes into his mouth and asked, "What's your favorite ride?"

"Oh, I haven't been to an amusement park since I was a kid," I said.

"Where'd you grow up?" Nathan asked.

"Cottonwood," Paul answered.

All heads turned to him. I assumed no one, including Paul, had told the cast that Paul and I had once been an item. So he got a few strange looks from the others, but he simply drank his wine and said nothing.

"I grew up near Anderson," Scott said.

I studied him for a moment. "We were practically neighbors, then."

Scott nodded. "Place gave me nightmares."

"Is that why you write horror stories?" I joked.

He studied me, giving me an appraising look, as if he didn't know how to answer, or maybe wasn't sure if I'd understand his answer. "No, I write for another reason altogether."

"What's that?" I probed.

"Oh, God," Richard said. "Let's not get into the deep, dark psyche of a thriller writer." He held up his glass. "Instead, I propose a toast to Georgia."

The others raised their glasses.

My skin began to crawl. I couldn't shake the feeling that the entire production was eerie. Really, all these men had come on the show to meet me?

It didn't feel right. It never had.

But then again, in front of me was sitting the one man I'd thought I'd marry in real life and he was clink-clinking along with the rest of them and pretending to be an insurance salesman, no less.

"Georgia, I think I can win you a penguin," Derek said, wiggling his eyebrows at me.

I jumped up. "As long as I can go barefoot, I'll follow you anywhere," I said, heaving him to his feet.

His cane was laying on the plaid blanket and he bent to retrieve it.

I held out my arm. "Don't worry about the cane. You can lean on me."

He smiled and wrapped an arm around my waist. This drew protests from the others. "Aw, man, what a ploy!" and "I wish I had a bum leg."

We ignored them and headed over to the ring toss booth.

The man working the booth was wearing a red apron with deep pockets. He had a handlebar mustache and was standing with his hands folded in front of him.

He eagerly welcomed us, yelling out, "Five bucks gets you three tries."

"Five bucks!" I laughed. "That's kind of stiff. When I was a kid it was a quarter or something."

Derek reached into his pocket. "I think I can cover it." He handed a five-dollar bill to the man, who in turn placed three silver rings in front of Derek.

Derek tossed one and missed, the silver ring clanging against the empty milk bottles.

"What was your time in Afghanistan like?" I asked.

"Oh, probably the same as the others'. A good day was when it was slow. When I was bored. That was a good day."

"And a bad day?"

"Worse than I could ever put into words. Complete chaos. I think you feel every emotion available to man either at the same time or in the course of an hour. Overwhelming really." He shrugged. "You were on the police force, so I think you know what I mean."

I reflected on my very short term as a beat officer in San Francisco. "I don't think it compares. I couldn't do what you did."

Heck, I could barely do what I'd done, hence my unfortunate and premature termination from SFPD.

"You're not giving yourself enough credit," he said, tossing another ring and missing. "Pfft. I'm terrible at this game."

I laughed. "*You're* not giving *yourself* enough credit!"

He flashed a winning smile. "Third time's a charm, right?"

"Sure," I said. "Go for it."

I hoped he'd make it soon. I imagined Cheryl might make him keep trying until she got her "shot." Derek tossed the third ring into the air and it landed neatly around the neck of a bottle.

Good! Now they won't have to reshoot the scene or keep filming.

I leaned into Derek and he smiled.

The man running the booth reached up and pulled the penguin down. He handed it to Derek, who in turn presented it to me. The penguin wore a purple necktie and had a big fuzzy head of rainbow-colored hair. We both giggled.

"It's the cutest penguin I've ever seen!" I kissed Derek on the cheek. "Thank you."

Before Derek had a chance to reply I felt someone brush against my elbow.

Scott was standing next to me and asked, "Want to ride the Ferris wheel?"

Derek took it as his cue to return to the picnic blanket.

I hugged the penguin to me for protection. "I don't really like carnival rides," I confessed. "They scare me."

Scott's eyes widened. "They scare you?" He smiled. "Fear! You're barking right up my alley," he said. "I love things that go bump in the night. Anything that makes you feel that chill. You know you're alive then! Don't worry about anything. You just snuggle up to me. I'll keep you safe."

I hesitated, but you only live once and of course there would be nothing dangerous about the ride. I knew that was an irrational fear on my part. Besides, I didn't want to look like a complete chicken on national TV.

"Actually the Ferris wheel is my least favorite ride ever," I said.

Scott clapped a hand to his forehead, then rubbed at his shaved head. "Don't say that! It's so un-American. And right now you're looking so patriotic, what with entertaining one of our veterans." He took the penguin and carried it for me. "You have to go on the Ferris wheel."

"The Ferris wheel is not American," I said.

"It isn't?" he asked.

"No. It's French or Turkish or something," I said.

Scott chuckled.

"What?" I asked.

"The original Ferris wheel was designed by George Washington."

I stopped in my tracks and looked at him. "You're kidding, right?"

He smiled in a way that made my stomach flutter a bit. Only one side of his mouth quirked up and his eyes twinkled. "Not *the* George Washington. Another one. He designed it for the Chicago World's Fair."

We began to move again toward the ride.

"You're a walking encyclopedia, huh?" I asked.

He shrugged. "Aw, I'm a geek that way. Writer, you know. I like to research stuff."

The man working the Ferris wheel appeared in front of us. "Step right up, step right up. You'll get a view of the entire park from up top."

Scott and I both burst out laughing. It was hard to imagine a fake studio view being enticing, but surely the TV audience would get a screen montage of downtown L.A. or Venice Beach at sunset or something else completely fabulous. Scott and I would get a view of a wall of blinding lights.

Scott helped me into the gondola that was parked in place at the base of the ride. He handed me the giant penguin and

I placed him on the floor of the car, so only his beak and hilariously wild rainbow hair were visible.

Scott jumped in next to me and the attendant secured the bar in place. The car jolted as the man pulled on the lever to put the ride in motion. Our gondola rose up a level. We rocked to a stop as a cameraman boarded the car below us.

"Don't rock the car," I said to Scott.

He smirked, his face lighting up like a little boy's on Christmas. "You think I'd try to scare you on purpose?"

He leaned ever so slightly forward.

I grabbed at his shirt.

He grabbed my hand. "You can trust me." His voice was low and rumbling, the sound sending delicious little goose bumps up my arms.

"I don't trust you!" I said.

He winked. "You will."

"Lean back," I said through gritted teeth.

He eased back into the seat. "Don't be scared," he said.

"Isn't that what you want?"

He shook his head. "It's only fun when people are enjoying the feeling."

"How could anyone possibly enjoy it?"

The gondola rocked and started to rise again.

Scott squeezed my hand. "Most people enjoy a little thrill."

"Thrills are different from being terrified."

He frowned. "Really?"

Suddenly the ride jerked and images of Aaron slamming into the San Francisco Bay flashed before my eyes.

I yelped and grabbed at Scott again. He put an arm around me, laughing, and said, "Now, that's what I'm talking about."

I pinched his arm. "Shut up!"

"Hey, hey. It's fine," he said. "The ride always jerks up at the top."

He was right, of course, and now I was starting to feel like an idiot.

The ride was fine.

It was probably perfectly fine. I'm sure it'd been tested . . .

Tested by . . . whom?

Who had tested any of the equipment?

I took a deep breath.

"I'm skittish today."

"I understand," he said.

There was a look of compassion on his face that intrigued me and I decided getting my mind off the ride might be the best thing. "Have you been in love before?" I asked.

He raised his hands as the car descended. It was comical. The ride was so smooth, I wondered why the heck I'd been scared in the first place. I raised my arms alongside him and whooped.

He laughed. "Yeah. Her name was Jean. She was a total babe. I was crazy about her."

"What happened? She dumped you?" I asked.

He turned to me and said, "No, we married."

"Oh?"

"Then she got cancer about six months later." His eyes glossed over and he said quickly, "She went so fast. Didn't suffer."

My heart suddenly felt heavy. "I'm so sorry."

"My first book hit the *New York Times* list the day after she died," Scott said.

I gasped.

"Life is but a dream, huh?"

Our car reached the bottom and the smiling attendant welcomed us. "Beautiful view, eh?"

Scott picked up the penguin and helped me out of the gondola. We walked in silence toward the group. I felt I needed to say something, somehow try to soothe the wound I'd so carelessly opened up.

"How long ago?" I asked.

Scott handed me back the penguin, a far-off look in his eyes. "Five years ago."

"I'm so sorry," I said again.

He reached out and stroked my cheek. "Don't be sorry; you didn't know. These are some of the things we have to learn about each other." There was mischief in his eyes again as he said, "I mean, how else are we going to end up together?"

Thirteen

Nathan was practically jumping out of his skin. "Bumper cars! They have bumper cars! Can we ride, huh, can we?"

I hooked an arm through his. "Lead the way!"

The small bumper car ring had mini versions of Nascar racers and I realized the network would be covering the races around the time the show aired. No way was Hollywood going to miss a perfectly good promotional opportunity.

Nathan raced toward the cars and I couldn't help but feel he was more interested in them than me.

That's okay, I reminded myself. After all, I was supposed to be trying to figure out who was on the show for the money. I needed to get my mind off the horrific events of the past few days and get my head in the game.

Derek, the vet, seemed sincere and obviously I didn't have a good handle on Scott yet.

I climbed into the small bumper cars and zoomed toward

Nathan. He maneuvered around and raced away from me, laughing.

"I'm gonna getcha," I yelled.

I sped toward him and missed.

"Ha! What a woman driver," he screamed at me, then he tilted his head back and his blond curls bounced as he laughed so hard. The word *jackal* came to mind.

I whirled the car around and followed him. He seemed like such a kid. He had to be on the show for the money. He didn't seem to have the maturity to be looking for a real relationship.

Then again, does anyone go on a reality show looking for a real relationship?

"What're you looking for in life, Nathan?" I asked as my car connected with his bumper.

He bumped my car back. "Fun!"

"What else?" I asked, as I rammed into his mini racecar.

He grinned. "Love."

"What else?"

He bumped my car again, this time softer. "A friend. A best friend, I think," he said, laughing.

"Money?" I asked.

"Sure, lots of that. Fame, too. But love is more important than those things."

"You're a walking cliché," I said.

He drove his car away from me. "I'm not walking, sister. I'm racing."

I sped toward him. "And I'm doing the chasing, is that right?"

Suddenly our cars lost speed and the whir of the power going off punctuated the end of the ride.

He popped out of his car and helped me out of mine. I was still barefoot and slid on the smooth surface of the bumper car arena floor. He caught me.

"Oh, girl. It's almost like you're surfing! Show me your best move."

"Are you kidding?" I chuckled. "I don't surf!"

He fell to his knees in a mock death. "You're killing me. Next date, let's go to the beach. I'll teach you!" He took off at a sprint and slid across the slick floor, arms extended in full surf mode.

If only I had control of the dates. I'd love to surf with this crazy guy.

Richard was standing near the exit of the bumper car ride. In an unspoken dance, each guy was patiently waiting his turn with me. Man, group dates were awkward. And what was I really learning?

Nathan wiggled his fingers at me and I blew him a kiss as he disappeared, presumably to return to the blanket picnic—or for all I knew maybe they were all relaxing in their dressing rooms. Suddenly the image of Pietro hanging in mine flashed before my eyes.

I felt off balance and grabbed for Richard's arm.

"What is it?" he asked. "You look a little pale."

I covered my face with my free hand and took a deep breath.

"Cut!" Cheryl yelled. "What's wrong now?"

"Nothing!" I said. "I just . . . I just need some water."

"I'll get you some," Richard offered.

But a crew member was already handing me a bottle of icy water. I nodded at him gratefully, took a swig, then wiped the condensation from the bottle off my hand. "I'm okay now."

Cheryl eyed me cautiously. "Why don't we take fifteen?"

I shook my head. "We don't have to stop on my account," I said.

Richard rubbed my arm. "It's okay if you need to take a break."

"I have to give the crew a break anyway," Cheryl said.

Oh, my! This was the first time she was actually being nice to me.

What was going on?

I walked down the corridor toward my dressing room. What should have been a walk to relax myself turned into a death march. I couldn't get the image of Pietro out of my mind and now walking to the dressing room only made it worse.

I stopped in front of the door, wishing someone were with me, but that was silly. I was a big girl now.

What were the chances of finding another heinous scene in my dressing room? Really? Probably slim to none.

I heard rustling behind the door.

My breath caught.

Was someone inside my dressing room?

I frantically turned the knob and pushed open the door. A man was seated in my makeup chair. He whirled around and I screamed.

I clapped a hand over my frenetically beating heart. "Daddy!"

My father leapt from the chair and embraced me. "Shh. Don't make too much noise. I'm not supposed to be in here."

"You scared me! I wasn't expecting you!" I said, as I buried my head into his chest, emotions overwhelming me.

My dad was in his early fifties and more handsome than

any Hollywood actor could get. He had a full head of black hair, with just a little gray around the temples and a wicked smile. My mother had passed away when I was young and the only family I had was Dad.

I cried into his flannel shirt and inhaled his scent.

He smelled like the outdoors, fresh and breezy and woodsy at the same time. He was as solid as an oak and was always, *always* in my corner.

Dad was an almond farmer. He'd been my champion since before I even knew what a champion was.

"What are you doing here?" I asked.

"I'm your surprise guest!"

I covered my heart with my hand. "Thank God. Part of me feared they'd pull out old Mrs. Windbag."

Dad laughed. Mrs. Windbag was the nickname we'd given my first grade teacher, who'd sent scads of notes home complaining about my inability to sit still at school.

Dad had ignored those notes, saying in his best hick voice, "Sitting all day ain't natural. Kids oughta be out running all day. Helping out with the farm."

And, of course, that was what I did every day of my life until the age of fifteen, when I'd suddenly discovered boys. Then the farm and our small town seemed like a waste of time. I'd set my sights on a city. I wanted to grow up to be a city girl.

Cosmopolitan allure.

Who knew it would turn out to be overrated?

Dad stroked my hair. "What's wrong, honey?"

"Oh, Dad! If only you knew! But I don't have time to fill you in right now. I have to be back on the set in a few minutes. When can I see you next?"

"Well, I'm free all afternoon," Dad said.

"Come to my Prevost coach after we finish filming here, okay?"

Dad nodded. "Oh! And remember, you're not supposed to know it's me. So act surprised when they announce me."

I glanced at my watch and smiled. "I have to go." I kissed his cheek. "I'm so glad you're here."

I turned toward the door of the dressing room. I couldn't wait to get my date over with so that I could sneak another chat with Dad. Seeing him had felt so right. Like a prayer answered by God. Now I suddenly felt I could continue with the charade of the show.

With Dad as my counsel, I might actually have a chance of winning. Not that I harbored any hopes of actually falling in love, but maybe if I figured out who was on the show for the right reasons we'd get to split the prize money. And maybe, just maybe, I could figure out what had happened to Pietro and Aaron.

I pulled open the door to exit my dressing room and ran right into Ophelia. She straightened when she saw my dad standing in the middle of the room.

I shut the door and stuttered.

"I didn't see a thing," Ophelia said. "Let's get back to the set and I'll do a quick touch-up on your hair there."

We walked in silence.

When we got back to the set, Ophelia straightened the ends of my hair and gave me a thumbs-up.

I resumed my position near Richard. He was smiling and

welcoming. I tried to look enthusiastic about our date and plastered a grin on my face.

Cheryl called, "Action!"

Richard linked his arm through mine and we strolled toward the popcorn booth.

"Want a snack?" he asked.

I didn't really, but felt bad saying so, so I conjured up a little excitement in my voice. "Yum. Popcorn."

I must not have done a great job, though, because Richard said, "You don't have to if you don't want it. We can sit on the bench and chat."

I glanced over toward the canoe rides. "Or, we can go for a ride."

He followed my gaze. "The canoe ride?" he asked, incredulity thick in his voice.

I giggled more from nervousness than anything else and then regretted it. Giggling always made me feel like a ninny.

"I don't think I'll fit in it," Richard said.

"You never know until you take a chance," I said over my shoulder, starting toward the canoes. My voice sounded more confident than I felt.

I approached the attendant and held up two fingers. He pulled over the nearest canoe, with an image of an Indian chief painted on the side, and motioned to us.

"I could sue for that, you know," Richard said.

"For me forcing you to ride a canoe?"

"No. For that! The image of the Indian chief on the side of the canoe. It's—"

"Cut!" screamed Cheryl.

We looked up, startled.

"Uh, let's not go with the lawsuit talk," Cheryl said. "We don't want to encourage any frivolous litigation."

"I assure you," Richard said, "to the peoples affected by discrimination and harassment it is anything but frivolous."

"Right," Cheryl said, managing to sound almost bored. She pointed back toward the vending booths. "Popcorn! Much safer. The lighting is better there anyway."

She gave Richard a curt look and I felt that either I was growing in her estimation or she had a name to add to her doghouse list.

We reassembled over at the popcorn booth. A crew member handed us both bags of salty, stale popcorn.

I popped the first few pieces in my mouth and tried not to make a face. "What kind of law do you practice?" I asked.

"Labor and employment law."

I feigned interest. I knew right then and there I was not a fan of Richard's. He seemed overly confident, bordering on arrogant. This guy had to be on the show for the money, and even if he was there for love, there was no way I'd want to split the prize with him. He continued to drone on as we took a seat on the park bench.

I popped a few more kernels into my mouth, then suddenly gagged. I had a coughing fit.

Cheryl yelled, "Cut!"

Richard clapped my back and I spit out the popcorn, realizing that it was actually packaging popcorn.

"Oh, God!" I yelled.

Cheryl and the crew were laughing.

"Is this some kind of joke?" Richard roared.

"Not at all," Cheryl said, still laughing. "No one actually

eats the stuff! We just put a few real ones on top for looks, but the bags are always filled with packaging popcorn."

"That way they last forever," a crew member said, "and we don't end up with greasy bags."

They all continued to laugh.

I began to giggle, too, but Richard was still fuming.

"I was making a critical point," he said.

Part of me wanted to say, "You were?" but that would have been rude.

Cheryl laughed even harder and said, "Really?"

Richard reddened.

Ah, suddenly I was beginning to soften toward Broom-Hilda—even she had a sense of humor.

Fourteen

Richard and I somehow stumbled through our torturous scene, or at least Cheryl finally felt she'd gotten enough footage to use and her shout of "Cut!" came at last.

I sauntered toward the picnic blanket and collapsed. All the men were there, smiling except for Paul. "When's my turn?" he scolded.

The men had propped up the giant penguin and stuffed part of the baguette under a wing. It looked comical, but I refrained from laughing because I didn't want Paul to think I was laughing at him.

I jumped up. "Oh, yes. Of course."

"Saved the best for last, huh?" he said, standing up to join me.

We strolled toward some benches. The crew had put on a wind fan and my hair blew around my face.

Paul stopped in his tracks, brushed my hair back, and cradled my face.

"Georgia," he said, "I'm here for love. I came to . . . I'm on the show for love," he repeated. Heat surged between us and he bent to kiss me.

Was it true?

Could he be trying to send me a signal or was he . . . was he only doing this all for show? The thought made me nauseous.

I put my hands on his chest, separating us and pushing him away gently.

"Thank you for sharing your feelings," I said guardedly, aware of the cameras all around me. "I don't expect anyone to tell me to my face that they're on the show for money."

"I know," he whispered. "Sometimes life gives us surprises we don't expect. Sometimes they're good—"

I dropped my hands, breaking our physical connection. "And sometimes those surprises aren't so good."

"Cut," Cheryl called.

Paul held out his hands. "What's going on?"

"We're done. It's a wrap for now. Thanks, gang."

The other men began to leave the set. The crew started to take down the lights.

"But that's not fair," Paul said. "The other guys got a lot more time with her. They got to go on rides and stuff."

Cheryl shrugged. "I'm not in the business of fair."

I was ecstatic to be back at my trailer. My face was scrubbed and I was in my sweatpants and tank top, waiting for my dad to sneak off.

The filming for the carnival group date had taken up most of the morning and afternoon, but I still had an hour before I needed to get to hair and makeup for my evening one-on-one date with the good doctor Edward.

A pebble hit the side of my trailer and a man's voice called out to me.

"Georgia?"

I jumped to open the door. "Daddy! In here."

He smiled broadly as he entered my trailer. "Aw, my little girl, living in a trailer!"

"Shut up and have a seat."

He chuckled, then seated himself in my eat-in area, only he looked squeezed in between the wall and the table, sort of like a jack-in-the-box.

"Although, I gotta say," Dad said, "this is a really nice trailer."

"Technically, it's not a trailer; you know that. It's an RV."

Dad winked at me. "Sure it is."

We both laughed.

"Why don't they have you staying in that fancy mansion next door?" he asked.

"The men are staying there. Apparently they negotiated better than I did."

"Well, if the comforts around these parts aren't so comfortable you can always come home." He looked at me hopefully.

"Don't think I haven't been thinking the same thing."

Dad sat up straighter. "Really?"

I opened the fridge and pulled out a Budweiser for him. "I don't know."

"Your room is ready for you."

I laughed. "Well, Dad, by going back home I didn't mean back to my old bedroom."

Dad chuckled. "No, no, of course you didn't."

I handed him the beer can. "The booth may not be comfy, but at least the beer is cold."

He nodded. "Aw, don't worry about the booth. I'm just glad to see you. When Becca called she said all sorts of strange stuff had been happening during the filming. What's going on?"

I told him about Aaron's accident while bungee jumping, then Pietro's alleged suicide and Teresa's look-alike going by the name of Florencia.

My father sat grim faced as he listened.

"And you'll never guess who showed up to replace Aaron," I said.

Dad looked at me blankly. "What?"

"When Aaron had the bungee-jumping accident off the bridge. They sent someone to replace him on the show."

"Oh," Dad said. "Okay, who?"

"Paul," I answered.

Dad's face turned white. "Paul Sanders?"

Of course, along with Becca, the other person at my side on that fateful day when Paul had stood me up was my father. Dad had dressed in a tux. It was no small feat, getting him to agree to take off his suspenders and replace them with tails, believe me, but he'd been so happy and proud to be walking me down the aisle that he'd have worn a clown outfit if I'd asked him to.

And then the torturous wait, which had been terribly awkward and had gone on far too long, until we finally realized that Paul was not coming.

It had fallen to Dad to have to announce to the guests that the wedding was "postponed," with the word "indefinitely" hanging in the air.

My guests had taken it in stride. Everyone making excuses for Paul. "Oh, well, with a police officer you never know—probably an emergency somewhere!"

Dad slammed a fist onto the small table and his beer bounced up and down, nearly toppling over. "I'm going to kill him!"

He leapt to his feet, this time bumping into the table so hard that the beer did spill.

"Dad, no! Come on, sit down. It was a long time ago—"

"It hasn't been that long, Georgia! No self-respecting man leaves a woman at the altar. That no-good—"

"I'm not concerned with him, Dad. I'm over him." Even as I said it, the words caught in my throat. "I need to focus on the accidents. Don't you see? That woman Teresa/Florencia is on the set . . . I was bungee jumping with Aaron. At the same time . . . It could have been me."

Dad's face lost some color and he sat down again. "Do you think she's trying to get to you?"

"Yeah," I said emphatically. "I think she saw me on the set and figured a little revenge would feel like just what the doctor ordered after serving five years behind bars. But somehow things got messed up and Aaron got the brunt of it instead of me. Then I bet Pietro must have seen something and she had to silence him because he told me he needed to speak with me. And he ends up dead in my dressing room. I think she's after me."

Dad's complexion went from pale to bright red. "You have to stop the show. Get out of here. Come back to Cottonwood—"

"No. I'm not running." The words rushed out before I knew I meant them, but I did. "I won't back down. If it is

Teresa who's after me, I need to know. I can't keep running from things."

"Honey, you never run from things. You—"

"I do. I did. I ran from the humiliation of losing my job and my fiancé. I ran right into the claws of Broom-Hilda."

"What?" Dad asked.

I grabbed a rag from the kitchen and wiped up the spilled beer. "Do you want another one?" I asked.

"You got any bourbon?"

I laughed. "I know I've given you a shock, but my gut is telling me to stay. I have to figure out who killed Pietro and tried to kill Aaron or—"

"You don't believe it was suicide?"

"No."

"Well, isn't Paul here to figure all that out?"

I fixed my dad with my best "I am woman; hear me roar" look.

"Oh, hell, Georgia, I know you can solve this, I just don't want you hurt in the process."

EXT. BEACH DAY

Nathan is in bright pink and orange surfer shorts. He is topless and sports a ripped six-pack of abs. He's holding a surfboard in one hand and with the other he shades his eyes from the sun.

NATHAN

(*big smile*) Welcome to my office.

CHERYL (O.S.)
Is that what you call it?

NATHAN
Absolutely. I do some of my best work out here.

CHERYL (O.S.)
Do you?

NATHAN
Sure.

CHERYL (O.S.)
Work, I mean.

NATHAN
Sha. I surf.

CHERYL (O.S.)
So, you're on the show for money?

NATHAN
(*shoulders dropping and a look of extreme displeasure on his face*) No. The big surf's gonna come in and I'm going to ride it.

CHERYL (O.S.)
Are you saying, in fact, that you're looking for love?

NATHAN
(big toothy smile) Yeah. I'm looking for a little surfer girl. *(He breaks out into song.)* Surfer girl, surfer girl . . .

The Lincoln Town Car ride was nice. I knew it was all for show. They needed to film me getting out of it—otherwise, they might have sent a Prius to pick me up—but as it was I was bound and determined to enjoy the ride.

Cheryl had arranged for a private room at MOCA, the Museum of Contemporary Art, Los Angeles, to be ours for the evening. I was meeting Edward. We'd get to tour the museum at night alone and then enjoy a candlelit dinner.

I was so exhausted from the emotions of the carnival date that I just hoped the evening would go smoothly.

The car rolled to a stop and the driver got out. I expected him to come around and open my door, but instead the door opened to reveal Edward standing there.

"Good evening," he said, offering his hand to me.

Butterflies danced in my stomach and I suddenly felt shy. I took his hand and stepped out.

He looked me up and down, taking in my citrine gown. It was strapless with a bow on the waist and a floor-sweeping hem. He pressed his lips to the back of my hand. "You look gorgeous," he said. "It's good to see you again."

"Likewise," I said, putting an arm through his as we walked toward the front door of the museum.

The downtown location's sandstone building opened in the late 1980s to international acclaim. MOCA is the only museum in Los Angeles dedicated to contemporary art.

The building seemed too modern and plain for my taste, but as soon as we walked down the courtyard steps, I could see what the fuss had been about. The chief exhibition spaces downstairs were lit from above by groups of pyramidal skylights.

We walked down a corridor and into a large room that had high ceilings punctuated with those amazing skylights. In the center of the room was a table set for two complete with a three-tiered silver candelabra. It would have been incredibly romantic, minus the camera crew and production staff.

They were a constant reminder of what I was here to do.

Edward and I decided to tour the exhibits around the room.

On one side were marble statues in an array of sizes and colors and an astounding and almost frightening spectrum of emotions.

The first statue was a man in agony, or at least part of a man. It was a pair of hands and a torso and head, struggling to free himself from the surrounding marble. It was called *Distress*, and I certainly felt distressed as I gazed upon it.

"Wow, that's something, huh?" I asked.

Edward chuckled. "Sort of how I felt in med school."

I laughed, but didn't want to say, "Sort of how I feel right now."

We moved on to the next statue, a little boy with a baseball bat in his hand and a look of complete joy and rapture on his face.

"That's more like it, right?" I said, looking up at Edward.

He smiled. "You want to have kids?"

"Sure, don't you?"

He nodded. "Definitely."

A warm, fuzzy feeling enveloped me as Edward put a hand on the small of my back and steered me toward the table in the center of the room.

He pulled out a chair for me.

"What manners!" I said.

"My mother would be horrified if she saw that I didn't pull out a chair for a lady."

"Especially on national television," I teased.

"Exactly," he said, taking a seat across from me. He examined the bottle of wine and then held it up for me to appreciate.

I wasn't really the hippest wine expert, but I liked that he'd shown me the bottle. Paul had always selected the different varieties we drank, with no regard to what I thought.

"Are you a wine guy?" I asked.

He shrugged. "I know a little. This one is from Glen Ellen, so my guess is it's gotta be good."

I flashed back to my popcorn episode that afternoon and wondered if there was actually wine in the bottle or if it was just colored water.

Edward filled my glass and the fragrant earth scent reassured me that the wine was indeed real.

I swirled my wine and watched the wine legs form on the sides of my glass. "Tell me about your mom."

He took the folded white napkin that was perched like a bird next to his wineglass and fanned it into his lap. "Ah, Mom! She's something else. She raised me and my brother alone. Single-handedly."

"No dad?" I asked.

"Dad walked out on us, while she was pregnant with my brother."

I felt a little pull inside my chest as I watched his melancholic expression. "I'm sorry about that."

He gave me a sad smile. "Men. Not reliable."

"Some men are," I said, thinking about my own dad.

"I'm glad you're confident about that."

I fiddled with my napkin, feeling uncomfortable. Edward was giving me a strange look.

Did he know I'd been stood up at the altar?

And if so, did he know it had been by Paul?

We carefully removed the silver platters covering our dishes to reveal delectable salmon slathered in a pesto and cream sauce.

"Looks delicious!" I glanced up at the camera that was closest to me. The lights were so bright by the camera that I couldn't see anything beyond it. "Can we eat this?" I asked into the white light.

I was answered by a snicker.

Cheryl appeared between the cameras. "You can eat. Take a few bites, but for God's sake, spice up the date a bit. You've got us bored to death."

"What?" I asked.

"Sit closer to him. Flirt. Feminine wiles—you know. Figure out why he's on the show. Grill him! Make it exciting for the viewer."

"Are you saying I'm boring?"

"Exactly," she answered.

I gave Edward a sheepish grin. "Sorry."

He chuckled. "I share the blame. I suppose I'm equally boring, although for the record I want you to know that *I* wasn't bored at all."

We took a few tentative bites of dinner and drank some

wine. I decided to go ahead and really sample the wine; after all, maybe it would loosen me up and I'd be more entertaining for the viewers—that, and the bottle of pinot noir was starting to open up and it was hard to pass up.

"Where do you want to live?" Edward asked suddenly.

"What do you mean?" I asked, caught a little off guard. The last thing I wanted to discuss on national television was all the reasons I wouldn't be returning to San Francisco.

"Well, I work in the Bay Area. You're happy in San Francisco, right? If we . . . if this . . . works out, then we'll want to be geographically close to each other . . ."

"Frankly, I've lived in San Francisco for six years now and I find myself not really wanting to return."

There was a disappointed look in his eyes and I struggled for something to say that would lift his spirits, but instead I said, "I grew up in Cottonwood. I think I'd like to raise a family in the country. On a farm."

His eyes twinkled. "On a farm? Sounds idyllic."

"In a lot of ways, it was."

He remained silent, but reached out and began rubbing his thumb across my wrist, the unasked question hanging between us: What kind of career growth would a small, Podunk town offer a surgeon?

Edward broke the silence by pulling me to him and kissing me. His lips were full on mine and I felt a delicious warmth spread from my chest into my belly.

"Cut, got the kiss," Cheryl yelled.

Edward pulled away from me, looking more than a little thwarted. "Oh, I . . . I was hoping we'd get longer."

I glanced down at my almost untouched salmon dinner. "Me, too!"

"Come on, we need a shot of you all walking out to the car."

My stomach grumbled as I bid adieu to a perfectly prepared gourmet meal that I wouldn't get to eat.

Edward escorted me to the Town Car. I was expecting a good-night kiss, but instead of pressing his lips to mine, he embraced me.

His lips brushed against my ear and a chill tickled my spine when he whispered urgently, "I need to talk to you, Georgia."

Fifteen

Edward's words wrapped around my heart like a sea creature's tentacles, digging and squeezing. My heart constricted and my breath caught.

He had something to tell me.

Just like Pietro!

I am in danger or he is in danger.

I grabbed at his neck. The camera was on us. I wanted to shout at them to leave us alone, but pressed my lips to Edward's instead.

"What is it?" I asked desperately between kisses, hoping my hair was obstructing the camera angle enough so that no one would be able to tell what we were saying.

"Not now," he said calmly. He stepped away from me and opened the car door. "Good night, Georgia."

His eyes were locked on mine. He seemed to be telling me to forget it. To get into the car.

"I had a great time," he prompted. "I hope you don't make me wait too long for the next date." He winked.

I nodded dumbly.

Date?

Is that code for something?

He tucked me into the car and then the driver was speeding away.

Darn!

I knew I couldn't very well have a conversation with Edward then, but it was still frustrating and frightening as hell.

The Town Car pulled into the spot next to my Prevost coach. I thanked the driver and hurried inside the coach to change. I was hoping Becca would take me to a place where I could have some greasy pub food along with the aforementioned and promised cocktail. Edward and I had finished our "date" in record time and I, of course, found myself still hungry. A few small bites of salmon wouldn't cut it for me for dinner.

I slipped out of the citrine gown and found that I could breathe again. These tight dresses had me holding my breath the entire time. But I knew better than to complain or they'd put me into a corset.

I grabbed a pair of my most comfortable jeans and sneakers and put them on. It was still early.

The telltale sound of gravel crunching around my Prevost alerted me that Becca was likely outside.

I peered through the blinds, just to confirm, and was rewarded by seeing my best friend practically skipping toward my door.

I flung open the door. "Why are you so happy?"

She laughed. "Am I?"

"You were floating across the parking lot."

She waved a hand. "Are you ready? I'm dying for a drink. I'll tell you on the way."

I grabbed my small purse, which held my wallet, lipstick, and keys, then looked around. Without my phone I always felt like I was forgetting something. I shrugged. "Okay, I guess I'm ready."

I locked the coach door, then followed Becca through the parking lot and side alley to her yellow Volkswagen Bug.

"So, what is it? Why are you glowing?"

She grinned. "It's nothing really." She shrugged. "It's just that I got to flirt with Ty a little while you were on your carnival date and he's hot."

"Oh, really? Sparks and all?"

She wiggled her eyebrows at me. "Yeah." She started the car and maneuvered through the L.A. streets. "We have to keep it on the down-low, though, because I don't want the barracuda hearing anything."

I nodded. "Well, she won't hear it from me."

I filled Becca in on my date with Edward and how strangely it had ended.

"I wonder what he wants to tell you. Any idea?" she asked.

"No! I have to find a way to talk to him."

"Well, don't look at me."

I bit my lip and fidgeted with her car radio.

"I'm probably gonna get busted for taking you out," she said.

"Right. Right," I mumbled.

"Don't look at me like that," she said.

"Like what? I'm not even looking at you. I'm looking at the radio!"

"Whatever, but I know you're all thinking, 'Why can't Becca help me?'"

"I'm not. I wasn't. I know you're not supposed to help me."

She sighed. "I'll see if I can get you time with Edward."

I smiled.

She poked me. "Shut it."

"I didn't even say anything!" I protested.

"Anyway, we're here now," Becca said. "Look for parking."

"Already? I was expecting traffic."

"No, not at this hour. Plus I picked somewhere close because you have to get up early tomorrow."

"Why do I have to get up early?"

"It's the elimination."

"Why can't we do those in the evening?"

Becca found a tight spot and slipped her car into it. "Because you have two more dates tomorrow."

"Why can't they be the next day?" As soon as I'd said it, I knew I was being whiny and that Becca would call me on it.

"What? We're made of money? You want a little cheese with that whine?"

I waved her off, but she persisted. "Do you know how much it costs to rent out the mansion? Plus it's got a lot of issues. There's an active leak and I don't know how long we can stay."

"Okay, okay," I said as we got out of the car and walked toward a small bar. There was a neon sign that read POOL and lots of signage for domestic beers.

"But it's not raining—how can a leak disrupt our filming schedule?"

Becca leaned into me as she pulled open the door to the bar. "Plumbing leak. It's the upstairs bathrooms and it's not the gray water, if you know what I mean."

"Yuk!" I said.

She made a face. "I know."

I shook my head at the irony. Hollywood would not delay a filming schedule due to a severe accident or suicide, but add in a little waste plumbing fiasco and everyone folded.

My eyes slowly adjusted to the dark bar. In the far corner was a pool table and alongside the bar was a wall that highlighted various celebrity headshots along with their autographs. We grabbed a seat at the bar. As soon as we ordered a couple of lemon drops, Becca took off to the ladies' room to freshen up.

I was looking forward to relaxing with her and catching up on things. Like telling her about seeing my dad and asking if she had an update on Teresa or maybe Aaron. Was he still in the hospital? Still in a coma?

I fiddled with my cocktail napkin as I wondered if there was a way to question Aaron. If he was still in a coma, it was unlikely, but if he was recovering maybe I could cash in a favor with an old coworker on SFPD and ask them to drop by and talk with him.

The bartender placed a chilled martini glass in front of me and one directly in front of the empty spot beside me. He poured the lemon drop from the shaker into the glasses.

I was ready to lick the sugar from around the rim of the glass, but sensed someone approaching from behind me.

I straightened and turned, my old cop senses firing.

Scott was standing directly behind me. "Hey, fancy meeting you here."

Ignoring the jolt of nervous energy that fluttered through my stomach, I said, "What are you doing here?" I asked.

"We followed you."

"Who? Who is we?" I asked, searching over his shoulder for another familiar face and praying that I wouldn't find my ex-fiancé, Paul.

"Ty and I." He motioned with his arm toward where Becca had disappeared.

I could see Becca and Ty talking in the hallway that led to the restrooms. Ty was leaning in toward her, pinning her to the wall between his muscular arms. Becca was laughing at something he said.

"Oh," I said.

"He likes her," Scott said in a confidential tone.

I smiled. "I can see that. Looks like he's going to eat her up on the spot."

Scott laughed.

"So, do you think he's on the show for the money?"

Scott wrinkled his nose. "Yeah, I think so."

"Do you know who's in it for the money? Can you just give me the names now and save me some grief?" I asked.

"I don't know for sure, but I have some guesses."

"You're one of them, right?"

"Are you kidding? If I was in it for the money why would I be here?" He opened his hand to encompass the bar.

"To fool me," I said.

"But I'm breaking the show's rules right now. I'd be risking getting kicked off."

"Well, look at Ty," I answered.

He raised an eyebrow. "Right. Okay, but he's not the sharpest tool in the shed. Please let's not compare me to him."

I laughed and he smiled openly. He looked irresistible, so cute and smart and confident.

I took a sip of my lemon drop, then asked, "How did you two get out of the house?"

He frowned. "Oh, that's not hard. There's no security or anything." He shrugged. "We just slipped out and didn't say anything to the other guys."

From across the room I could see Becca and Ty locking lips. I fought the urge to grab Scott and do the same.

Why does he have to be so sexy?

"So, what's up with you and the insurance guy?" he asked.

"Who?" I asked.

"Who?" Scott repeated. "Come on, don't act like you don't know who I'm talking about. The cop on the show pretending to be an insurance guy."

"Why do you think he's a cop?"

Scott hailed the bartender. "I wasn't born yesterday."

"Does it bother you that he's a cop?"

"No. Should it?"

"Not if you're not hiding anything."

He laughed. "I'm not hiding anything. You're the one hiding something." The bartender appeared in front of us and Scott ordered a manhattan, then turned to me. "May I buy you a drink?"

"I have one." I indicated the glass beside me, which I was shocked to find empty.

He chuckled. "You pretty much sucked it down as soon as you saw me. Do I make you nervous?"

"No. Uh . . ."

He ordered me another lemon drop and sat on Becca's stool. He was quiet for a moment, giving me the opportunity to study the contour of his jaw, which was strong and masculine. He suddenly smiled a lopsided grin, apparently indicating that he knew I was studying him and was pleased about it.

"You're incredible!" I said, embarrassed about being caught checking him out.

The chemistry between us was undeniable.

The bartender placed our drinks in front of us and left. I looked around and found that Becca and Ty had disappeared from the hallway.

"I can't believe she'd leave me alone with someone like you," I said.

"Someone like me?" Scott said. "Should I be offended by that remark?"

I shrugged, frightened by our connection and looking for any excuse to push him away. Was I really ready for relationship? "Someone who wants to rush off and see the videotape of a man plunging off the Golden Gate Bridge."

He shook his head. "No, no, no. You can't fault me for that."

I stared at him. "Please!"

He continued. "It was a shock. I was in shock. I mean, how often does that happen?"

"You going into shock? I don't know."

"Ah, you're one of those people who approach conversation like a sport. I like that about you. I meant the guy plunging into the ocean off the bridge. That part was a shock."

I sat up straighter suddenly. "Hey, wait a minute. Did you see the tape?"

"Yeah," Scott said.

"You did!" A bolt of excitement fired through me and I practically jumped off of my stool.

"What did you see?"

"Oh! Who's the ghoul now?" he said.

"No! I don't mean it like that." I shoved at his shoulder and he caught my hand, laughing.

"I mean—you know—did you see anything that might indicate it wasn't an accident?"

He shook his head. "No."

"How about with Pietro? Did you notice anything—"

"I don't know," Scott said, squeezing my hand and lacing his fingers through mine.

A warm, tingling sensation zipped up my arm and into my heart.

"Did you talk with him much?" I asked. "Did you know him at all? Do you think—"

"I didn't talk with him about anything significant. I've pretty much kept my distance from the others . . ." He tugged on my hand, gently pulling me forward. He leaned into me, tilting his head so that our foreheads and noses touched. "Why do you want to keep talking about all those other guys?" he said in a low voice.

My breath caught and something in my belly quivered as I looked into his dark eyes.

"I want to know what happened to them," I murmured.

"Forget about what happened to them," he whispered. "And think about what's happening now."

His mouth closed around mine, sending all synapses in my body into overdrive.

What is *happening now?*

Trouble.

Sixteen

INT. LIBRARY DAY

Richard is looking directly at the camera. Behind him are some nondescript bookshelves and a small low table with a lamp. He is about thirty, wearing a suit and tie.

CHERYL (O.S.)
So tell us, Richard, are you in this for love?

RICHARD
Well, let's just say I don't need any women in my life right now. I just passed the bar and I'm starting my law career. I need to be able to focus on my career.

CHERYL (O.S.)
So you came on the show for the prize money?

RICHARD
Oh, no, no. I didn't mean to imply that at all. What I said was I don't *need* any women in my life.

CHERYL (O.S.)
I'm sorry, I don't follow.

RICHARD
(*waving his hand around*) Well, there's clearly a distinction between need and want.

CHERYL (O.S.)
Right. So you would *like* a woman in your life, is that correct?

RICHARD
(*patronizing smile*) Now, what man wouldn't like a woman in his life?

CHERYL (O.S.)
(*laughter*) Okay.

RICHARD
What I'm saying is that I'd like a woman in my life that will, shall I say, *complement* my career.

CHERYL (O.S.)
All right, can you tell us in plain English and avoid all the legalese: Are you on the show for love or money?

RICHARD
(*a baffled expression on his face*) Love, of course.

The light pouring through the blinds in the trailer was enough to wake the dead. My head was pounding and I was angry with myself for staying out late. What was I thinking? And what had I accomplished?

Absolutely nothing, except now my body was betraying me every time I saw Scott or Edward—going all tingly and giddy and bubbly girly.

Ugh! I'm like a teenager!

I rolled out of bed and showered quickly, then presented myself in the makeshift makeup tent. Ophelia was already there waiting for me, arranging the brushes on the counter and plugging in the hair iron. She did my makeup in short order, stopping only to comment on the dark rings around my eyes.

"You need more sleep," she said. "There's only so much I can do with concealer."

When she was done with my hair and makeup she assisted me into a one-shouldered, emerald-colored gown. It had a tulle overlay that softened the underlay, which had a metallic sheen. The dress was gathered at the left hip and had a flared skirt with a dramatic train. It was stunning.

Ophelia handed me shockingly high matching stilettos. I felt like Cinderella stepping into the shoes—well, actually like one of her stepsisters, because I couldn't get my toes in past the heel.

Ophelia grabbed my ankle and tried to shove my foot into the shoe, demanding, "Aren't you a size seven?"

"Yes." I grimaced as she succeeded in squishing my foot into the shoe. I couldn't feel my toes and the arch of my foot was so badly compressed I feared standing up. "Uh, this isn't going to work."

She frowned and glanced at her watch. "We only have a few minutes. Come on." She tried to jam my left foot into the other shoe.

"Ouch!" I said.

"You only have to wear them for a minute. I'm not asking you to run a marathon in them!"

"I can't even stand!" I said.

She shook her head in disgust, clearly biting back what she wanted to say.

She reached for the walkie-talkie that was on the counter and squawked in a panicked voice to Kyle.

"The shoes make the dress!" she said.

She was right. Because of the flare on the skirt and the dramatic train, you had to have stunning shoes. It was as if the dress had been made to feature the unrealistically high, torturously tight stilettos.

Kyle's voice chirped back something inaudible, but Ophelia seemed to understand, because she muttered, "Okay, okay."

She leaned down and, reaching into one of her large duffel bags, pulled out a long, sharp object that glinted against the light, my cop brain instantly registering the weapon as a knife.

Oh, my God, is Ophelia working with Teresa?

I sprang to my feet and grabbed her wrist as she straightened, using her own momentum against her to roll her onto the floor. She fell face-first, the knife clattering out of her hand as she screamed.

I grabbed for the knife at the same time as I jammed my knees into her spine. The gown ripped at my back and the small room filled with the sound of tearing fabric.

"What are you doing?" she wailed.

"What are *you* doing?" I demanded.

She turned her head to the side and I could glimpse the look of horror mixed with fear on her face. "Oh, God! Don't kill me! It was you, wasn't it? You killed that poor man in your dressing room!"

Kyle appeared in the doorway of our tent. He was holding a pair of pink bunny slippers that sported a pair of wide eyes on the front that matched Kyle's own wide eyes. "What . . . what's going on?" he stuttered.

"Don't just stand there!" Ophelia yelled. "Tackle her! She's going to kill me."

I looked from Kyle to Ophelia. "I'm not going to kill you. You were going to attack me with a knife!"

"The knife was for the shoes," Kyle said.

"What?"

Ophelia laughed, a loud, stress-releasing cackle. "I wasn't going to attack you. I was only going to fix the shoes."

"With a knife?" I asked.

Kyle's face crinkled in disappointment. "We didn't have another pair in your size."

The adrenaline that had surged through my body dissipated, leaving me feeling shaky and stupid.

"There's been a lot of *mishaps*, for lack of a better word, on the set," I said. "I jumped the gun when I saw the knife." Still clutching the knife, I rolled off Ophelia.

"Well," Kyle said, "I can't blame you for that. I know cops, even ex-cops, get jumpy, but please, Ophelia wouldn't hurt a fly."

But people had been hurt, and I knew someone was behind it. I didn't believe that Aaron's fall was an accident or that Pietro had committed suicide. And who was more likely to be responsible for the incidents than a person with access to everything, like a makeup artist or hair stylist? Which made me think again . . .

Where was Teresa/Florencia?

Kyle handed me the bunny slippers, then scooped Ophelia off the floor. He assisted her into the makeup chair and then picked up one of the stilettos. Studying the back of the shoe, he said, "We're going to give it a slight modification for the shot and then we won't film your feet again. You can use the slippers."

Film the elimination scene in bunny slippers?

Part of me was relieved that I wouldn't have to wear the torturous shoes for long, but the other part of me felt ridiculous. How would anyone ever take me seriously?

Kyle stuck out his hand and I sheepishly gave him the knife. He sawed the back of the designer heel, creating a gap in the seam. Ophelia watched with a sour expression, massaging her elbow.

"Did I hurt you?" I asked.

She shook her head, her voice suddenly full of pride. "No, no. I'm fine."

"I'm sorry," I muttered.

She gave me a slight nod, letting me know my apology had been accepted but that we weren't exactly on buddy-buddy terms.

Kyle handed me the modified shoe. "Try this on for size."

I slipped it on. "I can get my foot in, but it's still tight. I mean, I can't walk."

"You can walk to the set in the slippers."

I felt a breeze through my open dress. "Uh-oh."

Kyle made a pouty face. "What now?"

"My dress is ripped."

Ophelia sighed. "If you hadn't attacked me—"

I held up a hand. "Listen, you should never pull a knife on someone without their knowing—"

"I wasn't pulling a knife on you. Don't say it like that."

Kyle inserted himself between us and made a circle with his finger. "Turn around, girlfriend, let me see the damage."

I bit my lip and turned around, mentally calculating the days I had left on the set. "Maybe I should just get another dress with shoes that fit."

"No time," Kyle said. "You're late as it is. I can fix this with duct tape."

Ophelia got out of the makeup chair and made a big show of reaching for her duffel bag. "I'm just getting out a roll of duct tape, ma'am, okay? No need to jujitsu me to the floor."

"Oh, stop it," I said.

"Well, I don't want you to think we're going to tie you up with it or anything," Ophelia said.

A chill danced up my spine. I couldn't afford to like or trust these people.

Liking and trusting the wrong person was a mistake that could cost me my life.

I stiffened while Kyle fixed the back of my dress, then I stepped into the bunny slippers, all the while watching both Ophelia and Kyle.

"Let's go. I'll walk you to the set," Kyle said.

I motioned to the door of the tent. "After you."

Kyle escorted me into a room set up to look like a library. Volumes of leather-bound books lined two mahogany bookshelves that were propped behind two gold chairs. Kyle vanished into the background and I suddenly felt alone and out of place even with all the crew members humming about.

Alone and vulnerable.

The lights were blinding me as I tried to look past them to see Kyle; I assumed he was still in the room clutching my high heels.

One of the techs approached me to connect my microphone pack. When I turned around so he could secure it, he laughed.

He patted the duct tape. "One doughnut too many, huh?"

I stiffened. "No! I . . . uh . . ."

He chuckled. "Sorry, I didn't mean to offend you. I mean, you're, like, a size two or something."

I laughed and the residue of the anxiety I'd felt in the hair and makeup tent disappeared. "No, I'm not offended. Let's just say the dress isn't really suited for jujitsu, and, for the record, I'm nowhere near a size two."

He indicated the gold chair. "You can have a seat. They want to work on the lights next."

I sat and waited for the magic to happen all around me, pondering the events in the dressing room.

Surely I had made a mistake.

But . . . if Teresa was out on parole and living as Florencia . . . and she wanted revenge on me for putting her behind bars, then it was realistic to think she could have help.

Could Ophelia be working with her? How well did they know each other? I'd have to dig deeper.

As I sat there ruminating, the rest of the crew entered the room, including Cheryl, followed by a cameraman. She took one look at my bunny slippers and turned beet red. "What's going on?" she asked.

"We had a wardrobe malfunction," Kyle said from the back of the room.

At least, it sounded like Kyle, but actually all I could see was a bright light in my face.

Cheryl shook her head. "I'm not going to film her feet in this scene, but she'll need shoes for the elimination scene."

"We have that covered," Kyle said.

Cheryl nodded. "Okay, Georgia, this scene is real simple. Harris is going to come in and have a chat with you and then we'll reveal our special guest."

Cheryl disappeared into the light and Harris Carlson entered the room. He took the other gold seat across from me. The man never ceased to amaze me: He hardly glanced over at me but as soon as Cheryl called "Action," he came to life and beamed a radiant smile at me as if we were lifelong confidants.

"Georgia, I know this has been quite a journey for you," Harris said.

"It has indeed," I said. Even if the audience was privy to only half of what we'd been through.

"You've had quite a few exotic dates, from rock climbing to taking in a carnival to visiting L.A.'s Museum of Contemporary Art."

It was strange to listen to him give a litany of my dates, but I realized he was providing a recap for viewers who might be tuning in to the show late. Also, I imagined they'd splice scenes from our dates into the promos and he was basically providing the voice-over for those commercials.

"That's right," I said.

"You're getting to know the men a bit more now. Nathan is a champion surfer; Edward, a handsome doctor; and Scott is a *New York Times* bestselling author. It's turning out to be quite a competition. Is there one in particular who's a forerunner for your heart?"

"They're all great guys," I said, fearing I was coming off a bit stiff.

"Right," Harris said. His expression basically confirmed that I was completely wooden, not to mention I could tell he thought I was hopeless.

He turned to the camera and spoke into it. "We know that with many contestants, there comes a time when they wish they could get some good old-fashioned advice from someone they know and love. And that's the reason why"—he swung toward me—"we have a surprise guest. Someone is here to help you through these difficult and life-altering decisions."

Harris Carlson stood and gestured toward the door. My dad entered the room. I sprang from my chair and rushed into his arms.

"Dad!"

Harris Carlson introduced my dad to the camera and then left, presumably to forage in the break room for chocolate croissants or an éclair at the food cart.

Cheryl said, "Keep rolling."

Dad squeezed my hands. "Hello, peaches."

We separated and sat in our respective chairs.

"I'm so glad you're here, Dad," I said.

Dad was dressed up for the camera. He wore slacks and a sweater vest that made his blue eyes sparkle. I knew he was handsome, but ordinarily he wore jeans and a work shirt with suspenders. Dressed up as he was, he was breathtaking, and a little part of me prickled as I spotted Cheryl studying him and licking her lips.

Dad didn't seem to notice the attention; instead, he steepled his fingers and smiled warmly at me. "I understand you're meeting some interesting young men."

"Uh, right," I said. "There's Richard, who's an attorney."

Dad nodded. "I see." He cocked his head, waiting for me to say more.

But did I really have anything more to say about Richard?

"He's very confident. Uh . . . a very confident type," I muttered.

Dad frowned, seemingly trying to follow my train of thought. "Do you think he's on the show for the right reasons?"

I shuddered to realize I didn't even care. So what if Richard was on the show for love? I wasn't feeling any connection to him, so at this point it didn't matter.

"I don't know, Dad, but I don't think I'm honestly interested—"

"Cut!" Cheryl screamed out.

I looked up, startled. "What?"

"You can't tell your dad you're not interested in one of the contestants."

"But I'm not interested in Richard," I protested.

"You're supposed to be building anticipation. The audience is supposed to be watching and trying to guess who you're going to eliminate. You can't tell them, 'I'm going to dump X and Y.' That's no fun. They won't watch the elimination scene then, because they'll already know who's out of the competition!"

"Right," Dad agreed.

I turned to him, horrified.

Now Dad is agreeing with Cheryl?

He reached out for my hand. "It's okay, honey—just create some questions in the mind of the viewer." He winked at me. "Like when you play poker and no one realizes you're about to zap the money straight out of their wallets."

"I'm not comfortable lying," I said.

Cheryl leaned in. "Don't think of it as *lying*. Think of it as, well, as not disclosing the whole truth."

When I made a face, she added, "Creating an illusion. See, I'm not *lying* to the audience about you being in bunny slippers, I'm just creating the illusion—"

I held up a hand. "I get it."

Much as I didn't like it, the more I resisted, the longer the filming would take, and I'd already had it about up to my eyeballs.

When I finished giving Dad a summary as best I could,

one that seemed to please Cheryl, he said, "Well, your eyes lit up when you talked about the writer and the doctor."

Seriously?

That was the same thing Becca had said.

Could I really be having feelings for two guys I'd just met on a reality TV show?

Seventeen

When I stepped back into the hall of the mansion, the stench from the leaking pipes was prominent. The crew was working feverishly. I suspected they wanted to film as quickly as possible and get out into the fresh air.

One of the runners on the set was spraying Febreze to no avail.

Cheryl led me toward the fireplace mantel. "We need a shot with your shoes on. The rest of the scene you can do with the slippers on."

"Right," I said, as Kyle slipped the high heels onto my feet.

"Don't move," he instructed, "or you could fall."

He arranged my feet in a ballerina's pose of third position with one heel snugged up tight into the other foot's arch.

"I don't think I could move if my life depended on it," I said.

Ophelia came in with Harris Carlson next to her. She

powdered his nose and sprayed his hair, then left without even a sideways glance toward me.

Cheryl instructed the crew to film me, then when they finished I was able to lose the stilettos while the men were called in.

Richard and Paul were the first to enter. They were dressed in tuxes and frowned when they saw my bunny slippers. Nathan and Ty followed. Nathan had on a suit with an orange plaid dress shirt and sneakers. He looked surfer dressy/casual with his longish blond hair bouncing as he walked. He flashed me the "hang loose" sign with his hand. Ty had on a baby blue suit with his signature cowboy hat and boots. He gave me a thumbs-up as he took his place next to Nathan.

Derek came in next, with his cane, and smiled warmly at me.

Edward and Scott brought up the rear.

Edward looked sophisticated in a dark suit. He said, "You look gorgeous, Georgia."

"Thank you," I said.

"I have a pair just like those at home," Scott said, as he winked.

I laughed. "Kind of you to notice. I guess my feet are too big for the petite shoes they have around here."

Scott crinkled his nose at me. "Mine are, too," he confessed. He swung his foot out, clad in a huge dark loafer, to show me.

We laughed together and I felt my heart soften as I looked into his brown eyes.

Cheryl clapped her hands. "Save the flirting for the camera!" she instructed.

Flirting?

Was I just flirting? And was it that obvious?

I glanced at Paul: he was scowling at Scott. I guess it had been obvious.

One of the show runners set up the tray of champagne. There were five flutes. Harris stepped close to me and took the lead as soon as Cheryl gave him the sign.

"Georgia, as you know, we have seven men remaining and only five champagne flutes to share." He made a dramatic gesture with his arm to encompass the table with the flutes. "It's time for you to say good-bye to two bachelors."

I nodded.

Harris reached out and squeezed my elbow. "I know it's a difficult decision." His face was composed in such a serious expression that I found it hard not to giggle. "But you've had time to consult with your special guest and I know you'll make the right choice."

"I'm ready," I said, taking a flute in hand. "Ty, will you accept a glass of champagne?"

Ty strolled over and tipped his cowboy hat. "I surely will, Miss Georgia."

He took the flute and then resumed his place next to Nathan.

One by one I called Paul, Edward, Scott, and Nathan. Each accepted his glass with a smile and then resumed his place in line.

Harris took a step forward and said, "Richard, Derek, I'm sorry. Please take a moment to say your good-byes."

Richard scowled, then stepped forward and shook my hand. "Georgia, I'm sorry it didn't work out. I . . . I simply don't know what to say."

I've left the attorney speechless?

Doubtful. I was sure he'd have a few choice words to say about me in the camera confessional.

"I'm sorry, too, Richard. I have to know. Were you on the show looking for love or money?"

His lips tweaked up, a mocking, condescending smirk on his face. "Georgia, I was looking for love."

Richard turned on a heel, then said over his shoulder, "At least now I can get some fresh air."

The group of men erupted in knowing chuckles. Then Derek moved closer to me, took my hand, and patted it. "It was a pleasure meeting you. I hope you find everything you're looking for."

"Thank you, Derek. And thank you for your service to our country."

I felt awful sending Derek away. After all, he was a war hero, but somehow I knew he wasn't the one for me and keeping him from home when he'd already done time abroad didn't feel right.

He nodded, then said, "And I know you have to ask, and I want you to know that I was here for love."

I struggled to catch my breath, feeling worse than I already did.

"It's okay," he said with a shy smile that looked like it was hiding a bit of hurt. "It's really okay. Good luck." Derek walked out of the mansion, leaning on his cane.

Before I had a moment to wallow in what I'd just done, Harris Carlson clapped his hands together. "Well, Georgia, only five men remain. Today you've eliminated two contestants who were on the show looking for love. And, as our viewers are aware from our confessional videos of the remaining five contestants, two are looking for love and three are on the show for the money."

The odds were against me.

I smiled at the remaining men. They were holding their champagne flutes and looking back at me expectantly.

I held up my flute, eager to finish the scene as the foul smell of the plumbing waste was beginning to choke us. "Well, gentlemen. Thank you for accepting this toast. I have a wonderful date planned for tomorrow." I felt so ridiculous; not only was I standing in front of the group of men in bunny slippers and a taped-on dress, but the date wasn't for tomorrow, it was for as soon as we could get changed and out of the house.

"There will be a group date for three of you and a one-on-one," Harris Carlson announced. "Unfortunately, that means someone will be left behind."

"We're going to the Santa Monica Pier," I said.

Nathan's eyes grew wide. "Ooh! I think that means I'm invited! I'm mean, I'm just sayin'."

Everyone clinked their glasses together, seemingly in as much of a hurry as I was to flee the mansion.

INT. LIBRARY DAY

Derek is looking directly at the camera. Behind him are bookshelves and, beside him, his cane is propped up against the small low table with a lamp. He is in his late twenties and wearing jeans and a green striped shirt.

CHERYL (O.S.)
So, Derek, are you looking for love or are you looking for money?

DEREK
Definitely looking for love. Just got back from Afghanistan. Really teaches you a life lesson that anything can happen at any time. People are here one minute and gone the next. You need to make the most out of life. Nothing really matters except for being with people you love. Sharing your life. After that, you know, having someone to memorialize you and your life and your experiences. What is money? Sure, it facilitates things and make things easier. You can afford a nice car, but does that nice car avoid traffic? No, you gotta sit in the same traffic along with everybody else. Just gotta get through life with somebody that you love and I'm really hoping to find that in . . . in someone soon and I am hoping this will be my time.

Eighteen

Even though the sun was high in the sky, it was a windy day in Santa Monica and the sand blowing against my bare shins was getting annoying fast.

I'd been happy to strip off the ruined dress, but now I was stuffed into a bikini that felt two sizes too small. Kyle had had to get creative with the duct tape, not only to ensure that the top stayed on, but also to make sure that Cheryl got the cleavage shots she was looking for.

I rubbed at my shins as I waited for the men to arrive.

Nathan, of course, had been right: He would be on the date today at the beach, along with Paul and Edward. My one-on-one date would be with Scott. I decided that Ty would be left off my date list again, giving Becca a chance to flirt with him.

The cameras were trained on me and I tried to smile, despite my hair sticking to my lip gloss every time the wind whipped it into my face.

I could see three men in the distance working their way toward me.

It was interesting to observe them walking side by side. Nathan was bouncing all around with energy that seemed immeasurable, a surfboard tucked under his arm. He wore blue surfer shorts that were covered in bright pink flowers. Edward, in contrast, was taller than both of the others and had a confident gait, sporting darker shorts with a lightning bolt across one leg. Paul just flat-out looked uptight and angry, his stride short and rapid. He wore a T-shirt with a print of the U.S. flag.

Nathan was the first to reach me. He flung his surfboard to the sand and swung me around in his arms, the same way he had every time he'd seen me.

"Hello!" I screamed as he flung me around.

"I knew you wanted to surf!" he said.

Paul joined us and kissed me chastely on the cheek. "Hello, Georgia."

The scent of his aftershave sent my nervous system into a frenzy as images of our old life together hollowed out my belly. Even though I was dying to grill him about any info he had from LAPD, I separated myself from him and murmured, "Hi, Paul."

I turned toward Edward, who wrapped his arms around me, enveloping me in a giant hug. In contrast to what I'd just experienced with Paul, Edward's touch left me feeling safe and warm.

"Good to see you again," he said.

"Likewise," I said, watching his face closely, hoping to communicate with him silently. I needed to get him alone as soon as possible. I had to know what he'd wanted to speak with me about the night before.

"Cut," Cheryl yelled. "We have what we need on the greetings. Let's do some shots in the water."

We all tramped down toward the surf like obedient children. Everyone except Nathan, who took off at a run. He was in the water, riding a wave, before anyone else could even get to the water's edge.

As soon as the water hit my toes I recoiled. "The water is freezing!"

Edward put an arm around my shoulder. "If you get cold you can snuggle with me."

Paul flashed us a mean look.

I moved closer to Edward, edging my mouth toward his ear. Because we were only in swimsuits and presumably going into the water, none of us were wearing microphones. If I got lucky maybe I could whisper to Edward and ask him what he wanted to talk to me about, but Nathan slid up next to us with his surfboard.

"Come on, Georgia," he said. "Give it a try."

"Oh, I don't know about that. Surfing's not my thing," I said.

"Here, like this." He put his belly down on the board and paddled out toward the middle of the ocean.

I laughed and looked at Paul and Edward. "I don't think there's any way I can do that."

"Cut!" Cheryl screamed.

We all turned to look at her. An assistant ran up to the three of us with surfboards.

"We need some good shots here, guys. If we're not

careful we're going to put our audience to sleep. Step it up!" Cheryl said.

Paul, Edward, and I tried to paddle toward Nathan but we tipped over multiple times. Water rushed into my ears and nose and salt scratched the back of my throat.

"I'm impressed with the guy," Edward admitted.

"It's harder than it looks," Paul said, begrudgingly.

I didn't say anything and just paddled toward the beach.

"Cut!" Cheryl said. "Are you done, Georgia?"

I grimaced, fearing she was going to yell at me and tell me to get back out there. "I can't feel any part of my body," I said. "I'm frozen."

Fortunately, before Cheryl could respond, a tech threw a thick polka-dotted beach towel at me.

Paul and Edward soon followed suit and emerged out of the ocean with their skin covered in goose bumps. The tech gave them towels as well.

Nathan was still in the distance surfing and hamming it up for the cameras. Paul was talking to the tech who'd handed him the towel. I grabbed Edward's hand and moved down the beach a bit, decidedly off camera for a moment.

"What's going on? What did you need to tell me?" I asked frantically.

He frowned and looked around; when he saw that we were alone he leaned into me. "It's about Ty," he said.

"What about him?" I asked.

Edward mumbled, "I don't think he's in it for the right reason. I know I shouldn't be saying this to you because at this point you don't even know if I'm in it for the right reason, but I just felt . . ." He shrugged.

"No, it's okay. Tell me what's on your mind."

"I saw him flirting with someone else."

Becca.

I hid my smile and tried to act serious. "So you think he's on the show for the money?"

"I know you don't have any reason to believe me and normally I wouldn't say anything. It's just that I'm really starting to fall for you and—"

My stomach did a mini flop, almost as if I were in the water again and toppling over, only this time it was pleasant. "You are?" I asked.

He smiled. "I think you're amazing and I don't want to see you get hurt."

"Right."

"I saw some things last night, before I took off for our one-on-one date, that maybe I shouldn't have."

"Like what?" I asked.

"I saw him kissing one of the assistant producers on the show."

Before I could respond, Paul spotted us talking alone and jogged over to us. "Hey, what's going on here?" he asked.

Edward did an uncomfortable shuffle. "Man, that guy's surfing is incredible. Look at him."

Instead of looking in the direction that Edward indicated, Paul studied us a minute. Clearly he didn't believe that we'd been huddled so close together talking about Nathan's surfing abilities, amazing as they were.

Edward seemed to feel guilty about having stolen my time. He made an excuse and walked toward the crew. Paul and I were alone.

I turned to him. "Do you have any information for me?"

He looked confused. "Like what?"

"I don't know. Have you heard anything from LAPD?"

"What? No." He rolled his shoulders in the way he did when he was hiding something. "What would I hear from them?" he asked.

"I don't know. Any news from forensics regarding Pietro's crime scene?"

Paul suddenly looked sick. He grabbed my hands. "Georgia, I made a mistake. I was a fool not to show up that day."

My heart felt like it was stuck in my throat and I found myself squeezing his hands.

Was Paul saying he was actually ready this time . . . ready for us?

"Can we stop this nonsense and go home?" he asked.

I pulled my hands away from his. "What nonsense?"

"This stupid show! It's a charade. Ridiculous! We need to go home and—" He waved a hand around.

"Go home and what?" I prompted.

"Get . . . you know . . . get . . ."

Married?

"Get on with our lives," he said.

Christ! He can't even say the word married.

"You left me at the altar," I said flatly.

"Right, yeah. Like I said, it was a mistake."

I studied him. Despite how cold he must have been after our dip in the ocean he looked like he was ready to break out into a sweat.

"It was a mistake? Are you saying you still want to marry me?" I asked.

Paul rocked back on his heels, then shifted his weight back to his toes. "Yeah. We need to get on with our lives."

"Get on with our lives, but does that include marriage?" I asked.

He bit his lip. "I suppose, if you think it *needs* to . . ."

My heart sank and I was certain I was about to vomit on the beach or preferably all over Paul. How could we be back at square one? It was bad enough that he proved in front our friends and family that he was a complete commitment-phobe, but if I wasn't careful he would air our dirty laundry in front of the nation,

Suddenly Nathan was back on the beach and Cheryl was motioning for us to return.

Paul nervously glanced toward the crew, then to me. "We'd better join the others."

Anger coiled through my stomach. "So you're back to telling me what to do?" I asked.

Paul looked hurt. "Telling you what to do? What do you mean?"

I stepped away from him and toward the crew. It was no use trying to talk to him. If we stayed in a relationship we'd talk ourselves around in circles, never quite understanding each other.

The camera crew had their cameras off their shoulders and the techs were packing up equipment.

"Thanks, gang, that's a wrap for this date," Cheryl said.

"A wrap for the date?" Nathan asked. "But I haven't even had a chance to talk to Georgia."

I felt bad for Nathan; clearly he'd thought we'd have an opportunity to get to know each other. Paul was right about one thing: The show was a charade.

What in the world was I doing here?

Nineteen

INT. LIBRARY DAY

Ty is seated, his cowboy hat hanging low on his forehead, casting a dark shadow on his eyes. He's in his late twenties and dressed in jeans and a western plaid shirt.

CHERYL (O.S.)
Hi, Ty, would you like to remove your hat?

TY
Oh. (*He removes the hat and runs a hand through his sandy blond hair.*) Is that better?

CHERYL (O.S.)
Much. We can see your eyes now.

TY
The windows to the soul.

CHERYL (O.S.)
Right. So, what's in your soul, Ty? Love or money?

TY
Oh, in my soul is definitely love. Lots of love.

CHERYL (O.S.)
Wait. Are you saying you're on the show for love?

TY
Oh, no. (*He puts his hat over his heart.*) In here there's lots of love, but right now my life situation is . . . well . . . (*He fingers the brim of the hat.*) Let's just say the cash prize is enough to warm a man's heart for a while.

Dressed in strappy sandals and bright teal capri pants, I waited on the tarmac for Scott.

Becca was directing and filling in for Cheryl, which put her in a bad mood because, I supposed, she'd rather have been back at the mansion making out with Ty or, if the mansion's stench was too much, lounging poolside and making out with him there.

"Where's the dragon lady?" I asked.

"She had a hot date, so I'm stuck filling in. Plus," Becca said, "it's been a long day so she needed a break."

"So do the rest of us," I whined.

Becca waved a hand around. "Preaching to the choir. We shouldn't have stayed out so late last night."

A crackle came through Becca's walkie-talkie. She pressed it to her ear, then said, "He's here. This is perfect timing. We'll get some great sunset shots."

The wind had settled down and the L.A. skyline was filled with orange, red, violet, and even green streaks as the sun was setting low in the sky. Scott appeared in the distance, his gait cool and smooth. He was dressed in jeans and a cranberry-colored striped shirt.

Energy coursed through my body, anticipation tickling my spine.

He smiled broadly when he got close to me, then shimmed right up to me until he was standing directly in front of me, not saying a word and looking sexy as hell.

I looked up at him through my eyelashes, not trusting my voice.

It was like we were having a private staring competition, then he broke the stare by lowering his mouth to mine. I wrapped my hand around his neck and pulled him to me. Electricity shot through me as our mouths connected, his hands in my hair, our bodies pressing together.

"Cut," Becca yelled.

Thankfully, Scott didn't release me, only turned his face toward Becca and asked, "What?"

"Cut! You guys can't be so close together—we can't film the kiss that way. It ends up just looking like a mash of heads."

Scott laughed, but I pulled his mouth back to mine, saying, "I don't care."

He kissed me again and this time Becca got closer. When she yelled, "Cut!" it sounded like it was coming from a bullhorn, which, contrary to what'd I imagined, was rarely used on set.

"You're wasting my time," Becca said. "Your ride is going to get here any minute and I need you guys to focus."

Scott took a step back from me and kissed me chastely on the lips. He turned to Becca. "Is that better?"

"Yes," she said. "Continue."

Scott indicated the tarmac and asked me, "Are we going for a helicopter ride?"

"Would you like that?" I asked.

He shrugged. "I've only had one date on a helicopter. In Alaska, we flew over the glaciers." His voice softened and his eyes glassed over.

My stomach dropped.

He was remembering his wife. He was in pain and there wasn't really anything I could do about it.

He cleared his throat and the awkward moment between us passed. "Are we going anywhere in particular?" he asked.

"I really have no idea. It's a surprise for me, too," I said.

Then we noticed some of the crew tilting their cameras upward. Scott and I both looked into the sky to see three hot air balloons approaching.

"Is that our ride?" asked Scott.

A nervous giggle escaped my lips. "I guess so."

The pilots landed the first hot air balloon a few yards away from us. Scott and I walked hand in hand toward it. We got a safety lecture while being filmed and then we climbed into the basket. During our safety lecture the other balloons landed and cameramen boarded those along with Becca.

"Is it safe?" I asked as I got on.

Scott chuckled. "Are you kidding me? It's a balloon!"

"So does that mean it's safe?" I repeated.

"Let me get this right: You're scared of Ferris wheels and you're scared of balloons," he said.

I fixed him with a glare. After what we'd witnessed together on the Golden Gate Bridge he could hardly blame me, but he sidestepped the issue, asking, "Are you scared of falling in love?"

Why did this guy know how to hit my buttons?

"Wait, don't we need a pilot?"

"I'm a pilot," he said.

"You are? I thought you were a writer."

He chuckled. "So being a writer makes me incapable of knowing how to do anything else?"

"I didn't say that."

He gave me a look. "Maybe not out loud, but that's what you meant. I was in the air force right out of school. Stationed at Beale."

"Well, all right." I shrugged. "But do you even know how to navigate this thing?" I asked.

He shook his head. "Scared as you are, and you didn't even listen to the safety instructions."

"I listened!"

He folded his arms across his chest. "What does the propane valve do?"

I blinked at him.

"How about the parachute valve?"

"Okay, so it sounds like you know what you're doing," I said, dodging his questions. "Let's get this puppy off the ground."

He smiled at me, then obliged by throwing out the sandbags.

In the balloon basket was a bottle of champagne and two glasses. There was also some sparkling water. The rules stated that if I offered Scott a glass of champagne on a date, then he was safe from elimination at the next ceremony.

"Are you sure you know how to handle this thing?" I asked.

"Piece of cake," he said.

We rose into the air. I must confess, the feeling was actually exhilarating. I grasped the edge of the balloon, my knuckles turning white. I bent my knees slightly, lowering my center of gravity; still the sensation in my belly as we got airborne was enough to make me feel light-headed.

"We're in the air!" I screamed.

Scott laughed. "You don't have to yell, I'm right here." He came closer to me and, as he did, the weight in the balloon shifted slightly so that my side tipped a bit.

"No! Get over there to balance us out."

He smiled wickedly as he saw the panic on my face. "Over there? All the way over there? Then I can't kiss you."

He leaned in, but I pressed my hands to his chest and said firmly, "Over there! You can't navigate or whatever if you're kissing me."

"Okay," he said, still grinning. As he moved away, the weight distribution rebalanced the balloon.

I felt my shoulders relax.

The view of the L.A. skyline was breathtaking. We

watched the sun setting lower over the ocean in silence for a moment, the wind lightly buffeting my hair.

Scott rubbed his shaved head. "I love to feel the wind in my hair," he joked.

I laughed. "Why do you shave your head?"

My guess was Scott was in his late twenties or early thirties at the most, but a lot of the men I'd served with at the San Francisco Police Department were already balding, even in their late twenties.

"My hair gets super bushy," he said, "kind of like that penguin you got yesterday."

I laughed, a warm feeling spreading in my chest.

"And," he continued, "when Jean got sick and had to have treatments . . ."

"You shaved your hair because your sick wife was losing hers?"

He swallowed hard, his Adam's apple bobbing up and down. "It was a stupid thing to do. It didn't make her any better, but . . ." He shrugged.

"I'm sure she appreciated it," I said.

He glanced away from me. The cooler with the champagne between us was calling to me, an unspoken reminder of the goal of our date.

"Would you like to toast?" he asked.

"Why not?" I replied.

He nodded and reached for the bottle of sparkling water.

"No!" I said. "I want the good stuff."

He eyed me, a small smile playing on his full lips. "I see. The lady would like a glass of champagne."

I winked at him. "Exactly."

He replaced the bottle of bubbly water in the ice cooler

and pulled out the champagne. He uncorked it and poured some into a flute for me. He handed to me.

I was keenly aware of the cameras positioned on the hot air balloon next to us and could even see Becca's ponytail flapping in the wind.

"What about you?" I asked.

"Hm?" Scott asked.

"Aren't you going to pour yourself a glass?"

He smirked. "You know I can't do that. You have to offer it to me or it doesn't count."

I took a sip of my champagne. "It's delicious," I teased.

He snaked a hand around my waist. "I'm glad."

"Hey, hey!" I said, panicking as the balloon tilted.

He retreated to his side of the balloon, laughing. The balloon with Becca and the camera edged closer. Scott directed our balloon away from them. Then a power line came into view.

My breath caught.

Oh, God, we're going to crash right into the power line!

My hand flung up over my heart, and for a sickening second I thought I'd scream, but Scott smoothly lowered the balloon under the line until we sailed right below it.

I stared at him, my mouth agape.

He winked at me, a glint of mischief in his eyes.

"Well, you're not boring. I'll give you that," I said.

He laughed quietly to himself. "Thank you. I'd rather be dead than boring."

"Would you rather be dead than having some champagne?"

He raised an eyebrow. "Are you offering me a toast?"

I nodded.

A smile splashed across his face. "I thought you'd never ask," he said, pouring himself a glass.

We toasted, our flutes clicking together.

"Cut," Becca yelled from the other balloon. She gave me a thumbs-up. "Very cute, guys.

"Bring the balloon down now. We have to get over to the mansion and film the elimination scene."

Twenty

The dress I had on for the elimination ceremony itched. It was a designer number with only one sleeve and an open back, but the front had a pink lacy section that was scratchy. Either it was the dress or I was developing hives because of the show.

I'd have preferred the silver dress Ophelia had just had me try on, but she said the coloring was all wrong. Either that or she purposely wanted me to suffer in the itchy dress as payback for tackling her earlier. Now she was doing my makeup, while complaining about having to work late.

"It's against union rules, you know, to have me here all day *and* night."

"Why are you stuck here? Where's Teresa?" I asked.

"Who's Teresa?" Ophelia asked.

"I mean Florencia." I'd known she knew her as Florencia, but part of me had been hoping I'd catch Ophelia in a lie.

"She had to go up to San Francisco. Visit her mother in the hospital or something like that," she said.

I grunted, annoyed at having to work so late myself.

What was Florencia really doing in San Francisco? Was she even in San Francisco? Maybe she'd left the country.

As I tried to figure out how I could verify Teresa/Florencia's story about her mother without a cell phone, laptop, or computer access, Ophelia took a step back and evaluated my face.

Perhaps I could get time alone with Paul and let him know about Teresa/Florencia's trip to San Francisco.

The stench from the leaking bathrooms was immediately evident upon entering the mansion.

"We've got to get the cast out of here," Becca complained to no one in particular.

"It was worse yesterday," a cameraman answered her.

"I can't see how it was worse yesterday," Becca said. "It seems like it's getting more awful by the minute. Maybe I can convince Cheryl to do another outing. Maybe Carmel."

"I'd like to go to Carmel," I offered.

Becca turned to me with a smile. "Right, we'd be close to the city again."

"Then I can go check in on Aaron," I said. Although I was thinking about Teresa and hoping to check in on her, too. "I heard Teresa took some time off to head to San Francisco."

Becca gave me a strange look.

I realized Becca probably didn't want me to say anything about Teresa in front of the cameraman.

Was there a way I could interview the crew and find out what they knew about Teresa without raising eyebrows?

Becca and the cameraman led the way to the living room of the mansion, where the men were lounging around on the couch waiting for us. They jumped to attention as we entered.

"Hello, everyone," Becca said, immediately taking control of the crew and directing them in a way that would make Cheryl proud.

Edward came forward and embraced me.

It was very awkward now to see men I was developing real feelings for all together in the same room.

Paul stepped between Edward and me and said, "Evening, Georgia."

I hugged him and whispered into his ear, "Florencia has gone to San Francisco. She has to be Teresa, right?"

Paul pulled away from me and looked into my eyes. "How do you know?"

"Ophelia, the other makeup lady, told me."

"I'll look into it," Paul said.

I nodded, but before I could say anything Paul pressed his lips to mine and in between kisses said, "Will you ever forgive me, G?"

A mix of emotions threatened to overwhelm me and I broke away from him.

I'd actually been considering letting him go tonight. Fighting my volatile emotions every time I saw, touched, or smelled him was becoming difficult, but I needed him around to find out what had happened to Aaron and Pietro.

Scott stood behind Paul and shuffled his feet, apparently not knowing how to approach me after Paul and I had just kissed. He was holding the champagne glass I'd given him a few hours before. Someone had refilled it and he held it up in my direction, in a silent toast.

I smiled and winked at him.

"Everyone take your places, please," Becca said. "We've had a long day. I need to move the scene along."

The crew and cameramen got into position.

The champagne tray had already been set up. I felt awkward as I looked out toward the men all nicely dressed and lined up, waiting for my judgment.

As if I'm anyone to judge!

"You look beautiful," Nathan shouted, seemingly disappointed that I hadn't had a moment to greet him off camera.

"Thank you," I said.

Ty stood next to Nathan and wiggled his fingers at me. I waved back as Becca ushered in Harris Carlson.

"Hey, wait a minute," I said to Becca. "What about a conference with my dad?"

"Your dad?" Paul asked, suddenly alarmed.

I laughed, realizing the men didn't know that my dad was my special guest and that he was the last person Paul would want to face.

"We're not doing a consultation tonight," Becca said.

"Why not?" I asked.

Harris cleared his throat. "Look, we're all punching the OT clock now, can we get on with it?"

Becca nodded, putting on her headset and calling, "Action."

We ran a similar version of the elimination scene we'd done only that morning. It seemed a blur to me already. Harris asked me about the date on the Santa Monica Pier and then the hot air balloon ride. He indicated that Scott had already received a champagne toast and was therefore safe from elimination.

One of the cameras panned the other men in line, who seemed to scowl at Scott.

Today I would need to get rid of one bachelor.

I called out, "Edward."

Edward approached me.

"Will you accept this glass of champagne?" I asked.

He smiled. "Gladly." He took the glass of champagne and returned to his place in the line of men.

"Ty," I called out.

Ty blew out an exaggerated sigh as he walked toward me. He tipped his cowboy hat at me. "You called, Miss Georgia?"

I smiled. Becca would be very happy I was keeping her handsome cowboy around. "Will you accept this glass of champagne?"

Ty nodded and took the glass, then returned to his place in line.

Harris took a step forward. "Gentlemen," he said, staring into the camera instead of at the men, "there are two of you left and only one glass of champagne."

It was a tough call between Nathan and Paul, and I hesitated, evaluating my options. Nathan looked sharp in dark pants and a white jacket. His straw-colored hair was combed down with gel and his eyes danced. As always, a smile played on his lips. He looked jovial.

Paul stood stoic next to Nathan. His stiff stance betrayed him—at least to me. The cop in him would always be there, watchful, guarded, and, worst of all, cynical.

I took a deep breath. "Paul," I called out.

He gave me a strange look as he accepted the champagne. A cocky smirk crossed his face as though he always knew I would keep him. He hadn't understood how difficult the choice had been for me. I looked across the room at Nathan. His face was downturned and somehow his hair had escaped the confines of the gel and flopped into his eyes, making him look pitiful.

My heart broke.

"Nathan, please say your good-byes," Harris said.

Nathan seemed stunned as one by one he shook hands with the other men.

Ty pounded him on the back and said, "Good luck, man."

Nathan approached me and I said, "I'm sorry, Nathan, but you know I have to ask. Were you on the show for love or money?"

His shoulders dropped. "I was on the show for love, Georgia."

The air rushed out of my lungs. I felt completely defeated. I'd made a mistake.

I wanted to take it back. Send Paul home instead.

Now, of the four remaining bachelors I had only one shot. The rest were looking for the money.

I looked around the room and everyone seemed to be giving me the "wrap it up" look. We'd all had a long day and the sewer stench in the mansion was suffocating.

I felt foolish for letting Nathan go. I would've had a better chance at the prize money by keeping him but at this point finding out what had happened to Pietro and Aaron seemed more important than any prize money.

I swallowed back my regret.

"Can I walk you out, Nathan?" I asked.

He looked up at me. "Yeah, sure."

We walked out into the corridor, the camera following us. The awful sewer smell in the mansion seemed to mix with mold. It was difficult to breathe in the corridor and I raced toward the exit.

When we emerged out on the cobblestone path, I turned to Nathan. "I'm so sorry to let you go. It's nothing personal," I said. "It's just that I don't think we're a match."

He grabbed my hand. "Why not? Why does this keep happening to me?"

I shrugged. "I don't know, Nathan, but it's not you. It's me. I'm so sorry." I gave him a hug. "You're going to find the right girl. I'm sorry to say, it's not me. But, please believe me when I say, you're amazing and whoever lands you will be one lucky woman."

When I returned through the corridor back to the main room the men were drinking their champagne and looking happy, despite the overwhelming stench.

Edward wrapped a hand around my waist. "Thank you for selecting me."

I smiled.

Paul grumbled at Edward's closeness and stepped toward us. Edward released me.

"Me, too," Paul said. "Thank you for selecting me as well." He gave Edward and me a nasty look.

I searched for Becca. "Am I allowed to announce the Carmel thing?" I asked into the bright lights.

Ty quirked an eyebrow. "Carmel?"

"It's not for certain," Becca said as she stepped out of the lights and into my line of vision. "I still have to clear it with Cheryl. Why don't we end the scene on a toast?"

"Good idea," Harris said, glancing at his watch. "I have to get out of here. I'm already into overtime and I won't even mention the smell."

Everyone grumbled about the smell.

Becca held up her hands. "Doing what I can, people. Doing what I can."

"Where's Cheryl?" Harris asked.

"Hot date," one cameraman said with a snicker.

"That's the second one in a row," the other cameraman said.

"Who is she with? Who's the lucky guy?" Paul asked.

Becca shrugged and made a face. I got a bad feeling in the pit of my stomach.

Where exactly was Dad?

I was awakened by pounding at my door. I jumped out of bed, glancing at the clock. It was six in the morning.

"Who's there?" I asked.

"Becca," came the reply.

"What's up?" I flung open the door of the trailer.

Becca was standing there, in jeans and a white top, her auburn hair pulled back in a ponytail.

"What?" I asked. "Why are you here so early? I haven't even had a chance to get coffee going," I said, hobbling over to the kitchenette and pulling out the coffee beans.

"I have good news and I have bad news," she said.

I waved her into the trailer, groaning. "Start with the bad news," I said.

She plopped down into my kitchen booth. "No, I know you. You'll get wrapped up in the bad news and right now we need to move."

"What? Move where?"

"We're going to Carmel, via Solvang," she said.

"Great. I love Carmel and Solvang," I said.

"And hopefully I can get a day off and get to see—"

"Hey, if you get a day off maybe we can get up to San Francisco."

She wrinkled her nose at me. "San Francisco? What are you talking about? I want to get to Point Lobos and see the sea lion coves. That's been on my list forever."

"Well, I was hoping if we got up to San Francisco, maybe I can check in on Aaron."

She held up a hand. "That's my bad news."

I looked up from preparing the coffee and stared at Becca. Her expression was somber.

"He died last night. Passed away at the hospital," she said.

The weight of what Becca was saying hit me full force in the chest. I gasped and pressed my hand over my heart, feeling as if it might stop. "What! How? What happened? I was hoping to talk to him." Tears sprang to my eyes and Becca leapt to her feet.

Her arms were around me in a second and she rubbed my back. "I know, honey, I know. It's terrible."

I separated myself from her. "Teresa was there yesterday in San Francisco. What if she pulled the plug?"

Becca made a face. "What? How could she do that?"

"I don't know. I'm grasping at straws here, but it seems so fishy. Why all of a sudden does she have to go visit her mother in the hospital? What hospital is she in? Do we know? Was it the same one as Aaron?" I demanded.

"Seriously, that's your theory? That Teresa snuck up to S.F. to kill Aaron in the hospital? Why would she do that?"

I shrugged, collapsing into the booth. "Maybe she thought he could identify her. Maybe he saw her fussing with the bungee cords . . . or . . ."

It sounded pathetic even to my ears.

"But if he saw her fussing with the cords why would he jump? He jumped off the bridge voluntarily, remember? Would he have taken that chance if he'd seen her fussing with the cords?"

"I'm glad I didn't get rid of Paul now! Does he know about this? How did you find out?" I asked.

"Cheryl told me. She got a call from the hospital. I don't know if Paul knows. I haven't been to the mansion yet." Becca stepped into my kitchen to finish the coffee preparation.

I held my head in my hands and racked my brain for answers.

Could Aaron's death have anything to do with Pietro's?

Had Pietro seen anything? Were the two deaths even connected?

I sprang from the table. "I have to talk to Paul. Is Cheryl going to make any announcement to the cast?"

"Not likely," Becca said. "She doesn't think it has anything to do with the show now. She told me not to tell anyone, so please don't—"

"I won't mention it to anyone. Only Paul—"

Becca was about to protest, but I held up my hand. "He won't say anything to the other members of the cast. I can tell he doesn't like them and, you know, he's not the chatty sort."

"We need to get moving to Carmel," she said. "Get some jeans on and let's see if I can get to Paul. You have one more group date on the way. Everyone gets to go, including Ty." She held up a warning finger.

I laughed. "Don't worry, your cowboy is safe with me."

Twenty-one

Solvang was a small Danish village located in the heart of Santa Barbara's wine country, near the Santa Ynez Mountains. I'd fallen in love with Solvang when I was just a little girl. Dad and I had come through on our way to Santa Barbara one summer and I'd had the time of my life, not to mention I got to indulge in the best pastries this side of the Mississippi.

The town was founded by a group of Danish teachers and the name Solvang meant "sunny field." It was full of windmills and home to the Hans Christian Andersen Park. There was a cute little town square with quiet, tree-lined streets that housed quaint, family-owned shops, bakeries, and restaurants.

I'd always wanted to move there. It seemed the perfect combination of small town and city. Plus the weather was gorgeous.

The crew parked my trailer on the outskirts of town and

I got to wend my way around the cobblestone streets looking for Scott, Edward, and Ty.

I was anxious to talk to Paul about the new developments but I wouldn't get to see him until the evening date in Carmel. I was looking forward to our date with a certain trepidation.

Part of me was still in love with him, of course. It's hard to get over someone, especially someone you thought you'd spend the rest of your life with . . .

Tonight, I'd look into his eyes and still feel the same charge I'd felt when I waited for him on our wedding day. It was hard to believe that our relationship could really be over. And at the same time I was excited to see Scott and Edward in Solvang.

How could I have so many mixed-up emotions?

And then the awful thought came that at least one of them was on the show for the money, if not both. Could Edward be trying to pay his medical school bills?

And what about Scott? He was an enigma to me. He was sexy as hell, sure, but was he really ready to move on after his wife's death?

As I rounded the corner I saw Scott, Edward, and Ty looking into a window. It was a designer shop with different men's apparel on display. The camera crew was across the street filming a few shots of the town.

The men hadn't seen me, but Becca had and she nodded for me to approach them, giving the cameraman a signal to film our exchange.

I snuck up behind Edward and tapped his shoulder.

"Hey, you!" he cried happily as he embraced me.

Scott snaked a possessive arm around my waist. "What

about the rest of us?" he said, pulling me away from Edward and planting a kiss on my cheek.

I hugged him. "Don't worry, there's plenty of love to go around," I teased.

Ty tipped his hat at me. "Miss Georgia," he said, winking.

I hugged him next, feeling his muscular shoulders through his thin western plaid shirt. He smelled like an intoxicating mixture of the outdoor air and men's cologne. Becca was a lucky girl indeed!

Becca had instructed me earlier that we were to stroll along the streets, so the camera could capture Solvang's charm. We were to end up at the castle arch at the entrance to the Hans Christian Andersen Park.

The crew arranged for us to ride bikes down a narrow street, toward the park. We found the bicycles and proceeded to ride them through the castle arch into the park. There was a skatepark with cavernous half-pipes that would challenge even the best.

I felt a little pang as I rode past those obstacles. Nathan would have had a blast here in Solvang and I bet he'd have been as adept at skating as he'd been at surfing.

Scott seemed to read my mind. "Nathan would have been all over this place!"

I laughed. "Yeah, we wouldn't have been able to keep up."

We rode past large oak trees to a small wooden playground that opened up to a larger playground with ladders and curved tunnel slides. There was an area for making music, complete with chimes, and a rock-climbing wall.

We parked our bikes in a grassy spot where a picnic table had been set up for us. Some of the crew were already there setting up equipment.

Becca directed us toward the rock-climbing area. "Why don't you guys horse around over there for a bit and we'll get a few candid shots."

There was the unofficial dance that happened on the group dates, when one guy stepped forward and the others got busy doing something else.

As it was, Scott grabbed my hand and said, "I'll race you to the rock wall."

Edward and Ty leaned back and picked out goodies from the picnic basket.

Scott was a good climber. He reached the top in seconds. Of course, it was child's scale so the feat wasn't impossible, but nonetheless impressive. He looked down at me. "Are you coming up?"

I glanced up at him and shaded my eyes from the sun. "I kinda like the view from down here."

He snickered and wiggled his behind for the camera. "You're not afraid, are you?"

"Considering that it's a rock-climbing wall made for children, I can safely say I'm not afraid."

He jumped down from the top, about two meters, and landed on his feet. He grabbed my hands and leaned in close. "You've come so far," he said. "I'm so proud of you." His eyes were full of mischief as he said it and I found it hard to resist him.

We leaned in to kiss, shivers dancing up and down my spine as our lips met.

"Great, we got the shot we needed," Becca said, jarring me from my romantic moment with Scott.

He pulled away from me slowly, his hands lingering on

my waist. His mouth close to my ear, he whispered, "I don't want to let you go."

I sighed. "I know. I want to stay here frozen in the moment for—"

"Come on, lovebirds, we don't have all day!" Becca bellowed.

Scott laughed. "Okay, I'll walk you over to the others now."

Scott deposited me next to the picnic table. The crew was having some technical difficulties; they'd lost sound.

"Why don't you lounge on the blanket with Ty. I'll get some shots; even with no sound we can montage the film and make it look good. Otherwise, we're going to be too late to get to Carmel tonight," Becca said.

Ty wrapped an arm through mine and said, "I'm up for lounging."

"Can you lounge in a cowboy hat and boots?"

He lifted the hat off to reveal his full head of sandy blond hair. He placed the hat on my head and then flopped down on the blanket. I sat next to him and used the hat to shade my eyes.

There was a lone cameraman covering our shots. We weren't miked and it gave us a bit of freedom.

Ty traced the line of my face with a finger. "What's wrong, Georgia? You don't look so happy."

"Don't I?" I asked.

"Nope."

I shrugged. "I don't know. Part of me, most of me, just wants the show to be over with, you know?"

He smiled. "Who are you going to pick at the end?"

I glanced over at the crew; they were busy packing up gear and fussing with the sound system.

"You got any inside gossip for me?"

He cocked an eyebrow. "You mean you'd like me to tell? I would if I knew, but I don't. And anyway, you're good friends with Becca. Hasn't she told you yet who's on the show for love or money?"

"No way! She's an ethical girl. She wouldn't tell me if her life depended on it."

Suddenly I thought of Aaron and regretted my choice of words. "Did Becca tell you that Aaron died yesterday?"

He propped himself on an elbow and frowned. "I thought he was in a coma . . ."

"Yeah, I was hoping he would get better," I said. "I have to figure out what happened."

"Why do you think something happened? Wasn't it natural causes because of the accident? I mean, hitting the water the way he did." Ty stopped talking and shivered. "Awful, wasn't it? Maybe he just . . . you know."

I sat up. "I have reasons to think there might be something else going on."

A flash of concern crossed Ty's face. "Like what?" he asked.

I didn't want to tell him about Teresa. It wouldn't be helpful to put ideas in his head. If you tell a potential witness what you think they might have seen, they will inevitably talk themselves into having seen it. Instead I asked, "Did you notice anything on that day?"

"The day on the bridge?" he asked.

I nodded.

He gave me a charming smile. "That it was windy as hell."

"That's San Francisco for you."

He shrugged. "Seriously, though, I didn't notice anything. What would I have noticed?"

"I don't know. I'm grasping at straws, I guess. What about Pietro?" I asked. "When we were at the studio, did you see anything strange?"

Ty shrugged. "Not anything helpful, I'm sure. Didn't the cops think he killed himself? Suicide note and everything, right?"

Becca approached us. Ty's body language changed: He straightened and seemed to puff out his chest. Gave me a warm, fuzzy feeling that he was strutting his stuff in front of Becca. She deserved to have a guy totally into her and trying to impress her.

She gave him a little smile, something akin to "Hi, hot stuff, I'm working now, but catch me later."

Ty pulled a fistful of grass out of the park lawn and began to flick the blades around one by one, perhaps slightly disappointed that Becca had bigger fish to fry now.

"Okay, Georgia, we got our sound system back up, but I think I have the shots I need with Ty. Why don't we stop at the Lutheran church on the way back to our vehicles? You can look around the church with Edward and then we'll wrap this up, so we can get to Carmel before sunset."

We all rode the bikes out of the park and then Edward and I hopped off to film inside the Bethania Lutheran Church on the corner of Laurel Avenue. We were followed by a lone cameraman.

Becca yelled out to him, "Just go and get a few shots; make it snappy."

When we opened the church doors, it was like stepping

into the past. The church had a Scandinavian seafaring theme and from the ceiling hung an old ship.

"This is awesome," Edward said.

I had to agree.

I moved closer to him, hoping he felt as enthusiastic about me as he did about the ship, but he remained a little distant.

"Is something wrong?" I asked.

He shrugged. "It's hard to watch you flirting with all the other guys."

He's jealous?

I suddenly didn't know how to feel or what to say. Having competing emotions was part of the game. Was Edward really jealous and therefore on the show for love? Or was he simply acting jealous so that I would jump to that conclusion and completely miss the fact that he was on the show for the money?

"Are you the jealous type?" I asked.

He shrugged. "Not normally, but this whole situation is awkward. It's hard to see a girl you think you might be getting really into, flirting with other guys."

I took a seat in a pew and waited for him to sit next to me. The cameraman lowered the camera and said, "Guys, I'm not getting enough light. Give me a second."

He popped out of the church, leaving Edward and me alone for a moment.

"You know it's a game. I'm trying to figure out who's on the show for the right reasons," I said.

Edward nodded and looked away. He stuck his hand into his pocket. "There's something about Ty. I already told you. I don't think he's on the show for the right reasons . . ."

Oh. So he was back to being upset about Ty and Becca. It made sense. He had no way of knowing that they had my blessing.

"I know not everyone is on the show to fall in love with me," I said.

Edward pulled something out of his pocket. The church door opened and the cameraman appeared again, this time with a light strapped to the camera. He then walked around us so that the ship was in our background, practically blinding us with the light.

Edward sat back in the pew, outstretching his arms. I was hoping he might put his arm around me, but instead he drummed the fingers of his left hand on the back of the pew, his right hand balled in a fist.

I didn't need the bright light on the camera to see what was in front of me. Edward had pulled a pill out of his pocket. He'd probably take it as soon as the camera turned off. What had he called it?

His personal stash.

I sighed and leaned back.

Any student of body language watching this scene on TV would plainly see Edward and I had just missed a love connection.

Twenty-two

Carmel-by-the-Sea is arguably one of the most gorgeous towns in the world. Sure, there are a lot of beautiful places out there—Monte Carlo, Venice, Prague—but none of those have the Clint Eastwood charm.

I was seated in the outdoor patio of the restaurant he'd created, the Hog's Breath Inn, sipping a glass of chardonnay. There was also a bucket of champagne, tableside. Should I decide to invite my date to toast with me, then he would be safe at the next elimination ceremony.

I was exhausted. The drive from Solvang had been tiring and long, but fortunately we'd gotten to Carmel on schedule and I'd even had a moment to breathe.

Kyle had selected a white and red checkered top for me with loose-fitting white pants along with strappy low sandals, for which I was grateful. When I'd said, "What? Are you taking it easy on me? No kill-me stilettos?" he laughed and told me that in Carmel one needed a permit to wear high heels, for *liability* reasons.

Well, that was one more reason I loved Carmel!

My one-on-one date was scheduled with Paul. It was probably the only way I'd get to pump him for information. Becca had promised that she'd try to busy up the crew with something so that I could really talk to him and not have to do much inane blathering for the camera.

A cool breeze picked up on the patio and blew my paper napkin off the table. I stood to retrieve it and bumped right into Paul.

"Oh!" I said, as he grabbed my elbows.

"Sorry, honey," he said, "I didn't know you were going to jump up like that."

My heart raced at being in Paul's arms again and I tried to separate myself from him. "My napkin," I said lamely.

He didn't register what I was saying, only leaned in and kissed me.

My breath caught and my knees went weak, there was something so natural about kissing this man. I felt at home. He was familiar. I knew him.

We continued to kiss, at first tentatively then deeper, my arms wrapping around his neck and my fingers weaving into his hair, forgetting the cameras, forgetting the heartache he'd caused me, forgetting—

"Cut," Becca said. "The angle's all wrong for us."

Paul pulled away from me, but continued to stare into my eyes. "You still love me," he said, his voice husky and breathless.

"Cut, cut!" Becca yelled. "Take a seat, Paul, sip some wine. Give me a few shots I can use."

I stumbled away from him, feeling a little light-headed and a little love drunk.

Could it work between us again?

I took a seat across from him and stared at his handsome face.

Is it possible that we could make a go of our relationship after all?

He reached out across the table and took my hand. "It's so good to be with you, Georgia."

"Likewise," I said and suddenly I meant it.

"I've had time to think," he said. "Being on the show . . ." His eyes clouded over.

I could tell he was getting ready to say something in code to me.

He cleared his throat. "I've had time to think. I want you to know that I am looking for love. I know a lot of the men on the show have said the same thing to you. But I mean it this time. I really do."

The fact that he'd said *this time* stung. Obviously, it was clear he hadn't meant it before; and if he hadn't meant it before, why in world would he mean it now?

I felt myself grow cold and confused at the same time. How could I feel so close to this man and so distant at the same time?

I said, "It's a tough decision for me, you know. I've been thinking a lot, too. About so many things . . ."

"What have you been thinking?" he asked. "I want to know."

I took a deep breath. "Sometimes things just aren't meant to be."

A look of hurt flashed across his face. "No, that's not true; sometimes things—"

"Paul—"

"Wait!" He held up a hand. "I want to say that sometimes things happen, unfortunate things, awful things, but those events can make people realize they've made a mistake."

I grabbed my wine nervously and took a clumsy sip.

"A guy can realize that he's made a grave mistake." He took a moment to look around the patio. A waiter appeared and filled his glass with chardonnay. Paul glanced from the waiter to the champagne bottle between us, a calculating expression on his face.

He wanted the champagne, not the chardonnay, that much was clear.

The waiter took our order and I harbored the hope that I'd actually get to eat the sautéed sand dabs I'd just ordered. Maybe, if I was lucky, even sample one of Paul's Angus beef sliders.

"It's pretty here," he said. "I've always dreamed that I would come to a place like this on my honeymoon."

We hadn't planned a honeymoon. We'd spent too much money on our wedding and had thought perhaps we could go on a cruise over the Christmas holidays, but we'd never even figured out where we would go.

"Your honeymoon. Ha-ha," I said, feeling nervous again and trying to ignore the growing pit in my stomach.

"Cut!" Becca said.

"What's going on?" I asked.

"You look like you're about to cry," she said. "I can't film you like that. You're supposed to be looking happy and in love and trying to evaluate this guy."

"I am trying to evaluate this guy," I said.

"Well, you've got to look more happy about it," she said.

"Yeah, I really wish you would look more happy about it, too," Paul said.

I bit back my tears and finished our phony date. I sipped the chardonnay and made a stupid comment about the ocean. The waiter appeared with my sand dabs and Paul's sliders and placed the plates in front of us.

Paul sniffed my plate. "Looks yummy."

"Yours, too," I said.

"I think these Angus sliders would be killer with a little champagne," he said.

So he'd just come out and said it.

Well, I would, too.

"And a wedding works best when the groom shows up."

He dropped his fork.

Becca made a motion for the crew to keep filming. I supposed they'd edit out my comments; after all, they probably wouldn't make any sense to the audience.

Paul picked up his fork and gave me a tight smile. "I'm sure you're right. In fact, if memory serves, you're always right."

"Cut," Becca said. "I'm calling it a wrap before you two stab each other's eyes out with the forks."

The crew began to tear down the equipment. I reached around and took off my microphone and handed it to the sound guy, who nodded at me.

Paul looked miserable, but I ignored his pouty, sulky attitude and leaned into him, grabbing his arm and whispering in his ear, "Hey, did you know that Aaron died yesterday?"

He sat up straighter and pushed the glass of chardonnay out of his way. "Yeah, I know. I'm on it." He was all business now, his demeanor returning to the cold and stoic Paul that

I knew. "You shouldn't concern yourself with this. We're looking into it."

"Well, I am concerned," I said. "Have you looked into Teresa?"

"What about her?" Paul asked.

"Is she still behind bars or do you think she's the makeup artist Florencia? She was in San Francisco the day Aaron died. Isn't that strange? Why would she be there?"

"What are you suggesting?" Paul asked.

"For starters, I want to know what she was doing in San Francisco," I said.

"I'll check into it," he said. "As far as I know Aaron died of natural causes from the fall."

In Carmel, I was staying in my Prevost coach, while the men got to stay at the famous La Playa Carmel Hotel. It was a renovated luxury hotel that was built in the early 1900s by an artist for his wife, a member of the Ghirardelli family. The grounds of the hotel were meticulously tended gardens with soaring cypress trees, a terraced swimming pool, and breaktaking views of the Pacific.

Cheryl had made arrangements to film our elimination scene in a salon of the hotel that overlooked the ocean; it was exactly the kind of view Hollywood would feature when someone was getting dumped.

I had a few minutes to change in between scenes. Kyle had come on the road with us and had assisted me into a lacy, lilac-colored gown. He pinned my hair up and added extensions that gave the impression my hair had been meticulously curled and coiffed. In reality, I needed a hot shower and shampoo.

Dad and I were scheduled to have a brief meeting before the elimination ceremony and I was anxious to see him.

In one corner of the salon were two leather chairs set with the beach view behind them. We had precious little time before night fell, but as it was, the sunset on the beach cast a beautiful orange and blue hue on the set. I sat in one of the chairs and waited for Dad.

When he walked in, I leapt out of the chair and into his arms.

"Daddy," I said. "I've missed you."

"I've missed you, too, peaches," he said. "How have your dates been going?"

I quickly recapped for him the date in Solvang and the one-on-one date with Paul in Carmel. I remembered to smile and hopefully seemed to our audience as if I were excited about the whole process. At least, Cheryl hadn't stopped me a bunch of times to tell me to look happy, so that was progress.

"Sounds like you got a lot of nice young men interested in you," Dad said.

Cheryl signaled us that it was a wrap and both Dad and I stood up. She leaned into my father and said something.

A big smile crossed Dad's face and then he let out a belly laugh.

Something inside me buzzed.

Why was Cheryl being so friendly to my dad?

Why was he laughing at her jokes?

Dad said something and Cheryl laughed as if he were the funniest man in the world.

I got that now familiar sinking feeling in my stomach.

They were standing so close together . . .

Suddenly the penny dropped. Dad hadn't been around a lot the past two days . . . Cheryl had been on some hot dates . . .

Oh, God . . .

Could Cheryl's "hot date" possibly be . . . my dad?

An image of her as my stepmother formulated in my mind and a sour taste clawed at the back of my throat.

I tried to focus myself and put the thoughts of my dad and Cheryl out of my head.

After all, what did I really know? They'd been laughing together. Lots of people laughed together.

And, hey, Dad was a funny and charming man.

But how on earth could he possibly be attracted to the queen barracuda?

Harris Carlson entered and introduced the scene for the audience. There were three glasses of champagne left and one man would be eliminated.

My hands were shaking. I had no idea who I would eliminate. I was developing real feelings for Scott and Edward, despite some doubts, and I wanted to keep them around. Paul had confused me more than ever and I knew I couldn't let him go right now.

I tried to ignore my mixed-up emotions about him and rationalized that even though Paul hadn't exactly been forthcoming regarding the Aaron and Pietro investigations at least if I had him around then I might be privy to insider information on Teresa/Florencia.

I knew Becca would understand if I let Ty go, but I felt badly that I should be the one to ruin her fun.

"Scott, will you toast with me?" I asked.

A smile warmed up his face as he stepped toward me and said, "I thought you'd never ask."

Next I called, "Edward."

He stepped forward and hugged me. Finally, here was

the connection I'd been hoping for in the church. A warmth spread through my body as Edward accepted the glass of champagne. He returned to his place next to the other men.

"Gentlemen," Harris said, "only one glass remains."

I looked between Paul and Ty.

Paul stared at me, his eyes dark. He was too proud to show any expression on his face.

Ty glanced down at his cowboy boots.

"Paul," I said.

He stepped forward and rushed to me, his face next to mine. "What, honey? What do you want to say?"

I swallowed past the lump in my throat. "Will you toast with me?"

Relief washed over Paul's face. "Yes, yes. Of course I will."

He took a glass of champagne and then stepped back.

Ty shrugged. "I guess this is it."

"I'm so sorry, Ty." I said. "It's just not a match. Can you tell me, were you on the show looking for love or money?"

Ty smiled. "Well, I guess you made a good choice, darlin'. I was looking for money."

I breathed a sigh of relief.

At least I was still in the game.

Of my remaining three men, only one was looking for love, but at least I had a fighting chance.

Ty walked off the set and I saw Becca smile. Maybe he'd found love after all.

Paul, Scott, and Edward held up their champagne glasses and Harris Carlson handed me a glass. We came together and toasted.

"Cut," Cheryl said.

Twenty-three

Night had fallen and a sea breeze was picking up and I fought to keep my hair out of my eyes as I made my way toward my Prevost coach.

A dark figure stood outside my door and a jolt of fear flashed through my body. My senses were on high alert.

"Hey, there, Thorn," Martinez said.

I breathed a sigh of relief. At least there wasn't a stalker outside my bus. "What are you doing here?" I asked.

"How about, 'Hey! Nice to see you, Martinez'?"

"It's always nice to see you," I lied. "How's the wife?"

Martinez smiled. "Ah, thanks for asking. Brandi's fine. I'll let her know you care."

I wanted to snort, but figured Martinez wouldn't appreciate that and right now I didn't want to step on any more toes than I already had. Also, he was clutching a manila folder and I figured there might be some information in it I was itching for.

I jammed my key into the lock of the door and said, "Come on inside. I don't really want anyone to see you here."

He followed me inside and said, "Yeah, good idea." He waved the folder around. "Besides, I have something for you."

He didn't wait for me to offer him a seat or a beverage; he just plopped down on the bench at my small table and placed the folder in front of him.

"What is it?" I asked.

"I can't believe you're still on this show," he said.

I shrugged and sat across from him, reaching for the folder. "Do you have info for me or not?"

He laid a palm on top of the folder, keeping it in front of himself. "Oh, yeah, I have a full dossier."

"On who?" I asked.

He wiggled his eyebrows at me. "Tell me first why you're still on the show. Paul loves you. He wants you back."

This time I did snort, unable to contain myself any longer.

"He does," Martinez said. "You two were good together—"

"No, we really weren't. Now tell me what you've found. Is it about Aaron? Is it about Teresa Valens?"

Martinez was Paul's right-hand man and he'd been doing the footwork while Paul had been in L.A.

"Teresa Valens was released on parole eighteen months ago," Martinez said.

My blood rushed straight to my head, leaving me light-headed and a bit winded.

It's true, then?

All this time, I'd suspected that was the case, but part of me was in denial. I supposed I hadn't really thought it possible that she would be released.

"How come . . . how was it . . . I . . ." I pressed my hands to my temples and tried to form the right words. After a moment I asked, "Why wasn't I notified about her release?"

Martinez shrugged his shoulders. "Lots of stuff was going on in the department eighteen months ago. Remember?"

It was true. We'd had a change of chief of police and I'd rocked the boat a little too hard by releasing departmental overtime expenses to the public. The chief hadn't approved the release and it tarnished the reputation of the department. It had been a very stressful time, culminating in my Skelly hearing and then finally my termination.

My head was beginning to throb. "So do we know if Teresa Valens is going by the name Florencia these days?"

Martinez nodded. "Florencia Diaz."

My head began to ache on a whole new level and I pounded a fist on the table. "Damn!"

"I know," Martinez said. "I don't think anyone really thought she'd come after you. After all, you weren't the only arresting officer—"

"Well, she's been in L.A. working as a makeup stylist for the last year and a half. Maybe she was trying to start fresh, but then our paths crossed again—"

Martinez grumbled. "Maybe you should get off the show . . ."

I narrowed my eyes at him. "Just pick Paul and be done with it?"

He shrugged. "Wouldn't be the worst decision you made in your life."

Something inside me snapped. "What?"

Martinez ran a finger around the edge of the folder but said nothing.

"Listen," I said. "Can you find out if Teresa or Florencia, or whatever the heck her alias is now, was at S.F. General the night Aaron died? One of the other makeup ladies told me she'd gone to San Francisco to visit a sick mother in the hospital or something."

"I'm on it," Martinez said. "I've asked the sheriff's department to give me an accounting of everyone who went in and out of that hospital room."

"Have you checked SFO flights? Can we confirm that she was even in San Francisco?" I asked.

"I'm working on that now," Martinez said. "I've requested copies of records from LAX but that takes time."

"All right. Let me know what you dig up," I said, eyeing the folder and wondering why he wasn't offering it up.

When Martinez remained silent, I asked, "You'll let me know what you find out, right?"

He looked surprised. "Sure. Of course. You'll be the first to know."

Even as he said it, I could tell it was a lie.

Paul would be the first to know. Martinez was here for something altogether different. He was in it for Paul. For Paul to win. The money or me, I wasn't sure.

God, what an awful feeling.

If Aaron was on the show for the money and Paul had taken his place, according to the rules, Paul would get the prize money.

Considering all the effort that Paul was putting into getting me back, could it be he was interested in the prize money?

My stomach churned and suddenly I didn't feel good.

"What's in the folder?" I asked.

Martinez covered the folder with his palm. "Thorn, I wanted you to be able to make an informed decision—"

"You did, Martinez? What's it to you?"

His head bounced up and down quickly. "Well, I wanted you—"

I pushed his hand off the folder and grabbed at it. "Come on. You can't snow me. You don't care what kind of decision I make."

He slammed his palm down on the folder again. "I do. Of course I do. We're all rooting for you back at the station."

"What a load of b.s. They don't care about me at the station. They were happy I was fired."

Not everyone. I knew that. I'd made friends on the force during the time I'd served, but many of them hadn't shed a tear the day I left, and everyone who had been a friend of Paul's had seemed to draw a silent battle line when we'd broken up.

"Let me see the folder," I said.

He passed the folder to me and said, "I hope the information helps you, Thorn. I really do. I hope you make the right decision." He leaned closer to me as he got up. "And you and I both know the right decision is to pick Paul."

The Prevost door slammed behind Martinez and even though I was exhausted from the drive and filming, not to mention the emotional roller coaster of the day, I still got up and locked the door. It wouldn't do to be caught reviewing contraband information by Becca or one of the techs, or by anyone else, for that matter.

I put on some water to boil and waited for my tea to steep before sitting down with the file. Playing a little game with myself about guessing what I'd find in it. I'd been hoping it would be information on Teresa/Florencia, but, judging from Martinez's last comments . . . did he have information on the contestants? Could it be that I would actually know who was on the show for which motive?

The first pages were on Edward. He'd received excellent marks in medical school. Been recruited by the finest. Well regarded and well liked. Seemingly an outstanding citizen.

The only mark against him was his outstanding bills.

The dossier on Edward showed medical school bills of $250,000.

Exactly the amount of the prize money.

How convenient and easy it would be for him to win the prize and pay off his bills.

I sat with the information for a moment, sipping my tea.

I liked Edward. He seemed gentle and kind. But did I think we were a match in the long run? Probably not. He'd want a career in the city, and right now, living in the city was the last thing on my list. Not to mention, the pill popping. There was no future for me and a guy with a habit.

So if Edward was on the show for money, then the contest was really between Scott and Paul. Or better said, between Scott and Aaron.

The next pages in the dossier were on Aaron. He'd been a wealth management adviser, which, from what I gathered, was a fancy title for stockbroker. He also had a huge whopping bank account.

There's wasn't much information on his personal life, except that someone had filed suit against him. Well, if the guy had a lot of money, that wasn't so unusual. Lots of vultures out there . . .

So had he come on the show for love?

Impatiently I flipped the pages; the next part was on Ty. Martinez must have put this together before he'd known that Ty was out of the competition. I already knew Ty had been on the show looking for money, so I scanned the pages on him quickly. He'd won a few rodeos and invested the prize money poorly. His balance sheet and credit were ruined. I made a mental note to tell Becca.

She was a big girl and able to look out for herself, but still I felt it was something that I should at least share with her. Although, maybe she already knew. Who knew how much the contestants had already confessed in front of the cameras or otherwise?

The next pages were on Scott. My breath caught. I wanted so badly to find something in here that might justify my growing feelings for him. He was funny and smart and made me think, always keeping me on my toes with his unexpected remarks.

There was a list of his books. All bestsellers.

I breathed a sigh of relief.

He probably isn't on the show for money.

Except that the figures on the bank accounts were low. Had he also invested his money poorly like Ty? Lost it all?

A nervous sensation rumbled through my belly and I tried to focus on the following pages, more on his career. Then a credit and background check, all clean. There was something that caught my eye, though. In the marital status column, it read, "single."

Not widowed, not divorced, not married, but single . . .

Where was the marriage license record?

I flipped through the biography section near the list of his books. It said, "Scott lives in northern California with his beagle, Benny." No mention of his wife.

Suddenly I felt like a stone was sitting in my stomach. If I was reading this correctly Scott had never been married.

What was all the talk about his wife who died from cancer?

All a lie?

Why? Maybe his novels hadn't been so successful after all. Maybe he'd made bad investments like Ty. But one thing was clear: If he'd made up a dead wife, then he certainly wasn't on the show to find love.

I felt so distressed that I ran to the bathroom feeling as if I could vomit at any moment.

But that would've been a mercy not allowed for someone like me.

I only dry heaved into the toilet, making my throat hurt and my head pound.

I'd asked for this problem and now I had it. Feelings for a guy who was a complete and total liar. I remembered our date at the carnival when he first told me about her, how his eyes had teared up and his expression of complete sorrow.

Now I felt foolish. Scott, the only guy out of ten that I was actually developing real feelings for, was in it to win the money.

Of course he'd told me a complete fiction! He was a writer. A novelist—that was what he did for a living. How naive could I get?

My nausea disappeared, replaced by a feeling of rage. My body shook and it felt like my blood was boiling. He was a horror writer and had carried out the worst horror upon me. A complete lie about having been married to a cancer patient.

A complete lie about losing a beloved wife.

Is it all a joke to him?

I washed my face with cold water, yet the heat rising inside me seemed unquenchable.

I wanted to see him now. Demand answers from him, pound my fists into his chest, hurt him like he'd hurt me.

The worst part, of course, was that I'd believed him.

What a fool I'd been.

Tears exploded from my eyes and I wept into my hands feeling more alone than ever. Why was it that when I was finally feeling hopeful about finding love, something like this would have to come along and crush me?

Martinez's words echoed in my head. "Paul still loves you."

My hands shook when I thought of Scott, and anger coursed through my body, but now, in contrast, when I thought about Paul I felt nothing. No aching in my chest, no hope for reconciliation, not even a zing of attraction.

I was more sure than I'd ever been that Paul and I were done.

Of my three remaining bachelors, there was Edward, who was likely in it for the prize money. Scott, who I'd been on the verge of falling in love with but now suspected was a total liar. And my ex-fiancé, Paul, who'd replaced the guy most likely looking for a love connection. Certainly America would be laughing at me.

My date the next day was set with Edward and Scott. How would I get through it? And was I really supposed to pick my ex at the end of the show?

Cheryl would be having a field day with me in the editing room.

I suddenly felt a burning need to talk to her. I wanted to cancel the whole show. But I knew it would never fly. If they refused to cancel the show for two deaths, it seemed unlikely that my wanting to back out because someone had lied to me would be a good enough excuse.

I felt angry with myself. Of course Scott had lied to me—that was the whole premise of the show, to see who could fool the stupid girl and get away with it.

Well, I wasn't a stupid girl. I would get to the bottom of this. I may not have found love, but I wouldn't be duped.

And I would figure out who had killed Aaron and Pietro. I wasn't buying the Pietro suicide thing. The two deaths were connected, of that I was sure.

I was done following the rules. I'd get my dad to smuggle me in a smartphone. After all, he couldn't be fired like Becca. I glanced at my watch. It was only seven forty-five. Still early enough to pay him a visit.

Twenty-four

I pounded on the door of my father's hotel room and whispered, "Dad."

While the cast and producers were staying in luxury at La Playa Carmel, Dad and most of the crew were stuck at a budget hotel. I didn't want to be seen or heard by anyone, but I was desperate to see Dad. I knocked again on the door and called out a bit louder, "Dad!"

There was a significant amount of shuffling around behind the door, while all sorts of thoughts crept through my mind.

What if he isn't alone?

He opened the door, wearing slacks and a button-down shirt. Totally not my dad's normal farmer attire of flannel shirts and suspenders.

"Hey, peaches," he said.

"You're looking mighty spiffy tonight, Dad," I said.

He laughed. "I guess I got into the L.A. scene a little."

I squinted at him. "Are you going out tonight?"

"I am, honey, but I've always got time for you. Come in."

"Got a hot date, Dad?" I asked.

He smiled. "Yeah."

"With who?" I was already dreading his answer.

"With the little lady that's running the show, Cheryl. She's a hoot."

The now familiar pit in my stomach returned. "Oh, I'm glad you like her," I said, trying to remove the sarcasm from my tone. "I haven't really been getting along with her."

Dad seemed surprised. "Really? She seems to like you very much. Why aren't you getting along?"

"She's very domineering," I said.

Dad grinned. "Well, she has to run the show. Sometimes in order for people to listen you have to—"

"Don't go there," I said.

He laughed. "I'm just saying sometimes a man likes a woman who knows her own mind."

I narrowed my eyes at him. "Is it serious?"

I tried not to let my face show the trepidation I felt. Of course I wanted him to be happy. He had a right to it, more than most, but I couldn't picture Cheryl in my life after the show. A vision of her passing me the cranberry sauce at Thanksgiving was enough to send goose bumps up my spine.

He waved a hand at me. "I like her, but we just met, peaches."

While I was growing up, after my mom had passed, Dad hadn't dated very much, and while I certainly didn't want to stand in the way of his finding true happiness, I was relieved that he'd said it wasn't anything serious.

"I need a favor, Daddy."

Dad's face showed concern and he immediately replied, "What is it, honey?"

I sat on the edge of his bed and pulled out the dossier that Martinez had brought to me. I handed it to Dad.

He took the folder from me and asked, "Should I pour us a bourbon?"

I nodded.

He crossed over to the small hotel fridge and pulled out two mini bottles of Jim Beam.

I grabbed his ice bucket. "I'll get some ice."

He took it from me. "No. I'll go. It won't be good if anyone spots you. You stay here."

He returned quickly and I poured the bourbon while he opened the folder and peeked at the contents.

"What is this stuff on Teresa Valens?" he asked.

I brought Dad up to speed as best I could while medicating myself with bourbon.

He frowned when he came across Edward's bills. "What's this, Georgia?"

"The good doctor has medical school bills to the tune of $250,000," I said.

"Isn't that the same amount as the prize money?" Dad asked.

I nodded.

He took a sip of his drink. "Guess this means he's on the show for money?"

"I guess so."

He flipped over to Scott's page. "What about the writer?"

"Doesn't look like he has much money, either, but more importantly, he lied to me. Told me he'd been married and that his wife died of cancer."

Dad frowned. "Why do you think that's a lie?"

"The paperwork says he's never been married."

"Who put this together for you?" Dad asked.

"Martinez, Paul's old partner."

Dad frowned. "Oh. He's got a solid motive."

"What?"

"Can you trust this information?"

"Dad! Martinez isn't going to lie to me."

Dad's face remained neutral. "He's not? Didn't he lie to you before about Paul?"

"What do you mean?"

"Martinez was the only one, besides Paul, who knew Paul wasn't going to show up at the church. He stood there at the altar that day, playing us for fools."

"He thinks I should pick Paul in the end," I said.

Dad thumped a hand on the small hotel fridge. "No! Even if one of the others ends up with the prize money, so what? Better that than to pick Paul."

I grumbled and sipped my bourbon. I agreed with Dad. "Right now, I'd rather give Edward an opportunity to pay off his school bills than pick Paul at the end."

"And anyway," Dad said, "just because the doctor needs the money doesn't mean he came on the show to get it."

"It seems pretty likely, though," I argued.

The medical school bills plus a little pharmaceutical habit. That seemed enough for me not to select him in the end. Only I wouldn't tell Dad about the pills—that would freak him out and bring on another lecture.

Dad swirled the bourbon in his glass. "And just because Scott may have lied about being married doesn't mean he isn't looking for love."

I buried my head in my hands. "Are you helping, Dad?"

He laughed. "Well, honey, I'm considering all the angles. You know, you can't hurry the crop."

"I don't need pithy quotes from *The Farmers' Almanac* right now, Dad."

He chuckled. "Everyone needs pithy quotes at all times."

"What I need is an Internet connection, that's what I need. I'll do my own research. You have your phone on you?" I asked.

Dad handed me his cell phone. I looked at it and laughed. "A flip phone? Really, Dad? I need Internet access!"

He shrugged. "I haven't needed to upgrade. They keep asking, believe me, but what the heck do I need Internet access on the farm for?"

"E-mail, texts—"

"I can text!" he said defensively.

I waved my hand around. "Never mind, I know that. I know I'm not going to convert you into High-Tech Man right now. Your Luddite ways are safe for the moment. Does the hotel have a business center?"

Dad laughed. "Are you seriously calling this place a hotel? It's at best a motel and, no, of course it doesn't have a business center."

I looked around the room. There were Internet cables on the desk to connect a laptop, but I didn't have a smartphone, much less a laptop. I rubbed my temples and moaned, willing my mind to connect the dots somehow.

"I can't believe I'm so trapped like this," I said.

Dad patted my back. "Come on, peaches. We're never trapped. We can think of something."

"The library?" I asked hopefully.

He nodded. "Sure, where's that?"

The idea hit me then, that not only were we stranded without a car, we didn't have access to Google or MapQuest to look up where the library was.

"How am I supposed to know? We don't even have—"

Dad opened the desk drawer and pulled out a brochure on Carmel. "Peaches, we do it old-school. What's the matter with you? Internet access doesn't replace your brain, does it?"

"Right. You're right," I said, suddenly cheered up. I was with Dad—he could pretty much figure out any town.

We rifled through the Carmel brochure; there was a map of the downtown area in the centerfold. Dad opened the map across the small desk and traced a finger along the yellow row of restaurants, cafés, and tourist attractions. He immediately found the main street of Carmel-by-the-Sea.

"Let's see," Dad said. "These old towns all have the main library near the courthouse . . ."

Bingo.

Next to the courthouse was a building labeled LIBRARY. A small code beside it said A6, corresponding to a legend on the other side of the map. We flipped it over; the hours for the library were listed: daily, ten A.M. to six P.M. I glanced at my watch. It was just past eight P.M.

"Argh!" I screamed and flopped onto the bed.

He watched me with amusement. "Are you going to have a temper tantrum now, peaches?"

"Isn't it just my luck that the library would be closed right now?"

He shrugged, one shoulder going higher than the other. "We need a plan B. That's all."

I sat up. "What's our plan B?" His phone rang in my hand and I glanced down at the caller ID. "Ick. Broom-Hilda."

Dad pulled the phone away from me; he wiggled his eyebrows and smiled as if to say, Watch this.

"Yel-low?"

I snickered into a pillow.

"Well, sure, Cheryl. I'm free right now."

Alarm coursed through me. "Dad! You can't leave me! We need a plan B!"

"Ten minutes? Okay, yeah, sure. I'll meet you in the lobby."

"Plan B!" I hissed.

He winked at me and ignored my frustration. "Sure thing, see you in a few." He hung up and looked at me. "How'd I do?"

"How did you do with what? You're abandoning me!"

"No, no. Don't look at it like that. See it as an opportunity."

"Opportunity for what?" I asked.

"Maybe you can borrow her phone, with the Internet access and all that stuff that you need."

"Please! It's against the rules for me to use the Internet. I'm not supposed to research these guys! She's never going to lend me her phone."

"I didn't say she'd have to know about it."

I cocked an eyebrow at him. "And just how am I supposed to borrow her phone without her knowing about it?"

He sipped his bourbon, then waved a hand in defeat. "I don't know, peaches. You're the one with all the bright ideas."

A moment of silence passed between us.

I cleared my throat. "What restaurant are you going to?"

"Place called the Vaca Loca on San Carlos Street."

"How far is that from here?" I asked.

He glanced down at the map. "About three blocks."

"Am I supposed to follow you guys there and steal her phone?"

He thought for a moment, scratching his chin. "Hm, okay, let's go down to the lobby and see if there is somewhere we can do a handoff." He moved toward the door.

"A handoff? Are you going to steal the phone from her?"

He stopped and glanced in the mirror on the back side of the door. He smoothed down the right side of his hair. "I'm going to try."

"My dad, the pickpocket. I'm so proud."

He smiled. "Please don't judge me."

I pulled open the door to the room. "Stop checking yourself out in the mirror; you look fine."

"Fine?"

"All right. Handsome, smashing. She's lucky to be in your company."

We laughed as he closed the door behind us. We walked down the red-carpeted corridor toward the elevators. He handed me a key card for his room. "Here, they gave me two cards when I checked in. You have to leave the phone on the desk when you're done with it. Be out of the room by ten."

I raised an eyebrow at him. "Are you going back to your room after dinner?"

He pushed the button for the elevator. "I might be able to entice her into a nightcap, but either way I guarantee she will be interested in getting her phone back."

The elevator doors opened. There were two businessmen in suits with severe expressions. We stepped into the elevator and the doors whooshed closed. We fell into the awkward silence of elevator rides and listened only to the pings of the floor numbers lighting up as we descended.

When the elevator doors opened, Dad and I stepped out together, followed by the businessmen. We let them pass us in silence. As soon as we were alone, we surveyed the lobby. There was a huge potted plant near the elevator doors, the front desk, and two benches on either wall.

"You can always hide behind the potted palm tree," Dad joked.

"I don't do a good impersonation of Lucy Ricardo."

Dad snickered. "You do it better than you think."

I whacked his arm. "Will you be serious? I need to figure things out."

He looked appropriately chastened. "Right. Serious biz. Show biz."

"Not the show biz. I don't care about that."

Dad leveled a look at me.

"Okay, okay. I care about that." I wanted to research Scott a bit more but I had bigger fish to fry. "I have to figure out where Teresa was on the night Aaron died."

The clerk working the front desk asked, "Can I help you folks?"

Dad suddenly turned to me. "Georgia, go upstairs to the room. I'll send the phone up to you."

"What? How are you going to do that?"

Dad's face warned me off. I nodded and turned toward the elevator. My finger pressed the button as I heard Cheryl screech, "Howdy, Gordon!"

Ack! I was almost caught by the dragon lady!

I stiffened and repeatedly pressed the elevator button.

"Well, hello, little lady," I heard Dad say.

There was the sound of kissy-kissy smooching noises and I was dying to turn around and look at them, but I simply dug my finger into the button instead. I tried to make myself a bit smaller and, yes, was tempted indeed to duck behind the potted palm.

"Now, now, none of that," I heard Dad say.

"Sorry, Gordon, I was only checking to see if . . . oh, wait, what are you doing?" Cheryl squealed.

"Can you live without your phone for a few hours?" Dad asked.

Cheryl giggled. "Of course I can. I just—"

"Good!" Dad said.

There was a moment of silence, then I heard Dad say, "Can you please put this in room 312 for safekeeping?"

"Certainly, sir."

The elevator dinged and the doors mercifully slid open. Thankfully, I slipped in as I heard Cheryl protesting. "Now, Gordon, don't be silly. I won't check it during—"

"No, no, no," I heard Dad say. "Now, let's hit the road. Got to make hay while the sun shines, or at least I gotta put in my order before they close the kitchen."

I pressed myself against the side of the elevator, out of view, and strained to listen as I held the Open Door button.

All I could hear was Cheryl giggling and then more kissing noises. I released the button to close the door and pressed the button for the third floor. If Dad was as much of a Casanova as he thought, the clerk should be arriving on the next elevator with the phone in hand.

Twenty-five

I was ready to slip the key card into the door when I heard the ding of the elevators. I turned to see the front desk clerk exiting the elevator.

In his hand was the key to my research. I smiled from my head to my toes.

"Howdy," I said.

"Evening, miss," he said.

I held my hand out to him. "Thank you. I'll take that."

He looked at me curiously. "Oh? You're in room 312?"

I could see his hesitation. "Don't worry. I'm not staying. It's my dad's room. I just need to fix a few things up for him." I leaned in toward him to snatch the phone away, but he slipped it into his pocket.

"I need the phone. He wants me to order his girlfriend some flowers."

"The front desk can do that, miss. Maybe I should hold the phone for him there."

"Give me the phone," I said, sounding more desperate than I'd intended.

"Oh!" he said, a look of surprise crossing his face. "I didn't . . . well . . . I just don't want to be giving the phone to the wrong person."

"It's okay—look, I have a key." I put the key card into the lock, only I did it upside down, so nothing happened. "Wait, wait." I jammed it into the card reader again and slipped it out too fast. The lights on the reader flashed yellow.

"Here," the clerk said, taking the card from me. He slid it into the reader and the lights turned green, a delightful little click sounding.

The door opened and he pulled the phone out of his pocket. "Here you are, miss. Sorry about the confusion," he said.

The phone was hot in my hand.

Finally things were going my way!

"No problem," I said over my shoulder. "Thank you!"

I breathed a sigh of relief as the door closed. Now I'd be able to get some answers. I kicked off my shoes and sat on the bed with my feet folded under me.

I tapped on the screen only to be greeted by a low battery message.

"Damn!" I screamed to no one in particular.

What kind of cursed life was I living?

A knock on the door jolted me, my heart racing. What now? Was Dad back so soon?

I dropped the phone like it was on fire and jumped off the bed, ready to hide in the bathroom.

Oh, God, what if Dad and Cheryl had decided to skip dinner and were ready to move right to the nightcap? Where was I supposed to hide? Eventually, she would need the bathroom. Maybe the closet would be better. I dove toward the closet.

"Gordon?" a voice called out.

A voice that stopped me in my tracks.

I turned toward the door and swung it open. Paul stood there, unshaven, hands in his pockets, and looking chagrined. He took a step back when he saw me, a surprised expression on his face.

"Georgia!"

"What are you doing here?" I hissed.

"I . . . I came to talk to your dad. What are you doing here?"

"About what?" I demanded.

He looked around the hallway. "Can I come in?"

"No!"

I had limited time, limited battery, and limited patience.

"Come on, G; don't make me beg for forgiveness from the hallway."

I must have made quite a face, albeit involuntarily, because Paul recoiled. "Beg for forgiveness?" I asked.

He took a step forward. "Honey, let me in."

"I'm not your honey and I'm not letting you in. I'm busy."

He looked over my shoulder and called, "Gordon?"

"Oh? You think he's going to be any nicer to you than I am? He's ready to break your legs."

Paul hung his head. "I don't know if I can explain but at least—"

"Save it." I closed the door in his face, my blood boiling.

He knocked again. "Georgia! Open the door. Don't be ridiculous!"

I flung the door open. "I'm not being ridiculous! You're

ridiculous! What kind of man leaves a woman at the altar and then tries to worm his way into her life again via a reality TV show, no less!"

"I'm not worming—"

"Worse, you're worse. You were going to try and talk to my dad—"

His brows furrowed and his eyes flicked to the left. "Because I didn't know how to find you."

"Oh, stop. You didn't even look for me."

He looked offended. "How do you know?"

"Because I know you! Tell the truth, you big liar, did you even go over to the Prevost to look for me?"

"Well, I—"

I slammed the door on him again and made my way back to the bed. I grabbed the phone and messed with the settings to use less battery; even still, it beeped obnoxiously in my hand at the same time that Paul pounded on the door.

"Georgia! We have to talk."

"No, we don't," I said from my position on the bed. I brought up a search engine. "I'm working."

"Open the door," he roared.

Suddenly I heard another voice in the hallway. "Hey, calm down, man. What's going on?"

"Nothing, buddy. Mind your own business," Paul said.

There was the sound of a door closing in the hallway. Paul pounded on my hotel room door again. "Georgia," he called.

The hotel phone rang. I picked it up.

"Hello, miss, this is the front desk. I got a call from your floor about a commotion. Is there . . ."

"An unwanted visitor, yes. Can you please send up security?"

"What?" Paul called from behind the door.

I hung up the phone and said, "Security is on the way."

I squinted through the peephole. Paul was leaning his forehead against the door. He was silent.

For a second I felt bad. Then the faces of our guests who had come to our wedding and waited for him flashed before my eyes and the feeling faded.

"What do you get from being on the show, Paul? Was Aaron on the show for the money? Do you get to keep the prize money?"

Through the peephole I saw him step away from the door. His eyes flicked back and forth, searching for an answer.

"It's over between us, Paul. I'm not your doormat anymore."

"G, you were never my doormat."

"No, but you treated me like one."

The ping of the elevator sounded faintly and then a voice said, "Sir."

Paul turned toward the elevator, then back toward the peephole. I could see his face plainly now. He didn't look half as miserable as he should. He didn't love me; he wasn't here to get me back. He was here for something different altogether.

What could it be?

He held up his hand and said to the security guard, "I'm going, I'm going."

Pressing my head against the door, I tried to let the feel of the cool wood calm me down. After a moment, I glanced out the peephole again. I couldn't see anything anymore, and the hall sounded quiet. I retreated to the phone and brought up the search engine. The low battery message flashed again.

I picked up the hotel phone and called the front desk. "Thank you for sending security," I said.

"You're welcome, miss," the clerk said.

"I need another favor."

"What is it?" the clerk asked.

"Do you have an iPhone charger handy?"

Silence greeted me.

"Hello?" I said.

"Sorry, miss, I was thinking. Let me check and if I find one I'll bring it right up."

I hung up and fiddled with the phone again. I didn't have access to any of the databases I did when I was a cop, so I did the next best thing.

Called a cop I trusted.

She picked up on the first ring. "Hey, who's calling?"

I laughed, realizing the information that showed up on her phone was Cheryl's name and number.

"Lisa, it's G."

She screamed. "Girl! Where are you? Are you okay? I've been trying to reach you."

"You have? Why?"

"Well, when the guy had the bungee-jumping accident off the Golden Gate, all hell broke loose here. We all knew it was your show and then Paul took time off to go to L.A. to be with you."

"What?"

"What?" she repeated.

"What do you mean, Paul took time off? He's working undercover—"

Lisa interrupted me with a snort. "Is that what he told you?"

The room seemed to close in on me. "I thought he was working the case."

"What case?"

"The guy falling while bungee jumping wasn't an accident. It was intentional."

"No, really? But we've had several departments looking into it. It doesn't appear to be a homicide."

"Teresa Valens showed up here, too. She was there on the bridge that day. I think she was trying to get to me. And then a guy hung himself. Or was hung . . . he'd seen something. And she was in San Francisco when Aaron died in the hospital—"

"Whoa, slow down. What are you saying about Teresa Valens? Isn't she in jail?"

"No. Martinez confirmed that she was paroled eighteen months ago."

"Martinez? You've been in touch with him and not me?"

"Don't get snippety. I haven't been in touch with him. He found me. I haven't had a phone, but I need you to look up some stuff now."

"Oh, sure, what a fair-weather friend you are."

The phone beeped another low battery warning.

"Save the guilt trip for when we can get drunk together," I said. "I owe you, but I really need—"

"How's the show going? Any hotties that you like?"

I thought of Scott.

"Plenty of hotties, but I think I'm lacking guys with integrity."

"Integrity is so overrated," Lisa joked. "Besides, it's a dog-eat-dog world. You need to think like a man: Pick the hottest guy there that can win you the prize; take a nice little trip with him to Jamaica or the Caribbean or wherever they send you; then, when all the photo ops are done, you break up with him and split the prize money."

An angry buzz from the battery sounded.

"Right, uh, Lisa, I got limited time here. Can you please look up flights from L.A. to S.F., see if Teresa Valens—or Florencia Diaz—was on one of them?"

"Who's Florencia Diaz?"

"That's what Teresa Valens is going by these days, her alias."

Lisa sighed. "Okay, but it'll have to wait until morning. I have a life, you know. It may not be as exciting as yours with a bunch of men vying for my attention, but Stinky's here."

I laughed out loud. Stinky, who weighed about as much as a mouse, had been in love with Lisa from the moment he laid eyes on her ten years ago. Lisa, however, was happily married with elementary school age kids and had never given Stinky the time of day.

It's seemed like maybe my luck was turning, though, because Stinky was the department's computer hack. If there was information to be found between the zero and ones, Stinky would find it.

"Where are you guys at?" I asked.

"Annie Get Your Gun."

Annie Get Your Gun was a popular cop bar near the hall of justice.

"Well, ask Stinky to look it up for me. He doesn't have a life," I joked.

Lisa made a retching sound. "You know what kind of payment I have to give him for favors."

"I know. You actually have to be nice to him and flash him your pearly whites."

"Hold on," she said. "Stinky, G needs a favor."

For a moment, all I could hear was the hubbub of the bar. Glasses and bottles clinking in the background along with the noise of a baseball game broadcast from the bar's big screen.

Stinky came on the line. "G! What's going on?"

The phone beeped again loudly. "Stink, I got a dying battery. I gotta go. Lisa will bring you up to speed. Need flight info and a little look-see into a death at S.F. General."

"What number can we call you back at? The one you called on?"

"Oh! No, no, don't call this number. Call my dad's number; it's 530—"

A loud tone buzzed in my ear. I glanced at the phone, the red battery line flashing up at me. I'd lost the call.

Shoot!

I knew Stinky would get the information for me, and I'd have to hope he was smart enough to pull Dad's info and call me at the right number.

I fiddled with the phone. I had 1 percent remaining. I thought of Scott and pulled up his Web page. His handsome author photo stared up at me. My heart hurt a bit. I'd just been starting to fall for this guy.

I clicked on the Buy Now button for his book and paid to have it shipped the next day to my Prevost, feeling justified that it was all in the name of research.

Twenty-six

The clerk never arrived with the phone charger and I felt the need to slip out of Dad's room before he showed up with Cheryl. I left the now dead phone on the desk, being careful to wipe my prints off it. Not that I figured she carried a fingerprint kit around with her, but, hey, why take a chance?

I put my shoes on and made it out of the room, feeling a sense of relief. The entire time I'd been in the room, the stress of Paul's visit and the thought of Dad and Cheryl returning and catching me red-handed with her phone had drained me.

I woke up groggy. The fog was hanging over the coast in a way reminiscent of San Francisco, and I was a bit disoriented. Then the image of Martinez sitting in the little coach's kitchen and showing me a folder flashed into my mind.

The events of the past few days came rushing back to me

and immediately I felt depressed. I glanced at the clock, knowing that I needed to be on the set early. Cheryl had succeeded in getting us into the Monterey Bay Aquarium an hour before opening; this meant our call time was six A.M.

I rolled out of bed and into the shower. I knew the drill now: If I arrived with a fresh face and wet hair to the makeup tent, then the day seemed to go smoother. I secured my wet hair into a ponytail and slipped on sweatpants and a jacket.

The temperatures in the valley were to be over a hundred all week; therefore, the air on the coast would be frigid, something to do with a marine layer getting propelled inland by the intense heat in the valley, so we would be blanketed in fog and the valley would be enjoying sunshine and orange juice.

I just couldn't catch a break!

When I arrived at the aquarium, I found the catering cart outside and immediately grabbed some fruit and coffee. Cheryl was there wearing dark sunglasses and speaking softly to one of the show's runners. She hugged her coffee mug to her as if defending the elixir of life.

Hm. Looks like she had a late night.

I wondered if she'd figured out that I'd used her phone.

"Good morning, Georgia," she said to me pleasantly.

Well, she was being nice to me, so my guess was she hadn't put two and two together.

Something buzzed from inside her pocket and she fussed with her jacket, handing me her cup of coffee to hold.

She pulled out her phone and swore under her breath.

"What is it?" I asked, panic rippling up into my throat.

Oh, God. Lisa wouldn't call Cheryl's phone with a message for me, would she?

"Makeup gal overslept," she said, putting the phone back into her pocket and pulling me toward the makeup tent. "I'll have to do it."

I held my breath. Just because she was being nice to me now didn't mean I wanted her up close and personal. She tossed me a pair of hot pink Capri pants and white blouse that fit like a second skin.

After I shrugged into the costume, she told me to take a seat, and immediately got out the blow-dryer. She gave me a voluptuous hairdo in a matter of minutes. Then she moved on to the makeup and tilted my chin, her hands cold on my face. "You have nice bone structure."

"I do?"

She nodded as she turned to get the foundation out. "I have to work fast; the men need someone, too."

"What happened to the makeup girl?" I asked. "Are you shorthanded?"

"Yes, one of my makeup people quit this week."

"Florencia?" I asked.

She nodded as she brushed foundation on me. "One of her family members in Mexico is sick. Her mother, I think."

A likely story.

Hadn't Ophelia said Florencia's mother was in San Francisco? Lies were hard to keep track of.

She probably knew I was onto her. This was where she would get nervous and messy. She'd make mistakes and I'd get her again!

Cheryl moved on to my blusher then eye makeup. She

took off her sunglasses and focused in on my lashes. Her eyes were red rimmed.

"Late night?" I asked, unable to resist.

She blushed. "No, no. Not that late. I'm just . . . not a morning person . . ."

I suddenly felt ashamed of myself for trying to embarrass her. Dad deserved someone to get all swoony over him.

"You're fast at the makeup," I said as she was finishing up with the lipstick.

She laughed. "That's how I started."

"Really?"

"Oh, yeah, worked my way up. Nothing worthwhile comes easy."

I sighed. "Ain't that the truth," I said.

She stepped back and studied my face. "You're beautiful."

"Thank you."

"Are you developing any real feelings for any of these guys, Georgia?" she asked, concern brimming in her voice.

Oh, God!

Cheryl was actually worried about my feelings?

Maybe she was falling in love with Dad—what else would explain her sudden sensitivity to my plight?

My skin pebbled at the thought.

Surely Dad and Cheryl weren't that serious!

The thought of Scott lying to me broke my heart, and I suddenly felt sick. "I thought I was having some real feelings," I confessed. "But now I just don't know."

She leveled a gaze at me and it seemed for a moment as though she wanted to tell me something she probably shouldn't.

I smiled. "Do you have any advice?" I asked.

She straightened. "Hmm."

I waited for her words of wisdom, but all she offered was, "Be careful who you give your heart to."

Yeah, I've already learned that lesson.

Cheryl packed up the makeup case. "I have to get over to Paul and Edward. We only have an hour in the aquarium and we can't waste any time."

"What do you need from me in terms of the shoot?" I asked.

She looked surprised. "You mean you're going to cooperate?"

"We only have an hour," I said.

"Good." She leaned over and undid the top button on my blouse. "This will get things started."

The Monterey Bay Aquarium, built in 1984, was located on the site of a former sardine cannery on Cannery Row. The aquarium was large, with hundreds of displays, but Cheryl had decided to film our scene in front of the awesome jellyfish display.

I waited for the men by the round tank of jellyfish, staring in wonderment at the array of colors they offered. The fish glowed and glided through the water; in contrast, I felt like I had the weight of the world on my shoulders. Stress and tension emanated all the way down my back and up my neck, giving me a throbbing headache.

My plan had been to eliminate Edward tonight. I was sure he was in it for the money. But that would leave me choosing between Scott and Paul. And if Scott couldn't be trusted, then I'd have to select Paul at the end . . . and that thought made me sick.

I guess I was hoping for a miracle. That somehow Edward would convince me he hadn't come on the show looking for the prize money and wasn't a prescription pill addict.

"Action," Cheryl called.

I turned away from the tank in time to see Edward round the corner first, followed by Paul.

Edward approached me quickly. "Hey, there, gorgeous," he said, kissing my cheek. He stepped aside to let Paul greet me.

Paul kissed my cheek, just as Edward had; only he put his hand on my shoulder and squeezed. "Hi, sweetheart," he said, his fingers finding a knot in my trapezius muscle. He manipulated the muscles, sending chills up and down my neck.

Edward seemed to notice Paul's hand lingering on me because he looped an arm through mine and said, "Can I breeze you away to look at some of these amazing fish?"

Paul lifted his hand off my shoulder, annoyed and eager to show Edward his displeasure. Edward, for his part, sloughed it off.

We walked through a corridor into the main exhibit room, where the crew had spent a good amount of time setting up the equipment.

The display in this room covered the entire wall from floor to ceiling. It was like peering directly into the ocean.

I turned toward Edward. "So, what are you going to do with the money?"

He blinked at me. "What?"

"The prize money. I mean, if you win. What are your plans?"

He snaked an arm around my waist. "Well, wouldn't we go to someplace exotic?"

"You mean, after you pay your medical school bills?"

His eyes clouded over. "See, that's where I'm lucky. I received an inheritance from a great-aunt right before med school. So I don't have any."

"Loans?"

"Right. I don't have any loans or bills. It's incredible, really." He shoved a hand into his jeans pocket and I wondered if he was already jonesing for the pill he always kept at the ready.

I studied the jellyfish. They were magnificent colors of magenta, lime green, and cinnabar. They looked electric and translucent at the same time.

Much like a lie. See-through and stinging all at once.

"What was her name?" I asked.

"Vivian," he said, without missing a beat.

It was a plausible story. Anyone could have told it. And I'm almost ashamed to admit that without the information from Martinez, I wouldn't have been able to tell it was a lie.

Although . . . there was a small bead of sweat forming on Edward's brow. Ever so slight and it would have been easy to miss if I hadn't been studying him so closely.

I leaned over and wiped his brow. "You have something here," I said, winking coquettishly. I made sure to pull my shoulder back and give the camera a shot of my cleavage, hoping Cheryl would be happy.

Edward didn't say anything, just brought his hand reflexively up to his neck. A universal body signal for distress.

"Med school must have been tough," I said. "I admire you."

His eyebrows dipped in the middle, forming a V. He was unsure why I'd suddenly thrown him a softball.

Basically, I'd gotten all the confirmation I needed: between the report from Martinez, the bead of sweat, and the pill popping, he was out of the running as far as I was concerned.

Now I knew I probably had to pick Paul in the finale. If I wanted a shot at the prize money. An incentive that was quickly becoming irrelevant.

Paul made an entrance, clearing his throat and strutting onto the set like a peacock. Edward excused himself and I was left alone with my ex.

He touched my elbow. "Good to see you, G. I especially like when you have to be nice to me."

Shame flared inside me. He wasn't a bad guy. He was a guy I'd been willing to—hell, wanting to—commit myself to for all eternity and, yet, now it felt like a guardian angel had been with me that day. Saving me from, what, marrying the wrong man?

It did feel wrong.

Our chemistry was adrift. His touch felt cold and when I looked into his eyes they seemed dead.

What had captured me so entirely just a few months prior?

Had it been the thought of a happy little marriage, in a city that I loved, with a job I'd found so fulfilling? Now all these things were worlds away. The city magic had worn off, the job lost its appeal, and Paul's charm suddenly faded.

It must be me.

It couldn't be that all those things were bad. I'd take responsibility. It was me that was the problem.

"Paul," I said in a hoarse whisper.

"I want to make it right," he said, his words too soft for the microphone to catch.

"You can't. It's over. It's me," I said.

"Cut!" Cheryl yelled out. "We can't hear you guys. Can you amp it up a notch?"

Paul nodded, but his eyes were watery.

"Ship sailed, Paul."

Part of me wanted to say I wished it were different, but the truth was I didn't.

I was different now.

I was a woman who'd been jilted at the altar. That experience had made me different. Damaged goods, in one respect. Paul had taken my innocence, yes. But I'd become stronger. I would survive. I'd be better because of it.

That which doesn't kill us makes us stronger.

Was that from *The Farmers' Almanac* or was that just Dad talk?

Well, at any rate, I finally knew that I wasn't in love with Paul any longer.

Twenty-seven

By the time we finished filming in the Monterey Bay Aquarium, it was only seven in the morning, but I felt like I'd already had a full day. However, I still had a one-on-one date to go, and then an elimination ceremony.

One of the techs dropped me off at my trailer; Cheryl had told me I was allowed up to a half hour of rest and then I needed to get ready for my one-on-one date with Scott.

I was ready to tuck myself back into bed and was already having sleepy thoughts as I jammed the key into the lock. When I realized the coach was unlocked, I automatically went into cop mode.

I pushed my shoulder into the door and leapt inside, screaming, "Freeze, freeze!"

Of course, this was probably why I made a bad cop. One should never rush into a situation unarmed, especially when they didn't know what they would find.

But this was my little place. My home away from home

and someone had been to visit without leaving a calling card.

No one was inside the coach, thankfully, but it had been trashed. All the kitchen cabinets were pulled open, their contents dumped on the floor. The drawers in my bedroom were also upturned; even the bathroom had been ransacked.

The feeling of being violated zipped through my body.

Someone had very deliberately gone through my stuff.

Was anything missing?

I felt I had to get out of the coach immediately. I didn't have anywhere to go and not even a phone to call for help!

Darn it, I couldn't wait to be done with this show! I hated not having any communication with the outside world. I exited the coach and walked toward the corner.

As I was about to cross the street, I spotted Becca's car advancing. She pulled over to the curb and rolled down the passenger-side window. "Hey, hot stuff, what are you doing out and about? Are you out of coffee?"

I pulled open the passenger door and hopped in. "No, I was looking for a pay phone to call you. Someone ransacked my Prevost."

Alarm showed on her face. "What? What do you mean, ransacked?"

"I'd show you, but I actually want it dusted for prints. Can you call the police?"

Becca put the car in park and dug out her cell phone. "Here, you call." She passed me the phone.

"Florencia didn't show up today on the set. Cheryl said she was going to Mexico, but my money is on her actually searching my trailer instead."

"Why would she do that? What would she be looking for?"

"The folder Martinez gave me is missing."

"What folder?" Becca asked.

A wave of guilt swept over me. Becca didn't know about Martinez's visit to me the night before. She didn't know that I'd actually cheated at the game and now suddenly I didn't want her to know.

If she knew, she might feel obligated to go to Cheryl and then she'd probably mess up her chance of getting promoted.

"Uh, he brought me some information on Teresa Valens," I said, only mildly wincing at the half lie.

Becca looked excited. "What did you find out? Do you think Florencia really is her?"

"Teresa was released on parole eighteen months ago."

Becca recoiled. "And they never told you she was being released? That's just wrong! It's crazy!"

"I know. Maybe I was notified. I can't say for sure, because everything was crazy at the department at that time. That's when we got our new chief and . . ."

Becca grabbed my hand. She knew that eighteen months ago was the start of my troubles. "Oh, God," Becca said. "What a mess. Call the cops."

"Is Cheryl going to be all right with that?" I asked.

"I'll call her after you talk to the police."

I dialed the police and it took a good fifteen minutes before I was able to connect with anyone who would come down to our set and look at my coach.

Becca and I bought lattes and hung around outside my Prevost, while she talked to Cheryl. Cheryl agreed that phoning the police was the only way to go, but before they even showed up we had the press to deal with.

"Did Cheryl call the news about this?" I asked.

Becca shrugged. "I don't know, but that'd be my guess. She wants publicity for our show and there's no publicity as good as the *National Enquirer*." She handed me the keys to her VW Bug. "Go hide out in my car. I'll fend them off."

I gratefully ducked into Becca's car and watched her expertly handle the press. No matter how much they begged for the scoop, she remained stone cold. Finally, she positioned them across the street, stating that my coach was part of the set and basically was private property.

She was able to hold them at bay long enough for the Carmel police to dispatch a lone officer. I ducked out of the VW Bug to greet her and pull her into the Prevost.

She had an angular face and looked haggard, but she listened patiently as Becca and I brought her up to speed.

Finally, she agreed to dust for prints and call LAPD to see if they had an update on Pietro's case.

A knock came at the door and we all jumped.

"Who's there?" the officer demanded, pushing me toward the back of the coach.

"FedEx," came the reply.

The officer turned toward me. "Are you expecting a package?"

I nodded, but Becca frowned. "You are?" she asked. "You know it better not be a disposable phone or tablet or—"

I waved a hand at her. "I can't believe after everything that's happened you're still such a stickler for the rules."

The officer looked from Becca to me, not sure what to do.

"He's probably legit," I said.

Nonetheless, the officer cracked the door and peeked out at the deliveryman. He wore a clean uniform and had a smile on his face as he quirked an eyebrow at her. "Georgia Thornton?"

"I'll take it," she said.

The deliveryman looked at his instructions, and then said, "Okay, I don't need a signature anyway."

The officer accepted the package, then closed the door behind him. She dropped the package onto my small kitchen table and said, "So, you don't need me to examine the package?"

"I don't think it's anthrax, but thanks."

Becca wrinkled her nose. "Well, I'm going to examine the package!" She swiped it out from under me and ripped open the tape. "What did you order?"

Scott's book *Death Thief* fell out of the package, his sexy author photo peeking up at us from the floor.

The officer picked up the book. "Oh! This is one of my favorites! I love this guy." She hugged the book to her chest and I suddenly felt possessive and embarrassed at the same time.

Becca broke into a fit of giggles.

The officer handed me the book. "It's a great read. You'll love it. The author's really twisted. Packs a punch."

I took the book and slipped it into my shoulder bag.

What did she meant about him being twisted?

The officer finally dismissed Becca and me from the Prevost, so she could dust for prints. She told Becca she would call her when her crew was done. It was well past ten thirty in the morning. We were totally behind schedule, but glad to be back on our way.

My date with Scott was scheduled to be a bay cruise, but with the foggy weather and the delay we'd had after the cops finished at my place, Cheryl had changed directions quickly.

Scott and I were going to have a simple date at a make-believe martini bar. The set looked immaculate and again I was impressed with what the crew could create in such a short amount of time. They'd designed a faux interior reminiscent of the 1940s. A huge red mahogany bar—well, it looked like mahogany; in reality it was painted polystyrene—polished brass bar stools, and mirrors framed in chrome. It was sexy and dark and breathtaking.

Until, of course, you touched the bar and realized it was all an illusion.

I was the first on the set; Kyle had only had to do a touch-up on my makeup from earlier in the day, but insisted I be crammed into a pair of black leather pants. When I complained, he said mom jeans were better left off TV and then pulled out a fuchsia halter top and told me to "fill it."

At least he'd let me wear decent shoes. They were flats that matched my top, with little beads all around them. Very cute and sassy, and, hey, I could even walk in these.

The sound guy fitted me with a microphone and then I was able to watch the lighting engineers go to work on wiring the set.

They worked around me, an unwritten rule somewhere that cast and crew didn't interact.

When I greeted them or tried to engage them in any conversation they only nodded politely and went about their business.

Cheryl came onto the set and examined their work; when they finished discussing booms and reflections and all sorts of other technical issues, she turned her attention to me.

"We have to make it snappy here, because we still want the scene with your dad and then the elimination scene tonight. How are you holding up?"

"I'm a disaster!" I admitted.

Cheryl's shoulders dropped and, for the first time since I'd met her, she looked overwhelmed. "I'm so sorry about your Prevost getting broken into. I thought our security was pretty tight. I can't imagine what happened."

Really?

How could she think the security was tight, with all the disasters going on around us left and right?

And she'd been the one to notify the press . . .

I stared at her, suddenly suspicious. She did have a lot riding on the success of the show. The way all the incidents were lining up she was going to be the one cashing in . . . Were there lines she wouldn't cross?

Before I could reply, Becca came onto the set. "Cheryl, we're ready on our end."

Cheryl nodded, abruptly back to business mode. "All right, places, please," she called.

A tall, bearded actor came onto the set; he was dressed as a bartender. He took a place behind the bar and looked up. "Is this good?"

"Yes," Becca said, "you're right on the money." She joined him behind the bar and gave him a quick orientation. She turned to me. "Martini bar only. Don't order anything else, or we'll just have to stop and start over. Martini, okay?"

I made a face at her. "I hate martinis."

"It's eleven in the morning," Becca said. "You're not getting a real martini, sister. Only ice water."

Cheryl motioned for Becca to put on her headphones and then called, "Action!"

Scott came on the set and my breath hitched. He had a magnetism that was undeniable. I felt sucked up into his aura and a little heartbroken at the same time.

Why did he have to lie to me?

He smiled as he approached and took the bar stool next to mine.

"Cut!" Cheryl screamed. She jabbed a hand out at me. "Get up! Greet him! Kiss!"

I stood up and moved the bar stool aside. "You want me to just throw myself at him?"

Scott and Cheryl said, "Yes," at the same time.

"Okay, okay," I said with more gaiety in my voice than I felt. Actually I didn't want to touch him—I was afraid of the sparks between us—but if listening to Cheryl got me out of this awkward situation faster, I would do it.

Scott walked off the set and came back in.

I moved toward him and he opened his arms to me.

"Hi," I said.

He said nothing, only wrapped his arms around me and lowered his mouth to mine.

I felt the electricity shoot through me, right down to my fuchsia-colored flats.

I closed my eyes for a minute to enjoy him, pretending I didn't know he'd lied to me about having a wife who died from cancer.

He moved from my mouth to my ear and whispered, "I've been looking forward to seeing you. I've missed you."

I pulled away from him, hoping to calm the hormone-induced frenzy that was zipping around my legs, making them quiver. I grabbed my bag from the floor and retrieved his book *Death Thief*. "Look what I got in the mail," I said.

"Aw, that makes for cozy bedtime reading." He smiled. "You shouldn't be reading it alone." He crinkled his nose at me. "Too scary. Maybe you need someone to cling to—"

"I haven't started it yet. I heard the author's twisted."

He laughed. "I take that as a compliment."

"You do?" I asked, surprised.

"Well, being that I'm a horror writer, I'd say so. You don't want your audience saying you're a nice guy when you write horror."

It occurred to me then that maybe the reason he'd come on the show was to promote sales, and a little piece of my heart hollowed out.

"I'm hoping you'll sign it for me," I said.

He patted his pockets. "I don't have a pen right now. But I promise I will."

We seated ourselves on the bar stools and ordered our fake martinis from the fake bartender. We watched him chill the glass and pour water from a gin-labeled bottle into the shakers.

"Do you like it dirty or dry?" Scott asked.

I wanted to say I didn't like it at all, but I knew Cheryl would make me suffer for it. So, because I didn't want to open myself up to any jokes, I answered, "Dry."

Scott didn't make a crack, though; he simply said, "I like a little olive juice."

I raised an eyebrow at him. "You do, huh?"

He smiled. "In fact, I love it. Love olive juice."

The bartender snickered. "Would you like to try it dirty?" he asked me.

"Dirty is with the olive juice?" I asked.

"Cut," Cheryl called.

I turned to her. "What?"

"Ask Scott the question, not the bartender."

I shrugged and repeated my question to Scott.

He nodded and smiled warmly at me, then reached out a hand and stroked my cheek. I stiffened, but he leaned in for a kiss anyway, saying, "Olive juice."

"It's a wrap," Cheryl called.

Scott leaned into me. "I love that you bought my book. That is so sweet. I'm kinda nervous now. I hope you like it."

"I'm sure I will," I said, although I wasn't sure I would. "Does it have lots of gore?"

He shook his head. "No, no. Let me know what you think, okay?"

I nodded.

"Are you okay? You seem distracted," he said.

I shrugged. "I'm getting tired of the pretending." I knocked on the rigid foam bar to make my point.

He straightened, a look of concern flashing across his face. "I hope you're not pretending with me. You're starting to feel something, right? That's not all just an act, right?"

"What do you mean?"

"You get a look in your eyes when I come close and you shake a little when we kiss."

"I do not."

He winked at me. "Okay, me neither."

Cheryl came up behind us. "We need to move things along. Georgia, you have a scene with your dad next. Scott, you have to go change for the elimination ceremony."

He glanced at me, a worried expression on his face.

Good, let him sweat.

"Georgia?" he said. "Olive juice."

Becca retrieved me from hair and makeup. I was dressed in a red cocktail gown that weighed more than a house. It had a strapless sweetheart neckline and a nude underlay but the bright black beading sewn into it was heavy. I'd complained to Kyle, but he'd simply said that I wouldn't be hiking in the dress and to suck it up.

Obviously, I'd lost any negotiating power I'd had with the hair and makeup people after I'd tackled Ophelia—if I'd ever had any negotiating power at all, which, actually, given my luck, seemed unlikely.

Becca and I walked together toward the set.

"What was the deal with the olive juice stuff?" I asked.

She laughed. "You still don't get it?"

"Fill me in."

Becca mouthed the words "olive juice" at me.

"Oh, my God!" I said. When mouthed it looked exactly like "I love you." "You're going to edit and splice that scene, aren't you? So it looks like Scott and I were declaring our undying love for each other, right?"

She laughed. "You got it, toots! Come on"—she grabbed my arm—"Gordon is waiting for you."

We strolled through the La Playa Carmel Hotel gardens and into the library salon. Dad was already seated in one of the leather chairs and chatting with Harris Carlson, who stood next to the empty chair, presumably waiting for me to occupy it.

Dad jumped up when he saw me and gave me a bear hug. “Peaches! Did you know Steve Jobs unveiled the Macintosh computer prototype to his development team here?”

“Uh, no. I didn’t know that.” I hugged him, feeling safe momentarily. I wanted to tell him I didn’t care right now about Macintosh computers, that I only cared if Lisa or Stinky had called with an update, but the room was filled with crew members and Cheryl was rapidly approaching me, so I bit my tongue.

A technician seated me and fitted me with a microphone.

Cheryl adjusted her headset and called, “Action.”

Dad squeezed my hand. “Only three men left, huh, honey? Anyone got your heart?”

“It’s a tough call, Dad,” I lied. I knew exactly who I’d be eliminating, but the viewing audience wouldn’t want to know until the final moment. Cheryl had made that clear already, so I blathered on, giving Dad and the audience a summary of the dates at the Monterey Bay Aquarium and the martini bar.

Dad listened attentively and then said, “Peaches, if you want a recommendation from me, get rid of the insurance guy.”

I smirked. Dad was no fan of Paul’s and he wanted the world to know it.

“You don’t like him, huh, Dad?” I asked.

Dad stroked his chin, clearly enjoying the invitation to publicly lash out at Paul. “I want you to pick someone *dependable*, Georgia. Someone you can *count* on.”

“Cut,” Cheryl called out. “Terrific, Gordon. You gave her

great advice. Let's move on to the courtyard for the elimination."

Cheryl led the crew outside toward the courtyard.

I grabbed Dad and whispered in his ear, "Daddy, did Lisa or Stinky call you and leave a message for me?"

He nodded, but before he could answer, Becca breezed past us, saying, "Your mike's still on."

Twenty-eight

INT. LIBRARY DAY

Edward is facing the camera but his eyes dart about. He looks ill at ease and, worse, appears as if he is trying to look relaxed. He is in his early thirties, wearing chinos and a white button-down shirt.

CHERYL (O.S.)
Edward, would you like to tell our audience a bit about yourself?

EDWARD
I'm a physician at University of California, San Francisco. Uh . . . what else would you like to know?

CHERYL (O.S.)
Are you looking for love or are you looking for money?

EDWARD
(*looking panic-stricken*) Love?

CHERYL (O.S.)
(*laughter*) Does that make you nervous?

EDWARD
I've studied science my entire life. How do you find love? How do you quantify it? How do you even know it's real?

Two champagne glasses were delicately laid out on a small butler's tray that was covered in red velvet. The scent of jasmine coming from the surrounding gardens was intoxicating and I wished I were here in this romantic paradise under different circumstances.

I stood before the champagne glasses and studied the bubbles floating up from the bottom and then popping when they reached the top. That was how I felt, I reflected. High at one moment and then my bubble bursting the next.

Harris Carlson joined me by the poolside. He said nothing until Cheryl called, "Action," then he said, "Well, Georgia. We're almost to the finale date. Tonight you will be releasing one of your eligible bachelors."

"Or not so eligible," I said.

I knew there was still one man left on the show for love.

What would happen if I released him today?

The show would basically be over, wouldn't it? I supposed Cheryl would make me continue—after all, there was still a prize to be won, even if I would be out of the running to win it.

Scott, Paul, and Edward entered the courtyard, all looking stunning in their tuxes. They lined up in front of me. Scott's eyes were full of mischief and he mouthed "olive juice" at me.

Paul kept shooting Scott dirty looks and Edward appeared uncomfortable.

I wondered about the dynamics between the men. Why did Paul have so much animosity toward Scott? Did he know Scott had lied to me?

I held up a glass of champagne. "Paul," I called.

Surprise splashed across his face. "Yes?"

I held the glass out to him. "Will you toast with me?"

He advanced quickly, looking relieved and nervous at the same time. I felt awful to be giving him false hope. I wasn't interested in a relationship with him at all, but I wasn't sure if Aaron had been on the show for love or money.

Paul accepted the glass of champagne from me.

Harris Carlson stepped up. "Gentlemen, only one glass remains."

The cameraman panned tightly on Scott and Edward.

I called out Scott's name.

He smiled, his shoulders dropping and a look of relief washing over his face. He came up to me and took a glass of champagne. "Thank you, Georgia."

Our hands touched as he took the glass from me and I fought the onslaught of butterflies in my stomach.

Paul and Scott stepped aside.

I lowered my eyes. "Edward, I'm sorry," I said.

He nodded. "I understand."

"I have to ask, were you in it for love or money?"

He swallowed, his Adam's apple bobbing up. "I was on the show for money, Georgia. I'm sorry. I needed to get a start on my medical school bills."

"No Great-Aunt Vivian?" I asked.

He laughed. "Oh, I have a great-aunt Viv, but she's poorer than dirt. Would have been happy to see me win the money."

"You're a nice guy, Edward. I hope you find what you're looking for," I said.

He smiled easily. "Well, in that case, I better get back to work. Good luck to you."

I looked back at Scott and Paul.

I was going to need it.

Becca drove me back to my coach as I moped. It had been put back together by a few runners on the show, so it was tidy, but still strange. Knowing somebody's gone through your underwear drawer without your permission always feels crummy.

"Want to get some drinks?" Becca asked.

"No, thanks. Sorry, but I'm beat and I feel . . ."

"I know. It's been a long day and tomorrow we have the finale," Becca said.

Relief wafted over me. After tomorrow I would be done with the show! Free to do whatever I wanted.

And what exactly was that?

"Who are you going to choose for the final date?" she

asked. "Or do I even need to ask?" She wiggled her eyebrows at me and a part of me ached. I was dying to tell her that Scott had lied to me, but that would only compromise her position at work.

"Who do you think I should ask?"

"Duh, the sexy writer. You're not thinking about Paul again, are you? I might have to bash your head in if you say yes."

I laughed. "Pfft. You couldn't bash my head in if you tried."

Becca laughed with me, and then fluttered her manicured fingers in my face. "I wouldn't want to break a nail. Anyway, since you're not up for drinks, then I'll have to call on a certain cowboy."

I smiled. "Is he still in town?"

"Yeah. Tomorrow I finish on the set and then I get a little time off. We might go to Cancún."

"Really? I'm shocked! You barely know each other!" I said.

Becca pushed open the door of the Prevost. "Look at you going all mother hen on me. Since when do you need to know someone to share a margarita on the beach?"

"I'm sure that's not all you'll be sharing."

Becca feigned a surprised expression. "I'm sure I don't know what you're talking about." She giggled as she leapt out into the parking lot. "Lock your door, okay, G?"

I leaned out into the parking lot and watched her get into her car. "I will. Stay out of trouble!"

She yelled over her shoulder as she pulled out of the lot, "Don't count on it."

After she drove away, I washed off the day's makeup and

slipped into a black top and sweatpants, waiting for night to fall. I wanted to run over to Dad's hotel and ask him about the message, but it seemed too risky. Better to wait until the crew had tucked themselves in for the night. It wouldn't do me any good to get caught cheating so late in the game.

To kill time, I pulled out Scott's book and curled up with it. The book began on a dark and stormy night.

How quaint.

The writing was tight, though, and I was immediately drawn into the story. A man haunted by demons, running for his life, then ending it prematurely by . . . I dropped the book suddenly as if bitten. The man in the story hung himself.

Oh, God!

What were the chances?

I grabbed the book and scanned the rest of the page. A suicide note! Panic overwhelmed me as I read: "Your indifference to me has made all the difference. I've tried so hard to make you notice me, but your plans don't include me."

What had Paul said, when I'd asked him about Pietro's note? Something about indifference.

Is it a coincidence?

I grabbed my sneakers and frantically shoved my feet into them.

I had to take my chances and get over to Dad's. I put the book into my shoulder bag and left the Prevost, locking the door carefully and looking over my shoulder out of habit.

A noise rang out across the parking lot. There was a border of shrubbery and it seemed to vibrate, as if someone were hiding in there.

My heart began to hammer out of my chest.

Someone was watching me, stalking me!

Why?

Waiting to get back into my Prevost coach for something?

Maybe they hadn't located whatever they were looking for the first time.

Plan!

I needed a plan. Retreating back into the Prevost was hopeless. I didn't have a phone in there and, more important, no gun.

Instead I took off in a mad dash toward a light post. The only thing on me that could conceivably be a weapon was my shoulder bag with Scott's hardcover book.

It'd have to do.

I wrapped the strap around my right hand as I ran. With my eye on the shrub, I pivoted at the light. Nobody was chasing me.

There was someone there in the shrubs, though. I had no doubt.

Teresa?

Whoever it was, I wasn't ready to confront them. Never willingly go into a situation you can't control; that was a mantra drummed into me at the police academy.

Funny, I didn't listen to that piece of advice when I signed up for this godforsaken reality show.

I raced out of the parking lot and down the street toward Dad's hotel. There were a few couples on the street, who seemed peeved when I rushed past them, but at least no one slowed me down.

The lobby of the hotel was empty, the clerk absent from the front desk. I sprinted toward the elevators but then took a detour into the stairwell instead. Better to have control than be caught standing still, waiting for an elevator. As I ran up the stairs, I pulled the key to Dad's room out of my shoulder bag.

Once on the third floor I raced toward his room and inserted the key, a vague thought squirming its way through my mind.

God, I hope Dad's alone!

The door came open almost in an instant. It was dark inside and it took only a few seconds for my eyes to adjust. The light was on in the bathroom and Dad called out, "Peaches?"

I stood in the dark in the main room and whispered, "It's me, Dad. Sorry to barge in on you."

He exited the bathroom. He was still in his dress clothes but was holding a hand towel and looking freshly scrubbed. "What's going on, honey?"

He moved to turn on the lights in the main room. My hand shot out and blocked his. "No, Don't. I'm being stalked. Let's keep them off for now."

I crossed the room and peeked out the drapes toward the street. The street was quiet: a few couples strolling by and a group of women, sharply dressed, looking like they were enjoying a girls' night out. I didn't see Teresa skulking around and certainly no one else on the street looked suspicious.

Dad stood next to me. He put a hand on my shoulder. "Georgia, you're white as a ghost!"

I stepped away from the window and out of the light. "Am I? I guess I'm spooked. I didn't get a chance to tell you earlier today, but someone broke into my Prevost and ransacked it this morning."

"We have to call the police!" Dad said.

"I did. They came to dust for prints. The only thing missing was the file Martinez gave me." I sat on the edge of Dad's bed. "Then when I got back tonight, I was reading Scott's book—that's a whole other story—anyway, I wanted to come here and see you and I saw someone hiding out in the bushes."

Dad crossed the room, his hand hovering over the light switch. "Is it okay for me to turn these on now?"

"Yeah."

Dad flicked on the lights in the main room and sighed. "Well, who do you think is following you?"

"I thought it could be Teresa Valens, since I know now that she's been paroled."

Dad sat next to me on the bed. "I have a message from Lisa and Stinky for you."

I bolted upright. "Right! What's the message?"

"Stinky got a hold of the LAX records. He shows Florencia Diaz traveling from LAX to Puerto Vallarta."

I collapsed back onto the bed. "Seriously? She's in Mexico?"

"Yeah, you'll love this part. There is a San Francisco in Mexico."

I moaned and buried my face in my hands. "I'm so stupid!"

"Don't say that!" Dad said, rubbing my arm. After a moment he asked, "So, if it isn't Florencia—Teresa—that's behind all this—"

I sat up, chills running through my body. "I came here to call Lisa or Stinky. I found something in Scott's book."

Dad scratched his chin. "What do you mean, you found something in his book? Like what?"

I grabbed my shoulder bag and pulled out Scott's novel. "There's a death in here that's very similar to Pietro's. The guy in the book leaves a note, and LAPD said there was a note in my dressing room—"

"Wait a minute." Dad held up a hand. "You think the writer is behind Pietro's death?"

My stomach knotted and I felt like I wanted to retch. "I don't know, Dad."

"And if he's responsible for Pietro's death, what about Aaron's?"

I cradled my head in my hands. "But how? He couldn't do it, right? He was on the show the entire time . . . it has to be someone behind the scenes—"

"Hold on," Dad said. "Scott was one of the people on the set at the Golden Gate Bridge, right?"

I nodded grimly.

"He was on the set when Pietro hung himself . . . or was hung . . . or whatever, right?"

"Yeah, but he couldn't have gone to San Francisco to pull the plug on Aaron in the hospital."

"Do we even know that happened?" Dad asked.

"It's an assumption on my part," I confessed. "I just thought Aaron was going to get better and figured someone was making sure that didn't happen. But that's when I suspected Florencia and now it looks like she wasn't in San Francisco at the time."

Dad walked to the small fridge and pulled out two mini bottles of bourbon. "I hope you're not making this a habit, Georgia."

"Making what a habit? Figuring out who the criminal is?"

Dad laughed as he cracked the bottles open and poured the drinks into the hotel glasses. "No, I know that's a habit." He handed me a glass. "I meant drinking bourbon late at night."

I laughed, too. "You're the enabler," I said, sipping the amber liquid and feeling the warmth in my throat.

I recalled Scott and Ty sneaking out of the house in L.A. to visit with Becca and me at the dive bar.

"God, Dad, he did sneak out of the house one night. He came to see me when I was out with Becca."

Dad frowned. "So, if it was easy for him to sneak out once, he could sneak out again, to either zip up to San Francisco or ransack your trailer or even hide in the bushes tonight."

"Uh, I feel sick, Dad. I really liked him."

Dad wrapped a protective arm around my shoulder. "Honey, we can't be sure of anything right now."

"I know. But I especially think I'm sick because I just got rid of Edward."

"What do you mean?" Dad asked.

"Well, obviously I can't pick Scott in the end. So that means I have to pick Paul."

Dad groaned.

"At least if I'd kept Edward—"

Dad finished his bourbon. "Well, let's cross that bridge when we get to it."

I stared at him. "You'd rather I select someone at the end who I suspect of murder over Paul."

Dad shrugged. "We can't try the guy right here and now. This is the United States of America. Everyone is innocent until proven guilty!"

"Oh, my God. You do prefer me to end up with—"

He held up a hand. "Now, honey, let's not get carried away. Why don't you call those cop friends of yours, Lisa and Dirty—"

"Stinky."

"Right. See if they can shed a little more light on things."

Twenty-nine

INT. LIBRARY DAY

Scott is looking into the camera; his eyes are twinkling and he has a smirk on his face as if he's in on some joke. His head is closely shaven and he's in his early thirties, wearing a plaid shirt with a dark vest over it and jeans, looking like he's slipped right off the cover of the latest fashion magazine.

CHERYL (O.S.)
Scott, can you tell us about yourself?

SCOTT
That's a loaded question.

CHERYL (O.S.)
Would you rather not?

SCOTT
(*shrugs*) What do you want to know?

CHERYL (O.S.)
The answer to the sixty-four-thousand-dollar question.

SCOTT
(*smiling*) I'm a Leo.

CHERYL (O.S.)
Love or money, Scott?

SCOTT
Ah. Money is so easy to come by these days, isn't it? Have an idea, like building a smartphone or tablet, or hell, just create a website where people can share their pet photos, and bingo—you're a billionaire. But love? That's a little more complicated, right?

The San Juan Bautista Mission was breathtaking. There were five historic buildings facing the center of an original Spanish-style plaza. The plaza was an immaculate grassy square and the adobe mission buildings seemed to glow against it.

Cheryl had requested the crew set up a tent for us along the northern side of the plaza where the chapel was. One tent had craft services and the other was for hair and makeup.

Kyle was present, putting the finishing touches on my "look."

"We have to take it up a notch, doll face," he said. "We're getting to the finale and I want you to look fabulous!"

He pulled out a ridiculous iridescent violet halter top that was covered in sequins. "Voilà!"

"What is that? You're going to make me look like one of the jellyfish from the—"

Kyle screamed out in shock. "Stop it! You're not going to look like a jellyfish! You're going to look hot!"

"But I'm not hot. It's forty degrees out, Kyle."

"I mean sexy, girl."

"The fog is rolling in, big time. I'm not going to look sexy in that; I'm going to look like an idiot. Give me a parka!"

Kyle prickled like a cat who'd just sniffed an electrical socket. "I'm not giving you a parka. Further, I secured a permit for these!" From one of his varied and multiple what I now considered "magician" bags he pulled out a pair of sequined stilettos.

I screamed.

A wicked and cunning laugh that chilled me to the bone escaped his lips.

"I'm sorry for tackling Ophelia, okay? Didn't I already say that? If I didn't, please let me say it again." I grabbed at his arm. "I'm so sorry, Kyle."

He remained stoic.

"Please don't make me wear the stilettos. I have blisters."

He waved a hand. "Pfft, what's a few blisters? Want me to call you a wambulance?"

Cheryl came over, a sour look on her face. "What's taking so long? The fog's going to whip us to kingdom come if we don't hurry up." She took me in. "Great top. Love it. Get the shoes on and move it!"

Kyle gave another evil laugh. "I'm going to craft services now to stuff my face."

"Good, I hope you choke," I called out after him.

He looked over his shoulder and smiled at me, wagging a finger. "Careful, honey, we still have the finale and things could get a lot worse!"

I took my place where Cheryl had instructed me to stand and waited for Scott. He appeared dressed in a wool crew-neck sweater and long pants. He looked warm and comfortable and happy.

"Hey, there, sexy," he said, closing in on me to give me a kiss on the lips, but getting my cheek instead.

"Hey, yourself," I said coolly.

He squinted at me, trying to figure out my mood, but I avoided his gaze by walking across the grassy square in front of the mission. The sky was beginning to darken and it emphasized the radiance of the row of white adobe arches. The mission was made famous in Alfred Hitchcock's *Vertigo*. There was a three-bell wall alongside the church. It was a beautiful campanario, high and majestic, and it loomed in our background.

"This looks different than I thought," I said.

"That's because there's no tower," Scott said.

I recalled the tower in *Vertigo*.

"How can there be no tower? It's where the girl fell from—"

Scott smiled. "Trick photography. Hitchcock did it in a studio in Hollywood."

I stopped walking, suddenly feeling as if I were the one with vertigo. Everything in my world was upside down, inside out.

Fake.

"You should know by now the tricks Hollywood plays," Scott said.

I searched his face. What was I looking for?

"Were you inspired by Hitchcock?" I asked.

"Of course. He was a master. I'd have to say most of today's thriller writers were inspired by him."

"The girl in the Hitchcock movie committed suicide," I said.

Scott shrugged. "I suppose she did. Remember her falling from the tower?" He gave a fake scream and windmilled his arms around as if he were falling off a forty-foot tower, one leg suspended in the air in a warrior pose.

A chill crept up my spine.

"It's sort of like what happened to Aaron," I said, trying to calm the alarms flashing through my body.

Scott straightened and put his foot back on the ground. He said nothing, but gave me a strange look.

"And Pietro killed himself, supposedly. Did you know that the note found by Pietro's body was like—"

"Cut," Cheryl yelled.

Ignoring her, I said to Scott, "A character in one of your books committed suicide, too."

He frowned. "What are you getting at?"

"Cut! Cut!" Cheryl screamed. "What are you doing? You two are supposed to be falling in love here!"

"Well, I'm not falling in love with this man. He's a liar, or worse," I spat out.

"What?" Scott asked, taking a small step away from me as if he feared I'd physically lash out at him.

"You were never married," I said. "Your sob story about your wife, Jean, dying of cancer. That was a complete fabrication!"

Scott looked like I'd just punched him in the chest. He stumbled backward in disbelief.

Probably couldn't believe I was onto his game.

"What do you mean, I was never married?" he asked. "Why would you say that?"

It was time for me to fess up about Martinez and the dossier.

"Someone researched it for me," I said. "You're not the only one who likes to play research games, you know."

"Someone who?" Cheryl demanded, her eyes blazing like flamethrowers right through me. She was thinking of Becca, of course. I had to come clean. I couldn't get Becca into trouble, but then again, I couldn't throw Martinez under the bus, either.

"LAPD," I lied.

"Everyone take five," Cheryl yelled. She shooed the cameramen away and approached me. "What are you doing here? We've got a scene to film here and we need to get on to the finale today. I can't afford another day at La Playa Carmel!"

"Hold up," Scott said. "Obviously she's got a few things to say to me. We need to clear the air. Can you give us a minute?"

Cheryl literally looked like her head might pop off, but some part of her must have recognized that the sooner Scott and I talked, the sooner she'd get her scene.

She held out her palm, fingers fanned out under Scott's

nose, and said between gritted teeth, "Five minutes!" She turned on a heel and walked toward the mission.

Scott turned toward me and I realized I was shaking.

"What's going on? Evidently someone's told you something that wasn't true—"

"Save it," I said, furious now. "When Pietro was found in my dressing room they gave me some information about his body."

"What's that got to do with me? With my being married? Why did you say you thought I'd never been married?"

"People talk. I know that you were lying about her," I said.

"But I wasn't!" he said. "I'm not. Why would I lie about something like that?"

"To get my affection or to win the stupid show. I have no idea!"

He shook his head. "No. No. I would never lie about something like that. Actually, I just don't lie. Lies are for people scared of the truth."

He reached out for me. I pulled away from him.

"Georgia! Please," he said. "I don't know who told you all this or why you believe it, but—"

"There's another reason to lie."

He cocked his head toward me. "What's that?"

"To hide something bigger."

He squinted at me. "Like what?"

"You killed Aaron and Pietro."

Scott's jaw dropped open, his eyes wide. "What?" he sputtered. "I don't know if I should laugh or cry. You're joking, right?"

"The note in my dressing room—"

"What note?"

Anger welled up inside me. "Don't pretend you don't know what I'm talking about! Pietro's suicide note was straight out of your book *Death Thief*!"

Scott frowned. "Are you saying that the—"

I jammed a finger into his chest. "The note in my dressing room was the same as the note in your book!" I repeated.

He recoiled from me. "Well, that's weird."

I leaned into him, my face close to his. "Weird? Is that all you have to say for yourself?"

His shoulders hunched up to his ears and he stepped back. "You think if I were going to kill someone I'd be stupid enough to plagiarize my own stuff? Leave a note that would directly point the finger at me?"

I stepped away from him, a nagging sensation making its way through my bones.

He did have a point.

"Anyway, the idea of murder is ludicrous," Scott said. "It was a crowded set with witnesses all around—"

"That didn't stop someone from killing Aaron! You couldn't have more witnesses than we did that day . . ."

I turned away from him, suddenly feeling defeated and confused.

"What?" he prodded.

When I remained silent he said, "Come on. Don't hold back on me now. You've already accused me of—"

"Pietro was killed because he knew something about that day on the bridge. I'm sure of it. He wanted to talk to me. Someone killed him to silence him." I turned back to Scott and studied his face.

His jaw was clenched and his eyes narrowed in thought. He rubbed at the stubble on his head. "Hmm. Why didn't you tell me this before?"

"What? Do you know something you want to tell me?"

"No." He shrugged. "Well, I don't know. That day on the bridge. It was me, you, Pietro, the doc, and the cowboy."

My mouth went dry.

"The day at the studio, it was the same people," he said.

"Plus the crew," I said.

He nodded. "Right, but . . ."

"What?" I asked.

"The night we drove back from San Francisco . . . Ty was asking a lot of questions . . . asking me about the tapes that I got to watch . . ."

A jolt of adrenaline blasted through me. "He knew about the note! You didn't know about the note. The police didn't say anything to anyone but Paul and me, but Ty knew about the note. He mentioned it to me in Solvang!"

Suddenly the world seemed to tilt and I lost my balance.

Scott grabbed my shoulders and righted me. "What's wrong?"

"Last night . . . Becca was going to go out with him!"

Scott and I raced toward the chapel. Cheryl was chatting with a tall, lean cameraman and eating a vegan wrap that the craft services had provided.

"Cheryl!" I screamed. "Call the police!"

She whirled around, a look of surprise on her face.

"What's happened?" she asked, a piece of lettuce peeking out from between her front teeth.

"It's Ty! He's with Becca. She's in danger. Where are they?" I yelled.

The cameraman came to the rescue. "I can get her right here," he said as he pulled out an iPhone from his pocket.

"Call her, call her!" I screamed. "We have to warn her."

"I can do better than that," he said. "I have her on my GPS phone locator."

I didn't want to ask. I was just happy that we'd be able to track her down quickly. He pushed a few buttons on the iPhone. We waited, the intensity mounting, until he said, "She's inside the chapel."

We ran toward the chapel together. Scott was the first to reach the heavy door. He pulled on the handle.

The door didn't budge.

"It's locked!" he said.

"There's another entrance around the side," the cameraman said.

We sprinted down the courtyard toward the three-bell wall. I swore under my breath about the stupid stilettos.

An image of Becca falling from the tower, like the woman in *Vertigo*, propelled my legs to move faster than I'd have thought possible, although logically I knew that there wasn't really a tower.

Part of me finally felt relieved that Hollywood did fabricate things.

The side door creaked open, revealing the inside of the chapel. The church smelled of incense and had three wide naves and a pulpit that jutted out from the wall. The ceiling and wall frescoes were repainted in native-influenced style with deep earthy tones that matched the reredos behind the main altar. In the reredos were six niches holding six statues. In the center bottom niche was the statue of the mission's patron saint, John the Baptist, that I found myself praying to intensely.

Please let us find Becca!

My stilettos clicked on the tile floor as we canvassed the church. Scott and Cheryl seemed to follow my lead and looked in the same areas as me, but it was the cameraman who said, "What's that?"

A flash of red on one of the pews in the front row caught my eye. I raced toward it, feeling sick to my stomach. The red thing was a lady's handbag, but I didn't recognize it as Becca's. I felt a mixture of frustration and hope. I grabbed at the bag and tore into it.

Becca's phone was inside the bag.

Cheryl let out a string of profanity that would've made a sailor blush, and then said, "Where, in the name of John the Baptist, is she?"

When no one answered Cheryl's rhetorical question, she said, "Why do you think it's Ty?"

"We don't have time to explain right now." I turned to Scott. "Did Ty say where they were going?"

Scott said, "I haven't talked to him since he was eliminated." He rubbed at his head a moment, closing his eyes. "Let's see. If I were him, where would I go?"

We all stared at him.

He made a face and shrugged his shoulders. "I have no idea. What does he want from her?"

"He must think she knows something," Cheryl said, turning to me. "What does he think she knows?"

I shrugged. "I don't know. Maybe she put a few things together like we just did." I pulled out Becca's phone and looked at the last missed and dialed calls. Cheryl squinted over my shoulder at the phone.

"Those top three calls were for the show. Reservations and such, but what is this?" She pointed at a call and pulled up the information on it.

"Car rental," the cameraman behind me said.

An awful feeling was building in my gut. They'd rented a car. Where had they gone and what was Ty going to do with my best friend?

Thirty

We all agreed that calling the Carmel police was our only option. Unfortunately they weren't exactly fast acting, and the fact that they had to coordinate with SFPD and LAPD made it all the more excruciating.

Paul had been brought in and I finally got to hear from his mouth that he hadn't been on official business during the show. Cheryl for her part looked completely perplexed that Paul was a cop.

"I wished I'd known that," she said.

I glanced at her. "Why, you wouldn't have put him on the show?"

"On the contrary," she said. "We could have used it. Imagine a real-life whodunit on TV. In fact, we could even have the viewers vote on who they think the bad guy is."

She had a faraway, pensive look on her face and I suddenly got the idea that she was plotting an entirely new show.

I buried my face in my hands, but wasn't able to hide my

frustration. "Becca is missing, right now! Do you understand that we need to get to her before anything happens?" I screamed.

Cheryl looked shocked. "Of course I understand that. I was only saying—"

Scott put a hand on my shoulder. "It's okay. We're going to find her."

Paul stepped up and said, "What do you mean, we're going to find her? The police will find her. You need to butt out."

Scott and Paul stood facing each other. It looked like a fight was about to break out. I stepped between them. "Hey, hold up. No fighting. We all have to work together."

"This is official business," Paul yelled.

"You're not on official business," I said. "You're on paid leave or whatever."

"Well, you're not official at all!" He sneered in my face.

I wanted to rip his throat out, right there and then, but the thought of Becca being God knows where with Ty snapped me back to reality. Anxiety grabbed at my chest and I feared I'd hyperventilate.

Scott placed a hand on the small of my back. "We need to collect ourselves. Focus and think. That's the only way we'll get your friend out of trouble."

I pressed my forehead into his chest and breathed in his scent. I could hear Paul grumble something, obviously angry that I'd decided to seek comfort in Scott rather than him.

The Carmel police officer who was helping us came into the room with a folder in his hand. "Well, we've been able to track down Ty's record." He placed it on the table in front of us. We all eagerly snapped for it, three pairs of hands working frantically to pull at the folder.

I noticed that Cheryl was busy tapping away at her iPhone and taking notes on a yellow pad.

I glanced at the sheet that Paul had scored on Ty. "Guy had problems," Paul said. "It look likes Ty had invested money with Aaron and Aaron lost it all."

"There's motive for you," I said.

"What's that got to do with Becca?" Scott asked.

In an unrehearsed dance, we all traded sheets of paper from the file and studied them.

"He lives in Texas," Scott observed.

"Check the flights in and out of Dallas and Austin," Paul said to the officer.

Cheryl looked up from her iPhone. "I can do that!" she said, swishing a finger across the screen on her phone.

Oh! She's going to help us now?

"Next flight out is in an hour," she said.

We all looked at each other and leapt up from the table.

The cop waved his hands around. "Wait, wait. I'll radio!"

"Do that," Paul said, leading the charge for us as he ran outside and looked for a vehicle. There was a crew van parked on the corner.

Cheryl called to a runner nearby. "Who has the keys to the van?"

The runner looked alarmed and confused. It was probably the first conversation he'd ever had with the boss. "I do, but why? It's parked legally . . ."

Cheryl waved a hand to quiet him. "Drive us to the airport, now!"

Scott, Paul, Cheryl, and I tumbled into the van.

My stomach was doing circles. If Ty was off to the

airport, then there was a good chance he'd already gotten rid of Becca. There was no way she'd leave and not tell me.

"We need to find her," I said. "I'm sure she's not at the airport."

Scott put a hand on my knee. "We have to find him first. Maybe we can figure out where she is from there."

Paul glared at us as he watched Scott's hand on my knee.

The nearest airport was in San Jose. Traffic was backed up on the 101. I felt like I would come out of my skin.

"It's not right," I said. "It's not right. I don't think he's there."

"Why don't we let Paul and the police try and track Ty down at the airport," Scott suggested. "And you and I can work on finding Becca. Divide and conquer."

"Yes," I said, relieved. Finally I felt like someone understood me. "Pull over, please," I said to the driver.

"Oh, stop it," Paul said. "You don't need to prove anything. You think you're going to find her any faster than we are? You have to let the professionals do their work." He leveled his gaze at me. "You've never been any good at investigations, Georgia. Face it. You thought Teresa Valens was the bad guy."

I felt rage building inside of me and fought the urge to lash out at him. Part of me wanted to bash his head in and make him pay for the hurt he'd caused me. But it didn't seem important right now. It was more important to find Becca and I wasn't going to argue with this man about my supposed incompetence.

"Pull over. Let me out," I said to the driver.

The driver glanced in his rearview mirror at me. "Uh,

I'd have to take the next exit and I have a mile of traffic ahead of me. Is that really what you want me to do?" He glanced at Cheryl for an answer.

Cheryl nodded. "Yeah. You can take Paul on to the airport. It's probably best if we split up. I'll arrange for another car."

She tapped again on her phone, bringing it to life. No wonder the thing didn't have any battery power left at the end of the day!

The next mile in traffic was excruciating, the three of us having a silent staring contest while Cheryl called a car service.

Finally the driver exited and let Scott, Cheryl, and me out. Paul barely glanced at us as we got out of the van.

"What now?" Cheryl asked as we climbed into the waiting Town Car.

"Let's get my dad," I said.

"Your dad?" Cheryl asked with more than a little trepidation in her voice.

I waved a hand around. "Don't worry. I know you two are an item."

Cheryl smoothed down her skirt, looking a little embarrassed, while Scott chuckled. "He's a very nice man, your father," she said.

"I know."

There wasn't much traffic southbound on 101, so we arrived at Dad's hotel relatively quickly. Cheryl had phoned him in advance and he was waiting for us in his room. We figured we'd be able to work there and at least focus.

I quickly introduced Dad to Scott.

Dad quirked an eyebrow and looked back and forth from Scott to me. "The writer?" he asked, not making an effort to mask his shock.

I frowned and brought a finger to my lips, trying to give Dad a signal not to repeat our earlier conversations.

Scott chuckled, not missing a beat.

Cheryl and I brought Dad up to speed on the details as best we could.

Scott got comfortable near the window and stared out at the street. He was lost in thought and I suddenly felt bad. I'd thought the worst about him. Thought he'd lied to me and accused him of being a killer.

He looked in my direction and caught me staring at him. He offered me a smile with a small nod. "I think we should head back to La Playa Carmel. Maybe one of the crew saw something. Saw them together or overheard their plans."

"Good idea," Dad said, clapping Scott on the back. He seemed glad to have something to do and eager to get on with it.

And if I were being honest, I'd say he was probably relieved that Scott was in my good graces and there was no chance of Paul winning the game now.

We all left the hotel and walked the short distance to La Playa Carmel. Cheryl was busy tapping on her phone the entire time, presumably rounding up the crew into the salon for a meeting. Dad held her elbow as she furiously tapped away, so she wouldn't trip. It was really too cute for words.

Scott took my hand and I felt the now familiar butterflies in my stomach.

When Cheryl finally finished on the phone, she squeezed

Dad's hand and I saw my own expression of schoolgirl delight reflected on her face.

We made it into the salon library; the staff members were already present with worried expressions and gossip afoot. It was a more skeletal staff than we'd had in Los Angeles, but still about twenty people, between the wardrobe and makeup crew, cameramen, lighting, sound engineers, and several runners.

Cheryl stepped in front of the group. "Gang, thank you all for your dedication to the show. We've had a bumpy and totally unprecedented ride together. I'm sorry to announce that Becca is missing and we need your help to locate her."

Kyle, the makeup artist, gasped and shrieked during Cheryl's talk so much that one of the runners had to hold him and pat his back. "I know, honey, I know. We all love Becca," she repeated over and over. "We'll find her."

I found myself annoyed. We all loved Becca, yes, that was true, but nobody loved her like I loved her. She was like a sister to me and I was going to find her or die trying.

"Stop blubbering!" I said. "We need to focus here, people! Did anyone see her and Ty last night or even this morning?"

"She wasn't with Ty last night," one of the runners said. She was wearing a long-sleeved black turtleneck, but I recognized her as the girl with tattoos down each arm. "She was with me. We went out to have a couple drinks. She was trying to hook up with him, but they didn't connect. In fact, I ended up with her phone. I had it this morning and took it to the mission to give it to her, but she wasn't there. And then someone stole the phone out of my bag," she whined.

"That was me," Cheryl said. "We found your bag with

her phone. We took it. Sorry. We were trying to locate her," Cheryl said.

One of the electricians sprang to attention. "Wait. I saw her this morning. I think it was around eight A.M. I was in early to prep for the elimination scene—"

"Is there still going to be an elimination scene?" Kyle asked, eyeing how Scott stood so close to me.

"Of course!" Cheryl said, practically screeching. "We have to have an elimination scene; we have to have a finale!"

"Hold up, hold up. Quiet!" I turned to the electrician. "What were you saying? You saw Becca this morning?"

"Yeah," he said. "Ty came to pick her up. They looked happy. He had an arm around her waist; they were giggling. I don't understand—"

"Did they say where they were going?" Scott said.

The electrician scratched his chin. "Coffee, I think. She was talking about a latte. He said he'd fix her up with one right away."

Scott and I exchanged glances, our minds already working together.

"There's a coffee shop on the corner!" he said.

"We need a phone." I tried to swipe Cheryl's out of her hand, but she screamed as if I'd stabbed her.

"No! You can't take mine."

Dad pulled his out of his pocket. "Here, peaches."

"I need a smartphone. GPS, Internet—"

One of the sound engineers handed his phone to Scott. "Here, take mine."

I stuffed Dad's phone into my pocket anyway.

Scott and I exited the building and ran to the coffee shop on the corner. The afternoon fog, blowing off the coast, was in full force. Goose bumps covered my skin.

Scott shrugged out of his wool crewneck sweater and gave it to me.

"Thank you," I said, taking his sweater and pulling it over my ridiculous sequined halter top. Now I was feeling more like me, but I would have loved to ditch the stilettos and put on a simple pair of Keds. "I can't run in these shoes," I complained.

"You look good in them," he said. "But you look good even in pink bunny slippers."

I laughed. "Now is not the time to win flattery points. Oh, and so you know, if I trip and kill myself on the streets of Carmel, I want you to sue. These shoes should be outlawed in every town!"

The coffee shop was open and the acrid smell of roasted coffee wafted toward us; despite it, I found myself craving something hot to drink. I skipped putting in an order, though; that would only slow us down.

"Were you working this morning around eight?" I asked the barista.

"Oh, yeah, been here since six."

I described Becca, suddenly wishing I had a photo of her or Ty, but as soon as I mentioned Ty wore a cowboy hat and boots, she said, "Yes, they were here! I thought they were so cute."

Relief flooded my body.

Scott jumped in. "Did they have their coffee here or—"

"Oh, no, they took it to go," she said.

Disappointment ran through me almost as quickly as the relief had.

"Do you happen to know where they were going?"
"No."

Of course things could never be easy for me. I felt like a great big loser. I collapsed at the closest table and banged my head against it. "Think, think, think," I repeated to myself.

Scott joined me with two foamy cappuccinos. "Caffeine. It stimulates the brain cells."

"I think you're lying," I said. "But I'll take you up on it anyway."

I sipped the hot coffee and closed my eyes.

Scott fiddled with the smartphone in his hands. "Okay, they grab coffee. She says something. Something that threatens him. He knows that she knows . . ." He stopped talking and quirked his head. "What does she know?"

"She doesn't know anything. I didn't tell her about the file."

Scott frowned. "What file?"

"The one that said you'd never been married and that Ty lost his rodeo money. The file that was stolen out of my coach."

"Oh." He was silent for a moment. "You've been holding back on me."

I sipped my cappuccino. "Fat lot of good it's done."

"For the record, I really was married. What I told you about Jean was all true."

The cappuccino swirled in my tummy, making me feel sick. I knew now that Martinez had messed with the information he'd provided me on Scott's record. He obviously wanted me to pick Paul at the end.

Had Paul been in on that decision?

It didn't seem to matter anymore.

"I am so sorry I didn't believe you. You were on the show looking for love?" I asked.

Scott smiled. "Yeah, definitely." Scott reached a hand across the table and laced his fingers through mine.

My throat felt thick and I found it hard to swallow.

"Did you find it?" I asked.

He laughed. "You can be really dense, huh?"

I pulled my fingers from his and stood. "Now, wait a minute."

He got up and took me into his arms. "Yes, I found it." He kissed me, our lips and bodies pressing together.

There was something so right about being in his arms. I must have been afraid of that from the beginning. It was no wonder he was the first one I'd wanted to eliminate from the show.

I was suddenly aware of someone watching us and I pulled away from Scott. Out the window and across the street, I saw him.

"Oh, God," I said.

"What?" Scott asked, following my line of vision.

Across the street was a photographer.

"It's the press. The *Enquirer.* I have a feeling I know who was hiding in the shrubbery last night."

"Now they have their story," Scott said. "They know who you're going to pick at the end of the show . . . at least . . . I hope you're going to pick—"

"Please." I pressed my lips to his, only pausing to say, "Now who's being dense?"

A tour bus pulled up in front of the café. I overhead

someone saying something about Point Lobos. A jolt surged through my body and I leapt away from Scott.

He frowned. "What? I'm sorry. I . . ."

"Point Lobos!"

"Huh?"

"The sea caves. Becca's always wanted to go." I ran out of the café and hurled myself into the tour bus. Scott followed.

"Can you take us to Sea Lion Cove?" I asked the driver.

The driver looked from Scott to me, but before he could answer, Scott pressed a wad of cash into his hand. "It's an emergency."

The driver gave a crooked smile. "Well, in that case, get in. I've been in love before, too, boy."

Thirty-one

It was a short ride to Point Lobos, about five miles south of Carmel. On the ride, I frantically texted the Carmel police, Paul, Dad, and Cheryl. I got various responses, from "We'll be right there" to "You always have to be right, don't you?"

The last one being from Paul.

When I grumbled about it, Scott leaned into me and said, "So, are you going to tell me the whole story about that guy or what?"

I flinched. Eventually, I knew I'd have to tell him, but I hated having such baggage.

"He left me at the altar."

Scott's eyes grew wide in disbelief and then he whispered, "What an idiot!"

I laughed. "Thank you. I'll take that as a compliment."

The driver pulled into the Point Lobos State Reserve. There was a smattering of trailhead postings along with amazing views of remarkable rock formations. "Where exactly do you want me to leave you?" he asked.

"Get us as close to Sea Lion Cove as you can," I said.

"All right, there's a parking lot up ahead. Then you can take a trail down. You want me to wait for you?"

"That's not necessary," Scott said. "The cops will be here soon."

A look of alarm crossed the driver's face as if he suddenly realized he'd gotten in over his head. "The cops? What are they coming here for?"

"Hopefully to arrest a cowboy," I said, flicking off my high heels and jumping out of the bus barefoot. "Thank you for the ride!"

Scott and I raced down the trail, the sound of crashing waves calling us. There were barking sea lions and chattering shorebirds, and a mist of fog that almost obscured the turquoise water of the cove.

As soon as I saw the dirt trail, I said, "Thank God I ditched the stilettos. There's no way I could have made it down there in those." Then under my breath I mumbled, "I hope I never have to wear another pair in my life."

Scott nodded. "Right."

I looked at him, surprised. "You don't like women in stilettos?"

The trail got narrower and more slick as we approached the cave. Scott grabbed my arm to steady me. "Well, you know, I'm a horror writer. I keep thinking you're going to get mad at me and bash me in the head with one."

I laughed. "Oh, God, we're never going to make it as a couple."

He smiled wickedly. "Are we a couple?"

"Yeah, a couple of knuckleheads, rushing in for a rescue unarmed."

"Right, what's our plan here?" he asked.

"I don't have a plan."

"I was afraid of that," he said.

"I just hope we find her." When we reached the cave, I called out, "Becca! Becca!"

The cave was cold and dark, and my voice echoed off the rocks. The tide was coming in and we slogged through ankle-deep water, calling her name over and over again as we searched the recesses of the cave.

"Becca!" I called out again, my voice hoarse from screaming. Then suddenly a lump near one of the rock formations moved. Tears sprang into my eyes.

It was Becca, bound and gagged.

Scott and I raced toward her in the ankle-deep water and unbound her as quickly as we could. Her eye was blackened and her lips were blue. She was soaked from sitting in water, the tide coming up all around us. But she was alive.

Thank God, she's alive!

She stood and hugged me, crying and trying to speak at the same time. She was shivering and her teeth were clattering so much we couldn't make anything out.

I hugged her to me. "It's okay, shhh, honey. It's okay. Let's get you out of here and get you into some warm clothes. We'll figure everything out."

"Ty," she wailed.

"I know. Can you walk?"

She nodded, but her knees buckled under her. Scott and I hooked our arms and carried her out of the cave in a two-person fireman carry. Hiking the narrow trail in that fashion was out of the question, so Scott put her over his shoulders and walked ahead of me.

When we reached the parking lot, emergency response vehicles were already there: a police cruiser with its lights flashing and an ambulance. Scott and I brought Becca over to the ambulance, where the crew immediately started treating her for hypothermia.

Sitting in fifty-five-degree water will bring on hypothermia in about an hour, and death in three. I shuddered to think how long Becca had been in the cave.

Cheryl came racing toward us, clapping her hands in delight. "You found her!"

Dad was right behind Cheryl, encircling Scott and me in a bear hug. "They got him!"

"What? How? Who?" I asked.

"The bus driver!" Cheryl said. "Apparently, the car they'd rented wouldn't start up again and Ty'd been hiding out in the parking lot looking for a way out, and when he saw you two, he knew he didn't have much time left, so he tried to hijack the bus."

"But the driver put two and two together," Dad said. "Gathered from what you all told him that Ty was a wanted man and clobbered him with one of your shoes!"

Scott, his eyes as wide as saucers, said, "I told you!"

I looked over at the police cruiser. The officer was taking a statement from the bus driver. We'd have to give our statements, too. I could make out a hatless, bandaged head in back of the cruiser. "Is that him?" I asked.

Dad nodded.

"He lost his hat, huh?" Scott asked.

"On the bus," Cheryl said. "That's how the driver knew it was him."

Another vehicle pulled into the lot.

"Oh, no!" I said, burying my face into Dad's shoulder. "It's the press!"

Cheryl's head swung around so fast, I feared it actually did a full three-sixty. "Scott, get into my car! We can't ruin our finale. Or our tell-all show and, boy, are we going to have one tell-all show! We're going to top the charts."

I didn't have the nerve to tell her they'd already got a shot of us together at the café, but I did muster one comment. "They've been hiding outside my Prevost."

Cheryl marched over to the reporter and exchanged terse words. When she returned, she ordered Dad and me to return to the set via the tour bus, which was still parked in the lot. She didn't want to chance Scott and I being seen together again.

The ambulance took off with Becca, the crew assuring me that she would be fine and released in twenty-four hours.

Dad and I climbed onto the bus and waited for the driver to finish with the police. When the driver finally got on the bus, he said, "Sorry, folks, I guess I have to drive you over to the police station so you can give your statement."

Thirty-two

Only one champagne glass remained. It was delicately laid out on the same small butler tray covered in red velvet, only this time it was oceanside instead of poolside. For the finale, Cheryl had made arrangements for us to film the scene on a balcony that overlooked the Pacific Ocean and I would be joined by each remaining contestant individually.

The set looked amazing and I was astonished at how professional the crew was. Everyone was going about their business rigging up lights and sound as if a murderer hadn't been on the set for the last week.

Ophelia had flown up from L.A. when she'd heard about the commotion. She said it was because she didn't want to miss my final choice, but I suspected she wanted to be part of the gossip.

This evening, I was dressed in a midnight blue jacquard dress with silver accessories. My hair was pinned in a French twist and for the first time in a long time I felt pretty.

It was probably knowing that the show was coming to a close and that I'd found someone I could count on.

Harris Carlson joined me on the balcony. He was chatting, unlike his usual business self. "Heard there was a lot of drama last night," he said.

"Yup. We got the bad guy."

He smiled. "I'm glad. It was terrible what happened. I hope he rots."

I looked at him, surprised. Harris had always been the epitome of control and yet, here he was showing real emotion.

"I think it was because of you," he said. "If you hadn't figured things out, the police sure wouldn't have, and that poor girl . . . she would have died in that cave."

"Well, that's what he wanted, that's for sure. He was hoping she'd be carried off when the tide returned and no one would be the wiser." Goose bumps rose on my arms and I immediately felt grateful for all the people in my life that I loved. "I'm just thankful we got there in time."

"What did she know?" Carlson asked. "Why would he want to hurt a lovely girl like Becca?"

"She been trying to reach him the night before, just for a date, you know. It turned out he was sleeping, or that's what he told her anyway, but when she started pressing him on stuff, like where he'd been the night Aaron died in the hospital . . . well . . . it turned out he didn't have an alibi and she put two and two together and that set him off. From what I gather it's the same thing that happened with Pietro. He must have been asking Ty a lot of questions and Ty figured he had to get rid of him."

Carlson shook his head, disgusted. "What a waste."

"He made a mistake though," I said, "by quoting Scott's

book in the suicide note. He'd done it as a ploy to throw the police off in case they starting really investigating, but in the end it cost him."

Cheryl popped into view from behind one of the glare screens.

"Are you all ready?" she asked.

We nodded and she called out, "Action."

Harris smiled into the camera even as he addressed me. "Well, Georgia. Tonight is the final decision. We've traveled across California, from San Francisco to Los Angeles, Solvang, and now Carmel-by-the-Sea. You've had your share of extraordinary and rather dramatic dates."

"That's right," I said.

"Do you feel like you've made a final decision?" Harris asked.

"I have," I said.

Harris crinkled his brow at me. "Do you need to have a final conversation with your father?" he asked.

"It's not necessary. My mind is made up."

Harris gave me a well-rehearsed patriarchal smirk. "Are you sure Daddy will approve?"

I laughed so as not to punch him in the nose.

"Well, I think my father just wants me to be happy," I said.

"Of course, of course," Harris squealed. "So, Georgia, as you know, we have only one glass of champagne and two bachelors. One has come on the show looking for love, the other money. Should you select a bachelor who was on the show for the monetary prize, he will win it altogether, and should you select a bachelor who was on the show to find love, you'll receive an all-expense-paid trip to an island of your choice and split the prize money."

"Right," I said, becoming a little impatient with the proceedings.

"Because this is the final elimination ceremony, you will be able to address each bachelor separately. Are you ready?"

"Yes."

Harris nodded. "All right. I'll bring out your first bachelor." With a dramatic wave of the hand he called out, "Paul?"

Harris disappeared and Paul stepped before me. He had a serious expression on his face and he eyed the glass of champagne cautiously. "Georgia," he said, his voice thick with emotion.

I suddenly wished that I'd had an opportunity to talk with him at the police station after Ty had been arrested. I knew Paul had given a statement, too, but Cheryl hadn't allowed me to be seen with either him or Scott for fear that paparazzi might photograph us.

"Paul," I began nervously and then stopped.

He gripped both my hands in his and stared into my eyes, reading for himself what I had to say. The edges of his eyes were red rimmed and swollen.

Has he been crying recently?

"Well," Paul said, "are you going to give me the boot or the champagne?" He smiled to let me know he was teasing, but the look in his eyes was all heartbreak.

I was heartbroken, too, and my eyes welled up with tears.

He released my hands and peace settled over me.

I had made the right decision.

Letting go of someone you've loved is hard, but we both knew it was over for real this time.

A tear rolled down my cheek and Paul reached for me, wiping the tear with his thumb and cradling my face.

"I'm sorry, Paul, I can't offer a toast today."

He released my face and bowed his head, his shoulders slumping forward. "I understand," he mumbled.

I cleared my throat, certain that my voice would crack. "I have to ask you if you were on the show for love or money."

He sighed, a look of misery on his face. "Money."

A gasp involuntarily left my mouth.

"Cut," Cheryl said. "Thank you, Paul. It's a wrap for you."

He grabbed my hand. "Not me, Georgia. You know that. You gotta know that. Aaron came on the show for money. As part of the rules I agreed to replace him, but—"

I pulled my hands away. "Martinez faked the report about Scott."

Paul was silent.

"Did you know that? Did you ask him to?"

Paul bit his lip, then said, "I had to try everything I could think of to get you back."

He grabbed at my shoulder but I shrugged him off. I knew for certain that what had happened with Paul was for the best because the people that mattered in life were the ones who always had your back.

"Come on," he said. "Don't be like that."

"Good-bye, Paul."

Ophelia stepped up to redo my makeup—crying in mascara on camera can really be brutal on a girl. She powdered my nose and cooed at me. "He was nothing to cry over, honey. I'm glad you picked the sexy hunky writer. Where will you go on the vacay?"

Cheryl appeared in my line of vision. "Great scene, Georgia. Those tears will be gold in our promos."

"Oh, my God," was all I could muster.

"Now," she said, ignoring my comment, "Scott doesn't know you've picked him, so give us a little to work with here. Make him sweat a bit. We can really use that kind of footage."

As soon as Ophelia finished freshening up my face and hair, Cheryl called, "Action."

Scott came onto the set and my body began to buzz and tingle just seeing him. He wore a serious expression but his aura emanated confidence. He glanced at the remaining flute of champagne on the small table then back to me. A slight smile played at his lips.

"Hi," I whispered, barely able to get the word out. My throat was dry and I longed to sip the champagne, but I knew I had to get through the scene first. "I read a really good book last night."

He laughed. "Really?"

"Yeah. *Death Thief*, have you heard about it?"

"I think I'm familiar with that book."

"The guy cheats death. And he ends up stealing the girl's heart in the end."

Scott studied my face, looking, I was sure, for confirmation of my decision. "I'm glad you liked it," he said.

"It's like what happened here."

He shook his head, clearly not knowing where I was going. "What happened here?"

"Guy stole my heart."

His eyes flicked to the champagne flute again, then back at me. "Which guy?"

My hands were shaking as I reached for the glass, praying I wouldn't drop it or I knew Cheryl would make me do the whole thing over and, really, once was enough.

"Scott," I called out, my voice warbling, "will you accept this glass of champagne?"

A huge smile broke out across Scott's face and he leapt toward me, picking me up in his embrace and pressing his lips to mine. The champagne sloshed out of the flute and down our legs, but I didn't let go of him.

I shook in his arms, glad to be done with the show, glad to have chosen right . . .

I'd thought coming on this stupid show was the worst decision of my life and now it turned out maybe it was the best.

"Scott, Scott," I said. Tears flooded my eyes and I fought to get the question out.

"What?" he asked.

"I have to ask. Were you on the show for love?" My breath caught. "Or money?"

"I came looking for love, silly, and I found you!" He kissed me again as confetti came down all around us.